*For George Koehler
and Bob Moran*

Cocktails and laughter,
But what comes after?
—"Poor Little Rich Girl," by Noel Coward

Chapter One

Everyone at Noel Coward's birthday party was watching the young couple dancing crazily across the floor. Not everyone was amused. Yes, some were, if I could judge by the indulgent smiles. A few partygoers, however, sat stone-faced, eyes dark with anger. A lovely party, ruined by drunken fools. Noel didn't seem to notice that his delightful party was fast degenerating into a bad scene from a British drawing-room melodrama penned by, perhaps, some fussy lady writer with three names.

But of course he did. Noel missed little, frankly.

At one point, leaning into Ellin Berlin, Irving's wife, and whispering something that made her laugh foolishly, he caught my eye from across the room—a slight nod toward Dougie Maddox and Belinda Ross. Knowing, that nod, and then—look, dear Ferber, at the cold breeze that's suddenly shivered off the East River into my cozy rooms.

I smiled back, but watched as Dougie waved across the crowded room at Noel, a boyish smile on his lips. Noel, shaking his head, shrugged his shoulders and walked away, placing his champagne flute on a sideboard.

The hour was getting late, and already I was planning my escape. A delightful time, yes, but too much party chatter, especially from some wide-eyed showgirl who'd come to the party draped on the arm of Tommy Stuyvesant, decades older and millions richer. Earlier I'd managed to escape her bubbly ramble only to have her find me hiding in a corner with the glass of red wine I'd barely touched—a batch of wine, Noel had confided earlier, freshly delivered from a Canadian rum-runner into Chelsea Harbor on the west side of town and delivered by a bootlegger to his apartment.

Irving Berlin, a little sheepishly, had been pressured to play Christmas carols on the white-lacquered grand piano Noel had positioned by the bank of bay windows that overlooked the icy East River. Christmas was days away. "They didn't name me Noel without reason," Noel had quipped when he invited us to his birthday bash. But Berlin's rousing "Joy to the World"—sung off-key and too loudly by the celebrants—had led to scattershot improvised parodies of other holiday chestnuts. "Hark! The Herald Square Merchants Sing!" That made me smile, though Leslie Howard laughed too long.

"I'm thirty-three years old," Noel had announced.

"The same age as Jesus Christ when he was crucified," Clifton Webb's voice had broken in.

"We all have our cross to bear." Noel had stretched out his arms and dipped his head to the side.

"Sacrilege," the showgirl with Tommy had sputtered. "That ain't right."

Everyone laughed.

But then Dougie Madden and Belinda Ross joined the party, and the temper of the room immediately shifted. They'd obviously come from another party—or maybe not—but both were tipsy, Dougie's voice crackling with humor as he slurred his words and Belinda, her squeaky little-girl timbre exaggerated from drinking, interrupting everyone's conversations. Irving Berlin stopped playing, with a final irritated run of his fingers up and down the keyboard. Noel put a seventy-eight on the gramophone, a scratchy "Good King Wenceslaus" that sounded like Rudy Vallee singing through a megaphone in a narrow hallway, and Belinda, almost as if hearing a stage cue, grabbed Dougie, and the two swirled around the room, bumping into folks, careening into chairs, demanding that Noel play the recording over and over.

Moss Hart leaned into me. "Edna, when no one's looking, smash that record into pieces."

"It doesn't matter," I told him. "I don't think that girl needs music to make a fool of herself."

Hart shook his head back and forth. A tall, slender man, handsome with that high forehead and slicked-back wavy hair and the ostentatious lavender bow-tie, Moss was a generation younger than most of us in the room, a man in his late twenties, the new *wunderkind* sensation on the Great White Way with his hit *Once in a Lifetime*. Bubbly, flamboyant, he was always overjoyed to be in the company of the likes of Cole Porter, Lawrence Olivier, and, surprisingly, me. Looking like a sparkling yeshiva boy from the Bronx in a pin-striped double-breasted suit with that vaudeville tie, he stood at my side much of the evening, watching, wryly commenting, and I feared the rollicking smart talk he was overhearing would shortly appear in a Broadway revue with or without George Kaufman as his co-conspirator. I said as little as possible.

"Why does Noel invite them?" he asked.

"Not *them*," I emphasized. "Him. Dougie. Noel told me he finds Dougie…fascinating. Doubtless a euphemism, but so be it. Moss, what he finds amusing is that Dougie, a thirty-five-year-old scion of old Manhattan money who safeguarded the family treasure after the Crash three years ago, seems to be discovering life outside a Wall Street office."

A year or so ago Dougie wandered into a party of theater folks, many jaundiced remnants of the old Algonquin Table crowd of the roaring twenties, and discovered that he *liked* theater—and, I gathered, the attention of Noel Coward. Dougie also discovered me, and we were friendly—I insisted that I *liked* him, despite his slavish interest in my life, my work, my conversation. He flattered me a little too much. "*So Big*—I read it—a masterpiece." Of course I agreed, but I only had to hear it once from him. A steady mantra, I could do without.

Dougie swirled past me, his face flushed, sweat beading on his brow as he clutched Belinda's slender waist. A boyish man, lanky though a little too bony, with a shock of gleaming straw-blond huckleberry hair slicked back from his forehead, a hint of a moustache over a thin upper lip. Blue-gray eyes spread too far apart over an elegant Roman nose. But what saved him was his infectious smile. His mouth was too big for his face, so his smile, toothy and wide, startled—and captivated. The sudden appearance of dimples also didn't hurt the charming package.

A celebrated bachelor, housed with an imperious mother in a Fifth Avenue castellated mansion, he famously avoided nightclubs, playboy binges at speakeasies, and serious thought. Suddenly he was investing his capital in Broadway shows, especially Noel's massive box-office smash *Private Lives*, which gave him entry to parties such as this one. Likeable, as I said, but I considered him negligible—just there in the room, the genial young man who flattered me too much when he didn't have to. Frankly, I didn't find in him the stuff of real friendship, a man lacking mettle. Last week, sipping cocktails in my apartment, Noel had argued the point with me.

"I like his wide-eyed innocence," he'd insisted. "A man without wit, true—dare I say witless?—but each experience he has seems to be a first-time experience. A child's reactions."

"And therefore tedious," I'd countered. "Dougie is…well, paper thin."

"Tedious, no!" His British inflection was exaggerated. *Teejus, no!*

"I choose my words carefully, dear Noel."

"But good-looking, dear Edna. That counts for something."

"I don't think so, Noel."

"We see the world differently, darling." He'd bowed at me.

"Yes, I have my eyes open." I'd wagged a finger at him. "And now he has love in his life."

Noel had grinned. "A man who experiences his first passionate love at thirty-five is like a goldfish in a glass bowl—a creature that swims deliriously in circles while those watching shake their heads in dismay."

I'd laughed then. "Let's hope he doesn't end up floating on the surface of that bowl."

"I thought you Americans believed in happy endings." Noel's eyes had brightened.

I'd pulled in my cheeks. "That is a happy ending."

Over the summer Dougie headed to Newport, yachting and doubtless wearing a straw boater and billowing white flannel trousers. Noel sailed from New York to England, then on to Egypt, madly writing fresh dialogue on board, and I traveled to France with my mother. Noel had returned to New York a few weeks back—twenty-seven pieces of luggage and a gramophone that played Sophie Tucker's "Some of These Days" till the wee hours of the morning. I returned with my mother and a case of jaundice—or was it simply bile?

A few weeks ago, everyone back from vacation, we learned that Dougie had become besotted with Belinda Ross, the dazzling new singer on Broadway. The boy who never gave in to the coy flirtations of debutantes was drunk in love.

"I was gone for the summer," Noel told me. "I come back a month ago, and Dougie is madly in love. What did I miss?"

Belinda now staggered against the piano, ran her fingers up the keys, seemed delighted at the invention of music, and started to warble some unintelligible lyrics, some garbled take on "Night and Day." Moss Hart, staring out the windows at the night river, swung around, caught my eye, and covered his ears in a deadpan Buster Keaton parody. Noel raised his voice as he tilted his long head. "Not now, dear Belinda."

She ignored him.

Dougie pulled at her arm, but she sloughed him off. "It's a party. A birthday." She pouted, "People know me now."

Of course, people did know her now. A year ago no one had heard of Belinda Ross. That was before her meteoric rise on Broadway, a trajectory dizzying to observe. September to now—a few months, and much attention. Her origins were admittedly obscure—especially given the press machinery of Broadway chroniclers who liked to cloak simple stories in Baroque legend and mystical rites-of-passage. F.P.A.'s "The Conning Tower" column described her as "the damsel in the gold dress." Walter Winchell offered her a ride in his Stutz-Bearcat convertible.

She'd been an anonymous performer in her brother's hole-in-the-wall theater somewhere in the hinterlands of Eleventh Avenue, so west of Broadway it could be Jersey, a shadowy old vaudeville house lost among the Chelsea Pier longshoremen and stevedores in Hell's Kitchen. Yes, a few long blocks from Times Square, but geography no one had heard of. The beautiful girl with a wonderful singing voice, equal parts thunder and whispered cooing, she sang and danced for the piddling crowd that somehow found its way onto that dark landscape. She could be a coy Mary Pickford, a vampish Theda Bara, even a smart-mouthed Fanny Brice, but she played to nearly empty houses.

Discovered there by Cyrus Meerdom, the powerhouse producer with the lascivious eye—rumor had it her greedy brother somehow orchestrated the serendipitous meeting—she quickly departed the ragtag company of actors and appeared in Meerdom's *Colleens* revue at the Mendes Theatre on Forty-third, an anemic show of half-baked numbers, except for Belinda's singing. Suddenly, the critics and audiences paid attention to the new star. For many, she epitomized the post-Crash femininity—gone the boyish, bobbed-hair flappers, the stick-figure mannequins. With her curvaceous body and hourglass figure that reminded some old-timers of an elegant Lillian Russell, Belinda captured a lot of fluttering hearts. She became a sensation.

But the revue wasn't. For one month, Cyrus was seen everywhere with Belinda on his arm. Dancing at El Morocco. At 21. Eating caviar *au blini* with Jimmy Durante at Les Ambassadeurs. Sipping Cel-Ray tonics at Hudnut's basement café. She clung to Cyrus' arm as though to let go would be to watch her treasure boat sail away. Rumors were everywhere. Supposedly someone overheard Cyrus whisper suggestions of Paris trips, a penthouse apartment at the Sherry Netherland, a yacht in the Hudson, talking too much so that his wife learned of the indiscretion. He didn't care.

Neither did Belinda. But the revue closed after four weeks. A flop. Two weeks later, Belinda found a new home. The success of *George White's Scandals* had ignited Broadway, with Rudy Vallee singing "Life is Just a Bowl of Cherries." Leggy beauties danced in syncopation. Imitating the revue, Tommy Stuyvesant, financed by an eager Dougie Maddox, opened his spectacular *Tommy's Temptations* at the New Beacon. Belinda Ross starred. The show was an instant smash—witty, sardonic sketches, yes, but mainly Belinda, showcased. Belinda's grinning face appeared on the cover of *Stage* and *Broadway Lights*. The *Daily News* featured her in a photogravure spread. Winchell's "On Broadway" in the *Mirror* wept with hyperbole. Her smiling face adorned calendars in gas stations across Brooklyn and Queens. Stage-door Johnnies left roses and phone numbers. George Kaufman, giddy, sent candy.

Cyrus Meerdom was a thing of the past.

Suddenly, Belinda was on the arm of Tommy Stuyvesant at Leon and Eddie's Famous Door, listening to the cool jazz of Wingy Mannone. A loudmouth with family millions, Tommy flaunted the vivacious Belinda, though he always wore a bemused look on his face, as though he understood the vagaries of such transitory romance. A bachelor who was also a notorious skinflint, he simply shrugged his shoulders when Belinda suddenly disappeared into the arms of his chief financial investor, the hapless Dougie Maddox. After all, she was still his moneymaker on Broadway.

When Dougie and Belinda arrived at the party, Tommy had been pontificating about the dire state of theater in these depressed years—"Those goddamn Hollywood movies suck the life outta Broadway"—but stopped when Belinda spotted him and threw a friendly half-wave in his direction. A tall, beefy man with a gleaming bald head and small dull eyes, who always looked uncomfortable in a suit, Tommy laughed out loud. Of course, everyone in that room who had followed the picayune melodrama of Belinda and her suitors shot glances at one another, but Tommy, shaking his head, turned away, indifferent. Belinda noisily gave Dougie a peck on the cheek.

Noel, a glass of cognac in his hand and a Turkish cigarette bobbing at the end of his long ivory holder, sidled up to me and nodded at the two. "Look, Edna. I've provided a floor show. The ingénue and the sybarite."

"But Tommy seems indifferent."

He grinned. "Look closely, darling. It's all a pose. A broken heart."

"You're a romantic, Noel."

He sighed. "I'm watching the death of my party."

"I think that happened a while ago, Noel—during Belinda's screechy rendition of Cole Porter."

"Tommy isn't happy his biggest star is filled with bathtub gin."

Watching the florid man as he gulped back his drink, I noticed a sudden flick of his head in Belinda's direction. Still that enigmatic smile on his face, that feigned indifference, but his eyes revealed something else: A trace of hurt? Or was it anger?

"Ah, Belinda," Noel laughed softly. "The girl who plans to ruin Dougie's life." Then, the smile disappearing, he said, "Such girls are commonplace, if captivating, and always fickle. Such girls are—doomed."

I raised my glass to him. "A dark romantic in the New World."

Noel narrowed his eyes. "Look at the two of them. The way they look at each other. They *love* each other."

"That surprises you, Noel?"

"Such raw love is dangerous in the young."

"Why?"

"They think they are the only ones who've ever been in love. It makes them…reckless." He chuckled as he raised his glass.

As the party went on, Noel's mood shifted. He stood by the piano but stared out into the black night. A gust of wind rattled the windows, snowflakes swirling. A hint of moonlight reflected on the choppy East River. His gaze shifting back to the room, Noel pursed his lips and frowned at the couple. He was watching Dougie, who kept telling Belinda to lower her voice. "Do you know where you are, for Christ's sake?"

She shot back. "Of course I know where I am. I'm not a fool."

Noel twisted his head to the side and drained his cognac. "A fool and Dougie's money are soon parted."

He stared back out into the black night.

A tall man, over six feet, lithe like a strapping young boy, that stark aristocratic face under the blond tousled hair, a few strands drifting onto his forehead, Noel leaned back against the piano, sadly resigned to a failed evening. He stifled a yawn, which surprised me, and he caught me looking. I walked over to him and looked up into his face. "Noel, you should ask them to leave."

His words were clipped, world-weary, very British: "Edna, love, I never ask anyone to leave my home." A thin smile. "In a moment I'll disappear and return in my red satin dressing gown and begin a recitation of homiletic bedtime stories."

I laughed. "'Twas the night before Christmas...'"

He finished. "And all through my house..." He smirked. "Design for living in Manhattan?"

After New Year's, he'd be headed to Cleveland with Lynn Fontaine and Alfred Lunt for tryouts of his new play, *Design for Living*, a new risqué comedy about a questionable—if engaging—*ménage a trois*.

Watching the drama in the room, Irving Berlin nudged Noel's elbow, made a *tsk tsk* sound, sat at the piano, and began a jazz-baby rendition of a song I didn't recognize, a mournful, down-and-out dirge that made Noel smile. "Someone is reading my mind," he said to Irving. "That's always dangerous."

But a few chords into the song, Belinda began humming loudly and, stopping abruptly, Berlin dropped his hands into his lap. He stared straight ahead, unhappy. Noel leaned over his shoulder. "Might I request the Mozart Requiem?"

There was a commotion at the front door. A raised voice, alarmed. A phony high-pitched laugh. Someone groaned.

"Oh, Christ," Tommy's voice boomed out.

The room went quiet.

Chapter Two

"Act two, scene one." Noel rolled his eyes.

Two men strode into the room, one of them already speaking loudly. As we all watched, our conversations stopped. Both were dressed in black-tie formal long cutaway jackets with white silk scarves, traces of light snow melting on their collars. Feathered fedoras held to their chests. They paused, as if uncertain of their welcome, and Noel breathed in, catching my eye. "Dramatis personae. The villains enter. The catastrophe. Are you ready for this, Edna?"

"Did you invite him?"

"Of course not." He paused. "Well, Buzzy Collins, yes. He's invited everywhere. It's almost an unwritten law in Manhattan society. But not Cyrus."

Buzzy Collins approached Noel, a nervous grin on his face. "Noel, we've just come from the Christmas concert at St. John the Divine, so far uptown I thought we were in Connecticut." He glanced back at the entrance where Cyrus Meerdom was slowly unwrapping the white scarf he'd worn over his tuxedo.

A smallish, round man with a cherubic face and a bulbous beet-red nose under a beetle-domed forehead, Buzzy demanded that everyone know him—everyone who possessed money and social position. He seemed to be connected to everyone in the Social Register—his mother was a distant Vanderbilt cousin, once a famous hostess—so he was invited everywhere, though no one understood how he fit into the social fabric of Manhattan, let alone the insular theatrical world of Schubert Alley.

"I hope you don't mind me bringing Cyrus. He tagged along and…"

Noel snapped, "Of course I mind, Buzzy. I choose who walks around my home."

Stunned, Buzzy shuffled away and lifted a glass of wine from someone standing near him, apologized, then downed it. "Good stuff." He spoke to himself. "Though I've had better."

Last spring Cyrus had passed on financing Noel's *Words and Music*, not unusual for a producer, especially in precarious times, but Cyrus made the mistake of commenting to Walter Winchell that Noel's snappy dialogue and rarefied characters smacked of empty posturing typical of an English dandy. Noel's words, he'd noted, were like sweetened plum pudding with the pits in the mix. Noel never forgave the barb, given Winchell's gleeful trumpeting of the remark in his column, and Noel purposely cut Cyrus at functions, at one point describing the small, officious man as a pus-filled canker sore. No love lost—and the rich stuff of Broadway gossip. And yet here was Cyrus standing in Noel's entrance with a smug look that said paradoxically—I wonder why this effete Britisher Noel Coward has dared crash *my* lovely party?

At that moment Belinda, tucked into Dougie's side, let out a harsh laugh. Slack-jawed, she never took her eyes off Cyrus. Every head turned to look. Hiccoughing now, she muttered something into Dougie's side, tittered a bit, then dipped her head into her chest.

Cyrus was frozen in that entryway, a look of surprise in his face. Doubtless he'd not expected to see Belinda at the party. With his index finger he drummed his lips, a silent *tap tap tap*, his stare unblinking. Then, tugging at the scarf in his hand, he looked over his shoulder, as if to escape, but finally, probably remembering how rich he was, he strutted into the center of the room. His eyes locked on Belinda. Eyes darting wildly here and there, Dougie cleared his throat, but faltered. Withering under the severity of Cyrus' look, Belinda turned away, bending her body and shielding herself behind Dougie.

Conscious of the room watching him, Cyrus ran his tongue into the corner of his mouth. "Harlot," he hissed.

Yet I noticed something in his eyes that belied his cruel attack: puppy-dog longing, hurt. Almost immediately, he seemed to regret what he'd said, breathing in and closing his eyes.

The explosive word stunned the room. Helpless, Dougie glanced from Cyrus to Belinda, who was still hiccoughing, and he seemed confused. "Cyrus, I think…" He took a step forward, wobbled on his heels, and gripped the edge of a chair.

Tommy Stuyvesant walked toward Cyrus. Nodding back at Belinda, a look that took in a nail-biting Dougie, he spoke into the awful silence. "Cyrus, perhaps you shouldn't be here."

Cyrus spoke over his words. "Hail, hail the gang's all here. What the hell do you care?"

A grumpy sound from Noel as he moved closer. "Gentlemen—"

He got no further. Tommy held up his hand. "Cyrus, you know how the game is played. Old men like you and me." A dismissive glance back at Belinda. "Pretty little things are like butterflies on flowers. They flit…"

Cyrus thundered, "This got nothing to do with you, Tommy. You stole her from my show. The day my revue closed, you swooped in and signed her. Unfair. I had plans. I took her from that Hell's Kitchen slag heap. You stole her from my…"

"Bed?" Tommy interrupted. "Really? I hope that's not what you were planning. Don't be absurd. A decoration at a table in a nightclub."

Emboldened, Dougie lunged forward. "This has nothing to do with both of you. Belinda and I are in love." A squeaky voice, breaking.

The simple romantic declaration sounded preposterous—a throwaway line from an old melodrama. Rudolph Valentino in flowing desert robes, wide-eyed into the camera. But it was said with such innocence that someone—a suave Leslie Howard, I realized, watching the antics with a glint in his eye—laughed outright.

"She loves your money," Cyrus said.

Dougie teetered, his hand bunched into a fist. He took another small step, rocked backward. For a second he closed his eyes, then snapped them open. "Goddamn it to hell."

Cyrus' eyes swept the room. "Is there a richer man in this room? Sign up for auditions. Anyone? A cattle call for a Broadway revue. All that glitters is not…"

Tommy inched closer to Dougie. He whispered something to him, but then his eyes swept to a frightened Belinda. The smile still plastered on his face, he watched her. Something shifted in the man—his breezy tone metamorphosed into a low rumble, darkness that belied his genial pose. "She can't help herself. None of these girls can."

Belinda threw back her head defiantly, teetered a bit, and brushed past Tommy. She stood in front of Cyrus, her face crimson. Then, after a quick glance back at Dougie, she threw out her hand.

A slap in his face.

He reeled, stunned, his mouth agape.

Silence in the room.

Wind off the East River, cold, cold.

"Well," Noel began slowly, "it's…" He snapped his fingers. "Perhaps a new and dreadful comedy of manners. Americans at play. Death by desertion. *Design for Dying*."

No one laughed.

Cyrus wrapped his white scarf around his neck, swiveled around, and headed to the door. As he rushed out, he mumbled over his shoulder, "Merry Christmas, you lost souls."

Again, the silence in the room was dark and heavy. No one moved. Irving Berlin began to pick quietly at the piano keys, a staccato *ping ping ping* that went on until his wife tapped him on the shoulder.

Moss Hart was in the hallway, calling for a cab.

I whispered, "Give me a lift uptown?"

He grinned. "Get your coat, Edna."

I said my quiet good-bye to Noel and avoided everyone else, though I nodded at Leslie Howard—he was staring at me as I apologized to Noel—and Noel reminded me that he'd pick me up the following afternoon for dinner at Neysa McMain's.

"Unfortunately," he whispered, "this will be our only topic of conversation."

Moss and I stood outside and waited for the taxi. Neither of us spoke for a while, me shivering in the frigid cold, my face pelted with ice pellets blown off the river. I pulled my scarf around my face. Yet after the dry heat of the apartment, the chill was oddly welcome. Moss stood in front of me, his face scrunched up. "Cocoon," he whispered.

I leaned into him. "What?"

"Cocoon." He pointed back to the apartment.

From where we stood we could look up at the brightly illuminated windows of Noel's apartment. A hidden-away enclave, this Beekman Place, a run of townhouses high on a river bluff called Cannon Point. Once derelict brownstones, cattle yards, fat-rendering plants, the neighborhood had undergone reinvention. The Campanile, with its Venetian Gothic façades. Noel Coward and Greta Garbo and Katherine Cornell could watch the snow fall on the East River against the backdrop of the Queensboro Bridge.

A shock of yellow, sharp against the dark night and the dark brick. Shadowy figures moved by the window. Even from the quiet street I could hear the piano. A rendition of "Silent Night," somber and majestic. All is calm. All is bright. The street was deserted, no passing cars, no one walking. The wind whistled off the East River.

Moss mumbled, "A rarefied world, Edna. A privileged desert, there." He pointed toward the apartment. In the dark I could see his bushy eyebrows twitch. "The games the rich play in a time of despair. Foolish, foolish. The bonfire of the vanities."

"Belinda and Dougie do bring out..."

He held up his hand. "I'm not talking about that petty scene." A pause. "Maybe I am—a little. It's just that..." A helpless shrug. "I'm as bad as the rest." From his pocket he extracted a solid gold cigarette case, flashed it before me. It glinted under the streetlight. "Privilege."

A taxi's headlights gleamed through the falling snow.

"What are you talking about, Moss?"

He got quiet after I gave the cabbie my East Fifty-sixth Street address, but then Moss tapped the man on the shoulder. "First, a detour."

The cabbie glanced back. A shaggy Irish driver with red curly hair under a slough boy cap, an unlit cigar tucked into the corner of his mouth, he narrowed his eyes at Moss. "Yeah?"

Quietly, Moss directed him downtown, away from the upscale neighborhood, until the cabbie pulled onto East Tenth Street and idled at a light. "What now, boss?"

For a second Moss said nothing, though he nodded at me, but finally he told the driver, "Just drive down the street. Slowly." He turned to me. "Edna, crack your window."

"Moss, it's December. It's snowing. It's…"

He reached over my lap and rolled down my window, though only a few inches. I shivered from the cold.

"Look."

I did. A deserted street at that late hour, mostly boarded-up business fronts, some covered with planks of wood. A pawn shop. A tobacco shop. Sagging brick tenements with zigzag fire escapes. A failed avenue, this bleak filthy street, with flickering streetlights that did nothing but exaggerate the sense of abandonment.

"Look." Moss said again, pointing.

A broken sidewalk littered with soggy cardboard boxes, garbage spilling out. Worse, upended apple crates, lopsided and ice-frozen. A chop suey joint on the corner. A brown rat slithered out of a trash barrel. At the end of the block, deep inside an alleyway, shadowy men bunched up, huddled, turned away from the street. Another block: a roaring fire in a barrel, its brilliant flames and cinders sparkling the sky. Bent over it, arms folded, a group of men. As we drove by, the cabbie clicked his tongue. We slowed—the spectral men peered at us, indifferent, blank expressions covering their faces. I shuddered. A dim-watt light in a storefront cast a purplish haze on the sidewalk. An old man, crouched down on the sidewalk, his feet planted over a subway grate that billowed up dark smoke, raised his fist against us. I turned away. The sudden shriek of tomcats at war.

"Lord, Moss."

"Cocoon," he said. "'Brother, can you spare a dime?'"

I closed my eyes, saw shafts of red and blue.

"Day after day." I choked up. "Apples for oblivion."

A wispy smile as Moss nudged the cabbie to head uptown. "A dose of reality before bedtime."

I said nothing.

When we pulled in front of the Lombardy, the doorman rushing out to open my door, I sat there, unmoving. When I faced Moss, I felt my eyes tear up. "Day after day," I repeated.

A church bell tolled in the neighborhood, and I waited as the chime struck twelve.

"Midnight," Moss said. "If I don't see you, Edna, have a merry Christmas."

I smiled at him. "We two Jews of Orient are."

He grasped my hand, squeezed it, then shooed me out of the cab. I leaned back in say goodnight. In a soft, buttery voice Moss whispered, "O little town of Gotham, how still we see thee die."

Chapter Three

"The slap heard up and down Schubert Alley."

Neysa McMein insisted she would not feed us until we told her all about that awful scene at Noel Coward's party.

"I didn't know people slapped each other anymore."

Noel had come by cab to pick me up at four, and we'd arrived at West Sixty-seventh, just off Central Park, in front of the stylish Hotel des Artistes building where Neysa had her art studio and living quarters.

"I've been on the phone with Ellin Berlin, who babbled about the brouhaha. But Ellin can go on and on and yet leaves out the juicy, scandalous details." Neysa grinned widely. "That's why you two are here." She hugged Noel. "Edna, was it really scandalous? I can't believe I missed the party. Noel, are you responsible?"

Noel leaned in, his voice confidential. "It was all Edna's fault, Neysa. She brings out the worst in men."

I shook my head back and forth, laughing. "It takes a lot of practice."

Neysa stood in the doorway of the room she used as her artist's studio, her hands fluttering around her face. Although she expected us, she seemed flustered by our arrival. That wasn't unusual—Neysa's chaotic Bohemian apartment attracted drifters and wanderers and ne'er-do-wells, as well as business titans and show people. She reveled in it—demanded it. I once walked in to hear a priest singing Irish tunes in a schoolboy treble while she matter-of-factly painted. Another time I found Cole Porter playing the grand piano—"Neysa's studio is the real Tin Pan Alley, Edna"—while she covered herself in pastel chalk. An eclectic crowd, she always insisted, was the best cure for Manhattan winter doldrums. Or, indeed, summer's fierce heat. Now, though she pointed toward a small dining room table already covered with dishes, she deserted us, walking back into her cluttered studio and tinkering with some pastel crayons. She dabbed at the artist board on her easel, considered it, then wiped it off. Neysa loved to work at her drawings while entertaining—and, incidentally, while drinking.

I peered over her shoulder. One more of her familiar American girl covers for *McCall's*. Or was it the *Saturday Evening Post*? Or *Coronet*? As a successful magazine illustrator, she produced endless romantic renderings of the all-American girl, a look that populated so much of the American imagination during these depressed years. Fair-haired, bright-eyed, cherubic—with a dash of coy maiden.

She looked back at me, then at Noel. "I fear Belinda Ross will be the death of poor Dougie." A comment thrown over her shoulder. "Tell me I'm wrong, Beauty."

This last endearing appellation was addressed not to me, to be sure, but to Noel—her own recent—and, in some quarters, derided—nickname for Noel, a reflection of their close friendship. A "deeply superficial" bond, to hear Noel describe it. When he was in America, he spent long hours sitting in her studio, watching her draw her pastel portraits, a cigarette locked into his long ivory holder, his eyes staring at the tall beautiful woman with the bushel-basket tawny hair, green eyes, and the wide, generous mouth. A face many men in the city declared the most beautiful since Helen launched those thousand misguided ships. She loved them all—or so she said more than once—as she snuggled with her Persian cat, Fifi, and tugged at the shapeless, untidy smock she lounged around in, a drizzle of chalk dust on her shoulders.

"For once, the man has to explore the romantic world," Noel commented.

Neysa shrugged. "With that rigid chin, that sunshine blond hair, and those Anglo-Saxon blue eyes, he could sit for Leyendecker."

I interrupted. "What I don't understand is everyone's fascination with Dougie Maddox. Yes, he is good-looking, but…"

Noel tittered. "Darling, Edna. My dear. It's the…the unknowing in his eyes. The wonder at a new world. Like a Greek statue with an imperfection."

"Nonsense," I said. "Admittedly a flatterer, and charming, if I can judge by the attention he gives me, but what you call wonder in his eye is, for me at least, embarrassing naïveté."

Neysa laughed. "Edna, you could be describing my husband."

I grumbled, "Frankly, I could be describing most men I've met.

"Except me, of course." Noel grinned. "By the way, where is that handsome soul?"

Neysa had married a striking man, over six feet tall, lithe, athletic, dripping with masculinity, a chiseled face, a man everyone happily called "Handsome Jack." He called himself that, unfortunately, though I found him to be a kind, gentle man. A witty man, as well. A nice combination. Neysa insisted she married him so she could look at him and experience hot anger when other women or men held his look too long. They smiled a lot at each other. A sudden marriage, surprising those of us who knew her. With absolutely no planning, she sailed to France on her honeymoon, accompanied by five other men, some said seven, including the rotund and chatty Aleck Woollcott. Unfortunately, she left Handsome Jack back in New York. The reason? He would have spoiled her good time.

"I like Dougie, but he lacks wit," I went on. "The only real deadly sin."

"No," Noel insisted, "that's boredom."

Neysa walked out of the studio, and we followed. A smear of rose pastel crayon graced her cheek, and she rubbed it with the back of her hand.

She was wearing a smeared painter's smock, broken shoes, and her fair hair, so beloved of her admirers, was a squirrel's nest of twists and turns. For a moment she dropped into a side chair, an overstuffed Victorian piece she insisted she'd dragged from the street. Mismatched tables, frayed Orientals on the floor, gaudy bric-a-brac, garish lamps that faced each other across a dumpy sofa. Sloping bookshelves. She threw her hands in the air, a gesture that suggested—Hey, my life, happy here, do I care what you think? Though she adored Noel, she also cultivated me, largely because I'd used her as the model for the free-spirited artist Dallas O'Mara in my celebrated *So Big* back in 1924. Her comment at the time: "Edna gives me the immortality my simple drawings refuse to do."

She loved the way I'd described her in my novel—a woman who could say nothing, pleasantly.

"I'm afraid Belinda might be a schemer," she announced now, standing up and moving us to the dining table. "But I really don't know her." She pointed at the food. "Eat."

A surprisingly good cook, though no one ever saw her in her kitchen, she served a honey-glazed ham smothered in slices of fresh pineapple. Thick slices fanned out on a turkey platter. Boiled potatoes loaded with butter and parsley, so shiny they could be objects for a still life. Carrots so emphatically orange I feared she'd dyed them. "Eat," she said again.

"Belinda may be a passing fancy," Noel said as he forked a slice of ham onto his plate. "Dougie's first infatuation." He rolled his eyes. "Arriving twenty years too late."

"Thirty-five is no time for puberty," I said, and Noel nodded.

Noel clicked his tongue. "We'll have to deal with the pain afterwards. When she moves on."

"Dougie in tears." Neysa smiled broadly. "Worthy of a painting. Michelangelo's *David* weeps."

Noel agreed. "The beautiful boy is sad—a poem."

I shuddered. "Perhaps I should leave the two of you alone to exchange mash notes."

Noel reached over and touched my wrist, "Edna, dear, you have to admit that my party was an unwritten act from your *Royal Family*. All that upper-crust *Sturm und Drang*."

I smiled back. "Perhaps."

Noel quipped, "The three not-so-wise men. Tommy Stuyvesant, Cyrus Meerdom, and our feckless Dougie. Lord. Or, maybe, that old children's fable—rub-a-dub-dub, three men in a tub."

"Tub," Neysa echoed. She jumped up. "That reminds me. New wine, fresh, delightful."

Neysa brewed bootleg wine in her bathtub, jugs and jugs of it. Prohibition hooch, celebrated. Red wine, hard whiskey, brandy. Her homemade scotch flavored with prune juice and grain alcohol. Her makeshift distillery was notorious—and coveted. Sometimes, stopping in, I was overpowered by the raw whiff of tannic acid or burnt creosote.

"Now that Roosevelt is elected President," she shivered, "my Republican heart quakes. Frankly, my Midwestern upbringing is branded in my soul. I'm sorry—his campaign pledge to repeat Prohibition next year will end this…this bliss." She pointed to the bottle she cradled in her arms. She poured goblets of dark red wine for us. "Drink up. FDR is breathing down my neck." She bit her tongue. "At least when the country is Wet again, I'll finally be able to take a bath."

"Delicious," Noel commented. "Tastes like illegality, my favorite diversion."

Neysa spooned some potatoes onto her plate. "I still don't understand what happened last night, Beauty."

I answered her. "Two old coots—one older and cootier than the other—suffer from late-life romantic dizziness, misreading an ambitious girl's slavish attention as her love for their wrinkles."

Noel brightened. "Money is an aphrodisiac." Then he added, "Dougie actually loves her."

"All the pity for him, then. Love doesn't conquer all."

Noel chuckled. "Ah, but the skirmishes in the field are delightful."

The phone rang and Neysa said loudly into the receiver, making certain we overheard, "Yes, about time. Noel and Edna tell me nothing I need to know. Edna masks her adoration for

Dougie with cynicism, and Noel talks like Mary Pickford getting her first blond ringlets."

She sat back at the table, her eyes gleaming, her hands folded into her lap.

"Yes?" asked Noel.

She ran her tongue over her lips. "Buzzy Collins is on his way up. I told him earlier to stop in. Demanded it." She caught my eye, noticed my disapproval. "Buzzy is a busybody, as we all know. But I cultivate busybodies." Her voice giddy. "My favorite little gnome come a-calling." She winked at Noel. He bowed toward her.

Buzzy seemed startled to see Noel and me at the table. He fumbled with the buttons on his fur-lined Chesterfield overcoat, his small pudgy fingers seemingly unable to loosen the buttons. Finally, he tossed the coat onto a divan but seemed to forget the feathered fedora gracing his round head. A vaudeville fall guy, I thought, the country bumpkin dressed up for a square dance at the Grange Hall. No—that was wrong. The dilettantish born-to-wealth layabout who always finagled an invitation to a cotillion, but never felt welcome there.

"Am I being ambushed?" His jittery first words, a glance that swept from me to Noel but landed finally on Neysa.

She laughed. "Of course, Buzzy. The town crier of the fading 400. The legendary and long-gone *the* Mrs. Astor's ghost quakes when you stroll by."

Buzzy walked to the sideboard and poured himself a glass of wine, toasted us. "Last night, right? Gunfight at the Nothing's-Really-OK Corral."

Noel laughed. "That's how you describe my Christmas party?"

"Hey, gang, I only arrived for the shootout."

Neysa rubbed her smudged face. A trace of peach pastel covered her fingertips. "Why would you drag along that hang-dog-faced Cyrus, dear Buzzy? You had to know Dougie would be there. He's Noel's current party favor." Then she mimicked one of Noel's favorite expressions—"Lots of fun!"

Noel frowned at her but his eyes twinkled. "Neysa, darling, you make me seem…without depth."

She raised her eyebrows but ignored him, addressing Buzzy. "Admit that you did it on purpose. You're a rabble-rouser."

Buzzy took a sip of the wine, rolled his tongue across his lips. "Not a bad batch, Neysa. You perfect your distillery talents at the penultimate moment the Feds take away your reason to live." He breathed in. "My old friend Cyrus is more sinned against than sinning, my friends."

Noel mumbled to me, "It's time for an old-fashioned Puritan apologia. The witch-burner begging for understanding."

Buzzy fretted. "I mean it. Cyrus is a friend of mine."

I laughed out loud. "Dear Cyrus, you've come with an agenda."

"Damn right," he snarled, then seemed to regret his snarky tone. He softened his voice. "You know, everyone is talking about it today. Winchell alluded to it in his column this morning. Talk about burning the midnight oil."

Noel looked puzzled. "A spy in the house of Coward?"

"A coward at the party of Coward," Buzzy said. "Someone obviously rushed from your party to the *Daily Mirror* newsroom to catch Winchell arriving from his favorite brothel and drunkenly typing his column."

"What did he say?" asked Neysa anxiously.

Buzzy paused. "'Broadway moneybags bested by beauty.'"

"Why does the *Daily Mirror* believe alliteration is an art form?" I wondered out loud.

Noel eyed me. "News hacks are horses'—ah…hindquarters."

Neysa chortled and pointed a happy finger at Noel.

Irritated, color rose in Buzzy's neck. "You know, Cyrus and I have known each other from grammar school. Both at Boston Latin ages ago. I was best man at his wedding. I'm five days short of sixty. He's three days over sixty."

Neysa looked perplexed. "I can't follow that math."

He blurted out, "All I'm saying is that he's a good man who discovered Belinda Ross—he *made* her famous—and stupidly got infatuated with the pretty girl. Sick with her—*sick*. Everyone seems to. Tommy Stuyvesant did. She has a way about her, that girl. Girls like her do that. The way she leans into you, coy-like, you know…" His words trailed off.

"Old men crumble," Noel said.

"And then there's Dougie," Neysa said.

Buzzy went on. "I know you're all members of the Dougie Maddox Adoration Society, but I never understood why. He's a vain, empty pretty-boy."

I interrupted. "I'm not a member of that club, sir. Neysa and Noel have exclusive access to that shrine."

Neysa leaned into Buzzy. "Edna condemns because he is too good-looking."

I insisted, "I have to repeat—a nice enough man, but one of hundreds of run-about swells in this jaded town."

Noel smiled at me. "Edna, darling, you're lying to me. I can always tell. Blood seeps out of your eye sockets."

"No matter. Dougie is hopelessly drunk with her," Neysa summed up. "I've never seen anything like it. You know, for years you'd see Lady Maud and devoted son at restaurants, at museums, mother and son. You saw one—you saw the other. Arm in arm. Even last year at the Waldorf-Astoria Charity Ball. Sitting together in the Italian tea garden at the Ritz-Carlton, or Dougie sitting in the Hispano-Suiza while Lady Maud had a dress fitting at Hattie Carnegie's. Lady Maud demanded he be at her side, living in that creaky mansion on Fifth Avenue. His devotion was total and a little frightening. He moved the family money around while she nodded at him, a beatific smile on her face."

Noel broke in. "My fault, I admit. Last spring I introduced him to theater. A casual invitation to a rehearsal party. Dinner with Helen Morgan. She sang a torch song at him over dessert, and he melted like an Eskimo pie on an August afternoon."

"Satan, you." Neysa twisted in her chair. "And there was Belinda Ross in the wings, dollar signs tattooed on her heart. Dougie topples. All fall down."

"And Mommy takes to her bed with a migraine," I added.

"I know a bit about her past," Buzzy confided, in a rush to talk. "And it's not pretty."

Neysa poured him more wine and blew him a kiss. "That's why you're here, Buzzy. It's not that we like your company. That you already know. Tell us." She wagged a finger at him, and he smiled back at her.

"A taxi girl," he said, simply. "Maybe. That's one rumor going around. Ten-cents-a-dance girl at the Orpheum Dance Palace on Forty-sixth and Broadway. Sailors and dock wallopers from the Chelsea Piers. Yeah, good singer, great legs. A stardust face that men moon over. C'mon, folks, Belinda Ross didn't come out of nowhere. She'd probably still be huffing it away with sentimental songs at her brother's derelict theatre in Hell's Kitchen if Cyrus hadn't taken her away."

"What about that?" I asked. "How did Cyrus…?"

Buzzy's cheeks puffed out. "Her brother, most likely, a shifty ambitious theater clown. Somehow he got Cyrus to venture off Broadway into that hovel called the Paradise, and there was Belinda, hands cupped under her chin, a twinkle in her eye, and an indecorous hand on Cyrus' wrist. End of story."

I sat back and considered. "No, there will be more acts in this play."

"A comedy?" Noel wondered.

I shook my head. "Not on your life. A tragicomedy at best."

For a while we sat in silence, watching one another. Finally, clearing his throat, Noel remarked, "A pretty girl with ice in her veins is the martini you crave only when the bar is closed for the night."

Neysa applauded.

The buzzer rang, and Neysa laughed. "Ah, I love my own theatrical timing. I should collaborate with George Kaufman. A comedy of manners—poor manners. Now—speaking of final acts."

Buzzy eyed her, not friendly. "Neysa, you're a beautiful schemer."

"Thank you, Buzzy. You finally noticed?"

Dougie Maddox, accompanied by another young man, shuffled into the apartment. Neysa half-rose from her seat, motioning him into the room, but Dougie, his eyes locking with Buzzy's, seemed at a loss. He backed up, colliding into his friend who whispered something in his ear. Then, eyes narrowing, Dougie stared vacantly at Neysa. "You said you were my friend."

Dougie looked haggard, as if he'd wasted the night away in an all-night dance club or at Tony Soma's notorious speakeasy, and now, late afternoon, emerged from his rumpled bed. Sadly, he was still dressed in the black cutaway formal suit he'd worn to Noel's party, but it was shabby now, unbuttoned, a collar flipped up against the side of his neck. His hair, usually so oiled and pampered and slicked back, was a frizzy chestnut ball.

His friend stepped around him and half-bowed, a snap-brim hat held against his chest. "I'm Corey Boynton." A pause, deliberate. "Dougie's old classmate from Yale. A thousand years ago." He faltered. "Friends for years. I…we…Dougie has rooms at the Stanhope Club, as you may know. Across from mine." Nervously he stared at Dougie. "I discovered him this morning in the lobby, sleeping like a baby in a chair." He waited for someone to say something, but when no one did he went on, a barely suppressed titter. "I took him out for air. He mentioned your invite…" He stopped, waved his hand helplessly in the air.

In his four-button brown spats and crisp Arrow shirt collar, Corey was a dapper young man, cultivated spit and polish. A chin so closely shaved it appeared to be polished. A head shorter than Dougie, a bit thick in the waist, he watched us, his cheeks becoming bright red. With his ginger hair and a wildly freckled face, he struck me as a jokester—but the look in his eyes suggested a man always calculating the odds.

"Welcome," Neysa mumbled, but she was staring at Dougie.

"I don't want to be here," he whined.

"Then you should leave," I said sharply.

He looked down at me, a sliver of a smile on his face. "Edna, I didn't realize you'd be here."

"What?"

"Nothing." A heartbeat. "You must think me a lout."

"Dougie, what I think…"

Noel broke in. "Dougie, sit down. Coffee. For God's sake, look at you."

Dougie's voice rose and cracked at the end. "I don't know what happened last night. And why Belinda is mad at me. What did I do?"

"Dougie, sit."

He shook his head. "Him." His voice thundered as he pointed a shaky finger at Buzzy. "Him. You made that happen. It was a goddamn birthday party"—he smiled stupidly at Noel—and Belinda and I were happy, dancing, laughing. Belinda told me she was happy to be at Noel's." His voice broke. "Happy." He dropped his voice. "Yeah, happy."

Noel stood up. "Come, sit. Mr. Boynton, you, too. Coffee. Coffee cures social embarrassment."

Corey Boynton stared into his face. "So does silence."

Noel's smile brightened as his hands fluttered around his head. "Good for you, Mr. Boynton." A pointed finger. "Bravo."

Corey didn't know how to read Noel's exaggerated hand movements—was he being made fun of?—so he sighed and looked away.

Neysa was curious. "Dougie, you moved out of Lady Maud's home?"

He waited a second. "Sort of. I—my rooms at the Stanhope are…"

"Quiet," Corey finished. "And mommy-free."

"I want people to leave Belinda alone," Doggie said loudly. "Leave us alone."

Neysa, the troublemaker. "The slap, Dougie. People don't slap people at Noel's decorous parties. They flirt and grope and gossip—and weep for their sins. But the slap. What did Belinda say afterwards?"

His eyes were narrow slits. "She said Cyrus got what he deserved, calling her a name like that."

"My, my," Neysa chuckled. "High noon at midnight."

Dougie scratched his cheek, appeared to lose his train of thought. "Then she said it was my fault. I brought her to a place where people wanted to hurt her."

"It was a birthday party," I interjected. "Sort of a Christmas party. It was…"

Dougie stared into my face. "It was a trap, Edna." He swiveled around. "Just like this invitation, Neysa. You—all of you are game players." His voice trembled. "I never used to know people who played games."

Buzzy spoke up. "The whole world plays games, Dougie boy."

Dougie sputtered, "Yeah, well, you're trying to break a girl's heart."

Noel started to walk toward Dougie, but the young man held up his hand, traffic-cop style. "I gotta go away from here. It's too damn hot in here. Do you people ever open windows?"

With that he spun around wildly, pushed against Corey's sleeve. Corey reached out to steady him.

"Well," Corey began, then gave a benedictory wave as he shuffled Dougie out the door.

"Lord," Neysa whispered, "that didn't go as I expected."

"What did you expect?" I asked.

Neysa clicked her tongue. "Fun and games."

"Maybe Dougie is right after all." I sat back. "Idle games, cruel."

Noel sat back down and looked unhappy. "Somehow Dougie comes off as the class dunce."

Buzzy nodded in agreement, taking a sip of wine, though he ignored Neysa's frown. Matter-of-factly, he reached across the table, grasped Neysa's fork from her plate, and speared a slice of ham. He held it in the air as though it was a campfire trophy from a hunt, and he munched on the edges like a feverish squirrel. A smear of red wine glistened his lips. "Do you still find that whiny brat fascinating, Noel?"

Noel sighed deeply. "A pouting child, yes." He sat back. "I like him. There's something about him that's—simple. And I mean no condescension by that. Fascinating."

"A simple man," I spoke up, "though born to incredible wealth, will never have a horse in any race being run."

Neysa squirmed. "Edna, that makes no sense."

"Of course it does."

"I like him, too," Neysa declared. Then, with a mischievous glint in her eye, she said, "A game. Give me one word that best describes our Dougie. Noel can no longer use—'fascinating.' Or 'simple.'"

Noel bit his lip. In an exaggerated British drawl, purposely effete, he announced, "Yes, 'fascinating' suggests some complexity of spirit. Children lack that."

"What word, then?" I probed.

"Dumb with wonder."

"That's three," I said.

"I can count, Edna. But—confused. Maybe. Or—love-besotted."

"Me now." Neysa raised her glass into the air. "Charming." A pause. "Still."

"Dangerous," I offered.

"Why?" Neysa wondered.

"Everything about him suggests disaster."

"Lord, Edna," Noel protested. "The prophetess of doom."

Buzzy was anxious to say something. "Boorish."

"I have the last word," Noel said with a smile on his face. "Lost."

Chapter Four

Noel phoned the next afternoon to warn me to expect an apology from Dougie. "He's on a tour of stammered regrets and can-you-ever-forgive-me performances. He acknowledges his boorish behavior at Neysa's."

Weary, I waited a moment. "It strikes me that it's habit-forming with him, Noel. Perhaps even part of his failed character."

Noel scoffed. "Edna, darling." I could hear the deep intake of cigarette smoke, the chuckle in his words. "You're so hard on people who try to make amends."

I'd spent the morning in my Spartan workroom, attempting a short story I'd promised *Ladies' Home Journal*. Nothing clicked—dark, unpleasant images of Dougie and Belinda overwhelmed me. Taking a break, sipping hot tea that Rebecca placed at my elbow, I listened as Noel lamented a world that was too severe on that infantile-though-striking young man.

"Noel, I'm not sure such gestures are genuine much of the time."

"He"—Noel paused a bit, reflecting—"I think he's not used to being out of control. I mean, a financial wizard in a time of financial chaos. Wall Street wonder drifting in the choppy sea of love."

"Forgive me, Noel. Your language is a little over the top, no?"

He laughed. "I've never been one for understatement." He clicked his tongue. "But suddenly this love for Belinda…"

I interrupted. "This schoolboy *crush*…" I emphasized the word.

He challenged me. "Whatever it is, dear Edna, doesn't *matter*. When your emotions get twisted into knots, common sense leaves town on the first bus."

"So you accepted his heartfelt apology."

"Lord, and I thought we Brits were cynical."

"You Brits are rank sentimentalists masquerading as world-weary souls." I stared at my typewriter and the blank sheet on the roller.

"That may be, but he offered tickets."

My fingers pecked at the keys—hieroglyphics appeared on the sheet. "To another staging of a fit of pique?"

"Tonight." I heard him striking a match, a deep intake of cigarette smoke, followed by a sigh. "To a show we've all avoided, despite the rave reviews—and Dougie's rhapsodic praise. *Tommy's Temptations* at the New Beacon Theater. To see the lovely Belinda dance and sing and feign coyness."

I shut my eyes. "And you said yes to this?"

"Actually, I told him you would be delighted to go, and reluctantly I would be your escort."

I smiled. "So you made up my mind?" Idly, I played with the space bar until the machine pinged.

"Dangerous territory for anyone, true?"

"Often lethal. I'm afraid."

"Third row center seats, dear Edna. A premium."

I glanced around my room. My wastebasket was filled with crumpled sheets. A few lines of a story, abandoned. Inky smudges on my fingertips. "Noel, everything comes with a price."

"Now who's being cynical."

I pulled the sheet from the typewriter, crumpled it, tossed it into the trash.

Noel laughed into the phone. "Edna, I can hear you battling with your typewriter. Do you ever *not* work?"

"Not since I was nineteen and a cub reporter in Appleton. Wisconsin."

"Edna, you know you cherish my company. You know you can't live without me at your side—or at least somewhere in the neighborhood. Once I travel to forsaken Cleveland—I hear it's dreadful in winter, snowdrifts higher than the Rockies, rivers of buckling ice—you may never lay eyes on me again. So, yes, darling, a call from Dougie—be nice to him—and then a call from me when I'm downstairs waiting for you in a taxi."

I shook my head. "You knew I'd say yes?"

"What I knew is that I'd have to reach you before Dougie phoned."

"Have I become that predictable?"

"As a matter of fact, yes."

The line went dead.

• • ● • •

I sat snugly between Noel and Dougie third row center at the New Beacon on Forty-third Street. I wasn't happy. On my left, Noel kept squirming in his seat, nodding at folks he claimed he knew, feigning surprise when a playgoer rudely slipped a program over reluctant heads and begged for his autograph. Each time he shuffled, his right shoulder banged into my arm and I twitched. No better was Dougie Maddox, one moment bubbly as a kindergarten mother watching her child sing "Row, Row, Row Your Boat," the next moment anxious, shoulders slumped, his teeth gnawing at a corner of a fingernail.

"Where's Neysa?" I asked. "How did she escape this royal fiat?"

Dougie didn't answer, his gaze suddenly intent on a party of nattily dressed businessmen filling seats to our right.

"She begged off," Noel answered. "Tickets to the Mite Club benefit. Handsome Jack is back in town. You've been there?"

I shook my head. "No."

The Mite Club, a popular spot, devoted one night a week to benefit the staggering numbers of unemployed and homeless of Manhattan, thousands strong, five dollars to get in, the money buying food and clothing for struggling families.

"We should be there," Noel commented.

"Isn't our being here enough of a charitable contribution?"

"Play nice, Edna."

Dougie nudged me, his voice frantic. "Do you see who's here?" He pointed to a pot-bellied man in a pinstriped suit, a gold-buttoned vest, watch fob, even a gold-tipped walking stick. A gaggle of men circled him.

I shook my head. "Should I know them?"

"The tall one with the walrus moustache—Wallace Benton."

I widened my eyes. "Of course."

Of course—the man whose florid face was splattered on the front pages of the *Times*, the *New York World*, the *Herald*, even the splashy subway tabloids. A ubiquitous grainy photograph that reminded those stumbling through the windy Manhattan streets looking for work that not everyone lost a fortune in the Crash. Wallace Benton had taken New York by storm just before that awful October day in 1929, splashing his cash around. But hadn't everyone been doing the same thing? The pink-cheeked elevator boy who lifted me to my nineteenth-floor oasis insisted that we discuss the stock market. "Gasoline Alley" in the funnies talked of bullish markets. The waitress at Rutley's Restaurant on Forty-first bragged about her stock market winnings.

Benton declared war on cautious city planners. In competition with the now-open—though largely unrented—Empire State Building, whose height challenged Walter Chrysler's own Art Deco confection, Benton began building the skyscraper to dwarf them all. Rising on the East Side like an unwanted child sticking his head into the clouds, the building was the talk of the town. His famous and ridiculed line—"Somebody gotta spend money in this dead town"—drew the spotlight on him when a Pathé newsreel captured his nails-on-glass Midwestern drawl that was equal parts smugness and wonder. In those dark theaters the haunted moviegoers who paid a nickel to escape their dead-end lives, and maybe win a cheap rose-tinted dinner plate on Dish Night if they were lucky—those souls nodded numbly. Yes, money to burn.

Like William Chrysler who ostentatiously bought his mistress a 134-karat diamond—"a skating rink," said the tabloids—or CBS's William Paley who flaunted his own ravishing mistress, the vampish Louise Brooks, Benton believed money needed beauty at its side, usually in a penthouse atop one of the new skyscrapers going up around town. You saw him in the tabloids, a Jean Harlow blonde attached to his money belt.

So here he sat, a large man with a neat barber trim, a man who repeatedly checked the gold pocket watch he held too close to his eyes. As I watched, hypnotized by his bluster and bulk, he said something to a man on his right, a remark that caused the young man to guffaw, too long and too hearty. A ripple effect because the other three men laughed loudly. Underlings, I thought, a servile claque.

Dougie wasn't happy, squirming in his seat.

"What?" I asked him.

He debated what to tell me. Finally, he hissed in my ear, "A dreadful man. He actually sent a note backstage to Belinda. He invited her to dinner at the King Cole Room at the St. Regis."

I whispered back, "I assume she said no."

He waited a heartbeat. "She said she did."

That remark bothered me because Dougie's face tightened, a scowl on his lips—the good-looking face, that of a spoiled child denied a treat.

"Hardly surprising," I began. "Belinda is the shiny Broadway light of the moment."

Noel, irritated, tapped me on the shoulder, as the curtain rose.

Tommy's Temptations was a musical revue that mimicked a run of current Broadway escapist shows. It stole from the notorious *George White's Scandals*, long-running and dizzyingly successful, in which barely clad beauties pranced about the stage provocatively while singing tunes that skirted the limits of censorship and common decency. But it also stole from Irving Berlin and Moss Hart's thunderous *Face the Music*, the satirical romp that skewered the rich in a time of Depression and gave the world songs to hum as they counted the pennies in their rainy-day jars.

Tommy Stuyvesant had not only stolen Belinda Ross from Cyrus Meerdom's short-lived revue the day after it closed, he'd also appropriated bits and pieces of other shows: a skit that mocked a snobbish society dame in ermine and cultured pearls trying to edge her way into a snake-like breadline outside the Grand Central Station depot, a song-and-dance number in blackface that echoed Al Jolson, high-stepping dancers in skimpy pink tutus, a sentimental Irish ditty that mourned the death of a sacrificing mother in Galway. I fully expected Rex the Wonder Horse to make an appearance. Breezy stage patter that was dangerously close to Noel's own satirical blasts. At one point Noel leaned into my neck and said, too loudly: "In the lovely gay years before the Crash, Mrs. Cartier never asked for cash." Behind us a playgoer applauded.

I whispered to Noel, who was yawning so dramatically and vocally he drew stares, "I don't understand." Yes, delightful, if humdrum inanity, but—rave reviews?

Dougie heard me, and simmered. "Just you wait." I stared into his face. His cheeks were flushed. "Just wait, Edna."

I waited. And then I understood the eager crowds that forked over their coins to sit in this dark theater. With perfect timing—an audience squirming, clutching watches—the curtain rose on Belinda Ross, the spotlight lingering on her curvaceous figure, dressed in glittery pink-spangled tights and an outrageous sequined boa. She danced a couple of energetic steps, recited a comic monologue, but then, approaching stage apron, simply stopped, one focused light on her face, and she began to sing. A spirited ditty about blighted love, a lyric that was mostly ribald and jesting, but also little-girl coy. My mind shot to Fanny Brice with a surprising dollop of Sophie Tucker as a chaser.

The audience sat up, a sudden stillness in the crowd as folks leaned forward in their seats. Then rounds of applause.

I marveled, frankly. Here was serendipitous metamorphosis. In Noel's living room, tipsy, gliding across the floor on Dougie's possessive arm, she struck me as one more ambitious showgirl, a modicum of talent perhaps, cookie-cutter good looks. One of the sleek blondes populating Manhattan, enchanting, expensive. All silk stockings, and no runs. But onstage her sweet melodic voice carried across the rows of seats. Belinda Ross was—mesmerizing. I hesitate to use that word but no other will do. The stage lights danced around her face, highlighted her wide mouth and high cheekbones. Stunning, another word that came to mind—breathtaking. With the stage makeup punctuating those dark eyes, that alabaster creamy skin, that long swan-like neck—a beauty. Lillian Russell with a dash of Jean Harlow. On my right, Dougie gasped, and I thought he'd weep.

Even Noel, fidgeting in his seat, got quiet, leaning forward, his face transfixed on the young performer.

The alluring magic of theater, I told myself—the primal, hypnotic power of performance beyond the proscenium arch that sometimes—with the coming together of heavenly forces—transforms the prosaic into wonder. That was Belinda Ross, something I never expected. The song ended, a languid bow and flashing eyes, and she disappeared into the wings.

"Lord," Noel sputtered, "this explains everything."

I nodded. "Talented," I said, a little breathless.

He shook his head. "More than that, Edna dear. A little rough at the edges, yes, new to this...adulation, but she is—I don't know—Eleanor Duse, maybe, Lily Langtry." An infectious smile on his face.

"You're foaming at the mouth, Noel."

He laughed out loud. "Look."

Wallace Benton, surrounded by his lackeys, struggled to his feet, his fat hands smacking together like a circus seal, sustained applause that covered the room, his head awash in a big grin.

Dougie fretted. "Goddamn it."

"But she's superb," I told him. "I didn't..."

"I don't care."

Dougie's only concern, I realized, was Belinda's devotion to him. He refused to share her with anyone—especially a fat cat builder who vaguely resembled a pompous William Howard Taft. A look of sickly possession covered Dougie's face. Yes, a man thrilled, not because of her sweet voice or her stage presence, but because she'd be on his arm dancing and hobnobbing late that night at Ciro's. Or dancing to Paul Whitman at the Palais Royal.

Dougie slipped away during intermission, so I stood in the lobby with Noel, chatting with theatergoers we knew. Aleck Woollcott, currently feuding with me, grunted as he walked by, swathed in silk scarf and red-satin-lined opera cape, an incongruous beret on his head, but he swiveled back to lean into Noel's shoulder, whispering, "Noel, the company you keep." An exaggerated shrug as he waddled away. At his side Helen Hayes *tsk*ed and tossed an apologetic glance at me, offering me a slight smile. We were old friends. Aleck grabbed her elbow and pushed through the crowd, loudly greeting Deems Taylor. "Music to my ears, that girl," he hummed to the music critic of the *World*.

"Louisa May Woollcott," I told Noel.

"Not nice, Edna," Noel said, but then he smiled at me. "But nicety is overrated, wouldn't you say?"

I drew my tongue into the corner of my mouth. "It's not my jibe, dear Noel. Dottie Parker owns the rights to it. And, oddly, Aleck found it—delightful."

"But I thought all your lines were original."

"Are yours?"

"Look over there," Noel pointed.

I found myself staring at a solitary man dressed in a sharp-cut seersucker suit a dismal shade of mottled gray, a pretentious tangerine ascot circling his neck, and a slicked-back haircut that gleamed under the overhead lights as though he were shellacked.

"A stage-door Johnny?" I wondered.

Noel shook his head. "Jackson Roswell." At my blank stare he went on. "Belinda's brother. The owner of the theater where she performed before stardust settled on her pretty shoulders. I had the misfortune to have lunch with him and Belinda and Dougie one afternoon. A let's-introduce-the-famous-Britisher-to-the-family occasion. Also unfortunate is that Dougie slipped him my phone number so he could discuss the future of Broadway. He's called once or twice about my writing some skits for his own revue. Lord, Edna, a bore. I ignore him."

"He's dressed like a drummer from Oshkosh," I said. "Out on the town in slick new duds. Babbitt from Keokuk. What's his story?"

The man was talking to no one, though his eyes surveyed the crowd, an anxious look on his face.

Noel pursed his lips. "What story, Edna? I understand he comes here to watch little sister outshine the others. Doubtless her dollar bills bought him that city-boy outfit he thinks is fashionable." Noel scratched his head. "An unstylish man wears a suit that you remember yourself not wearing the day before."

"He comes to watch his investment? The banker checking his deposit?"

"Dark, Edna, my dear. Such nasty thoughts." A quick grin. "So on-target."

"Buzzy did say that he maneuvered—maybe orchestrated—her discovery by the now-abandoned Cyrus Meerdom."

Jackson Roswell fascinated me: stiff, ramrod straight, except for the darting eyes. His arms crossed over his chest, he was a cigar-store Indian, a big, broad-shouldered man, dark hair parted down the middle. A Teddy Roosevelt moustache. When someone scooted by him, begging his pardon, he didn't move. Rather, feet planted, he compelled the woman to move sideways. She shot him an angry glance, lost on him because his gaze was fixated on the doors that opened to the theater.

Noel nudged me. "Really, Edna, do you always stare so relentlessly at folks?"

"Yes, as a matter of fact."

"Do folks ever call you rude?"

"All the time."

"And that doesn't bother you?"

"Not so far."

He held up his hand as his eyes swept the lobby. "We need to find our wandering boy, Edna."

At that moment I spotted Dougie as he leaned back into a glass-plated poster of the revue, Belinda's highlighted face towering over him. His shoulders hunched and his head tucked into his chest, his black bowtie slightly askew, his dinner jacket unbuttoned. Worse, he seemed to be muttering to himself.

"What in the world, Noel?" I said, pointing.

"Follow his steely eye."

Of course. Dougie's unrelenting stare was focused on Wallace Benton's party. The loud, blustery man's voice was celebrating Belinda Ross, and his acolytes were nodding and fawning and quietly—but, hopefully, diplomatically—shushing the noisy man. Of course, Benton was not alone in extolling Belinda's performance—all around us theatergoers talked of that show-stopping number, of their surprise. "They told me she was spectacular but, I mean, really..." But Benton was the loudest, and most authoritative. And, to be sure, he was the only one who caught Dougie's bitter attention.

"St. Bernard Coward to the rescue."

Concerned, Noel hustled over and mumbled something in Dougie's ear, but Dougie shrugged him off, though finally, nudged by the persuasive Noel, he smiled. Good Lord, I thought—not another farewell tour of apology. One thing was certain—the young man no longer needed to practice his lines. Luckily, a bell chimed twice, and Noel maneuvered Dougie into the theater. I followed. When we sat down, Dougie leaned into me, opening his mouth to say something, but I cut him off.

"No apologies," I said into his face.

He locked eyes with mine. "How did you know?"

I tapped his wrist. "It's not that difficult, Dougie. You seem to be working from the same script."

"Edna," Noel jabbed me in the forearm, "you're not nice."

Dougie laughed softly. "At least she tells me the truth, Noel."

A tick to his voice. "And I don't?"

"The truth is no fun for you." Dougie's eyes glistened. "You spend a lifetime making up your life."

As the curtain rose, I whispered to him. "Dougie, I may learn to like you, after all."

"Quiet," Noel muttered. "Why do Americans talk when the play is on?"

"Usually because we want to hear something interesting being said."

"Then you need to come to my parties."

"I do. And we know what happens there."

Bored now, the audience waited for Belinda's second-act appearance. Someone actually hissed at a roustabout vaudeville comic who delivered a string of tepid jokes. A fawning hotel clerk questioned a bedraggled Wall Street businessman. "A room for sleeping or jumping?" I cringed.

Tommy Stuyvesant had assembled a motley array of acts, but his dramatic sense was faultless. At the penultimate moment the lights dimmed, the orchestra began a teasing rumble of saxophone and midnight piano, a calculated pause, and Belinda appeared in a smoky purplish haze of light. Stretched out on a crushed-velvet chaise lounge, her face illuminated but shadowy, she sang a bittersweet lament of lost love, a surprising timbre to her voice, breaking at the end, a tear in her syllables. No longer Fanny Brice, now she bore echoes of Helen Morgan, the torch singer belting out "Can't Help Lovin' Dat Man" from *Show Boat*, the svelte saloon singer draped over a piano. A woman for all seasons, this fetching Circe. Two rows behind me a woman sobbed, then tittered with embarrassment.

And then it was over. The soft light on her face disappeared, a moment of silence as the purple fog dissipated, and the audience stood on its feet. Thunderous, overwhelming, in fact, and accompanied by shouts, huzzahs, and shrill whistles. Noel turned to me. "I never thought…" His voice trailed off.

"Why would we?" I answered, glancing at Dougie.

Still seated and dragging a white handkerchief across his moist cheeks, he looked up at me, puppy-dog wonder in his eyes, and mumbled, "She loves *me*." He stressed the last word. "She sings to me."

Backstage, huddled into a narrow hallway of the ancient theater, we watched as a stream of well-wishers and idle sycophants worked their way in and out of Belinda's dressing room.

Finally, signaled by an anxious Dougie, we walked in. Belinda was removing the last of her makeup, her face close to the mirror.

"I'm exhausted." Her first words to us, though said to the mirror.

Noel cleared his throat. "Belinda, my dear, you are a wonder of the world."

She barely nodded, her gaze still intent on rubbing some lipstick off her mouth. In the mirror's reflection, devoid of her stage makeup, Belinda looked like the pretty farm girl who stepped off a bus at Port Authority.

A small dressing room painted a dull metal-gray, doubtless the scene of hundreds of acts over its century, strings of vaudeville performers and Shakespearean troupes and Edwin Booth copycats who ignored the musty smell of old dry wood, the rancid smell of mouse droppings, the sudden *clank clank* of steam pulsing through old pipes. Such noxious odors warred with the heavy sweetness covering the room because of the bouquets of red roses and white carnations that covered the dressing table. A bowl of hothouse tulips rested on a shelf. No windows—a cell. In the cramped room the abundant flowers made the tight space funereal.

Dougie leaned in and she twisted her head upward so he could plant a peck on her cheek. A quick wink at him, a giggle. She tickled his side, and he jumped, delighted. He started to say something into her ear but she brushed him away. Instead, surprisingly, she glanced up at me, my back to the doorjamb, and said in a sweet voice, "Did I disappoint you, Miss Ferber?"

"Hardly," I answered, surprised. "Why would you say that?"

She smiled but looked uncertain what to say, her eyes cloudy. "Someone told me you're a...a difficult woman to please."

Dougie swallowed nervously while Noel, his eyes flashing, roared, delighted.

"Yes," I said quietly, "I noticed my nemesis Aleck Woollcott in the lobby. I fear he beat a sluggish path to your stage door and..."

A buttery innocence. "He warned me you'd find fault."

"Belinda, my dear, your performance was enchanting."

"Really?"

"A lovely voice."

Belinda sprang up and surprised me by pushing past Dougie, enveloping me in a quick but unwelcome hug. She smelled of a cloying gardenia perfume, so powerful my eyes teared.

She turned to Noel. "Did you enjoy it, Mr. Coward?"

"Madly."

Meanwhile, Dougie, watching this unexpected tableau, was smiling wanly, waiting for her attention. "Dinner at Jack White's," he announced. "They're expecting us. All of us." He pointed at Noel and me.

She shook her head. "I'm exhausted, Dougie. Not tonight. Please. I'm sorry. A good night's sleep. Every night, we go out…"

Dougie drew his lips into a thin line. "I've already reserved a table."

An edge to her voice. "I told you—not tonight."

He glanced at Noel and me, a helpless shrug of his shoulders.

An usher slinked behind me, rapped on the doorjamb so quickly that I jumped. "Sorry, ma'am." His cherubic face was ringed with laughter as he pushed by me. "More flowers for Miss Ross."

Indeed, he was carrying an oversized spray of deep-red roses, two dozen by my count, lacy baby's breath accents, tied up in an enormous satin bow. Gaudy, unnecessary, the huge arrangement dominated the small space. More appropriate, I considered, on the back of the winning horse at the Kentucky Derby. Belinda beamed, cradled the bouquet to her chest, buried her face in the lush blooms, and flashed her eyes at Dougie. "I warned you, Dougie. Stop this."

Dougie faltered. "I didn't. I…"

Belinda slipped the small white note from a creamy white envelope, and read the card. A lazy smile, almost dreamy. "Good Lord."

"Who?" Dougie's one word, sputtered.

Belinda faced me, a conspiratorial grin on her face. "Wallace Benton," she announced. "Again." Then, louder, a thrill in her voice, "Wallace Benton. The new skyscraper that…"

Suddenly Dougie lunged forward and ripped the card from her hand. Eyes blinking wildly, he stared at the printed words. He read out loud: "'You are Manhattan's newest and brightest angel.' Like hell." He tore the card into shreds and flung the pieces into the air. He grasped the bouquet from Belinda, swung it around the room so that red petals flew off, landed on the dressing table, on the floor, on Belinda's shoulders. Then, a maniac, he beat the bouquet on the edge of the vanity. The satin bow unraveled. Rose petals blanketed her cosmetics table.

Belinda started to cry.

Noel, flummoxed, said in a scratchy voice, "Dougie, for heaven's sake. Who knew you had such a fiery temper? Flowers are sent…"

Dougie held up his trembling hand. "I wasn't born yesterday."

"Frankly," Noel hissed, "you're acting as if you were."

Dougie sputtered. With a flash of embarrassment on his face, he shot by me, pushing his way into the hallway. Over his shoulder he yelled, "The hell with you all."

Quiet in the small dressing room, Noel shifting from foot to foot, a strange noise escaping his throat. I brushed rose petals off my shoulders, sighed, tired now, sick of the childish scene. I tried to think of something to say but finally stepped back, signaling to Noel: *Out of here. Now. Please.* He nodded back at me.

A rose petal was stuck in Noel's blond hair. A blood clot, dark.

Belinda faced her mirror, but her fingers played with a bunch of rose petals. "Wallace Benton," she whispered. Her eyes got wide with alarm. "But this isn't my fault. I didn't send *him* roses." She squeezed the petals. "He's—famous."

"And rich," Noel added. "In America, that's more important than fame."

Belinda narrowed her eyes as she watched Noel turn to leave. "Why can't a body have both?" She looked toward the empty doorway—the departed Dougie. "And love."

By the time Noel and I drifted into the lobby, the theater was empty, the crowds gone. Two bored ushers in sharp-creased pants and gold shoulder braids stood by the front doors, one of them bowing as he opened a door. At that moment I heard an unhappy grunt behind me.

Jackson Roswell stood by the box office window, his back to the glass, his arms folded. In the bright light of the lobby the seersucker suit looked shiny.

"What?" asked Noel.

Jackson sounded angry. "Dougie rushed by. Furious. He wouldn't stop." He took a step toward us, rushing his words. "Tell me what happened?"

I didn't answer, though I stared into his pale face. Noel answered him. "Talk to your sister, Jackson."

But he sputtered, "Tell me what happened?"

"They had a spat," I said. "A lover's quarrel."

The usher waited, holding the door open.

Jackson shook his head wildly. "I called out to him, but he looked right through me." His eyes searched the empty lobby, and then, peering toward the street, the dark sidewalk.

"It's not important." Noel nudged me forward. I approached the open door.

Anger in his voice. "Of course, it's important. Nothing can go wrong,"

I looked back, irritated. "What does that mean?"

His voice quivered. "We worked too hard for this."

"What?" I asked, but Noel, whispering in my ear that the man was a fool, maneuvered me onto the sidewalk. The usher closed the door behind us, though I noticed he watched Jackson warily.

Outside a gust of wind slapped me in the face, and I turned up the collar of my chinchilla coat. Noel stepped into the street to hail a cab while I huddled against the wall, my head turned away from the icy wind. Finally a black cab pulled up, and Noel and I slid into the backseat. The cab sputtered, the driver swore under his breath, a funny Yiddish curse that made me smile, but then he apologized. We turned onto Broadway, idled at a red light.

"Look," I said to Noel.

Jackson Roswell was slowly walking up the sidewalk, bent into the wind and the scattered snowflakes. He plodded along like an old man, his head dipped down. As our cab moved by him, I watched him absently brush against a street sweeper and, rousing himself from his trance, he raised an angry fist at the man. He turned the corner, headed toward Eleventh Avenue. Over his shoulder, angry, he was yelling something to the hapless sweeper. Jostled, the street cleaner paused, rattled. The man was pushing a straw broom, shuffling discarded programs into a heap by a trash bin. A fortyish man in a shabby, unbuttoned overcoat, he wore a rumpled business suit. A loose necktie. Kid gloves. A battered fedora on his head, pulled down against the chill. For a moment he gazed after the departed Jackson, but then, slowly turning, he stared back into the street. Our cabbie pressed the accelerator and we glided swiftly through the light. But I stared into the man's face—dull, haunted eyes that were so vacant they seemed drained of all life.

Chapter Five

Lady Maud once sat next to me at a charity auction at the Plaza Hotel's Palm Court. A number of authors, myself included, donated manuscripts for a silent auction to benefit homeless shelters and soup kitchens throughout the city. I parted with an early draft of *So Big*, boldly signed. Once she learned who I was—I was introduced to her as "Edna Ferber, you know, the *Show Boat* lady," an annoying introduction—she fussed and sputtered her pleasure. For the remainder of the dreary luncheon she monopolized me, a hailstorm of chatter about her dead husband, her Fifth Avenue mansion next to one of the Whitneys, her financial whiz kid Douglas—"he insists on being called Dougie, so Newport summer season, no?"—whom I'd not met at that time. And her devotion to the poor.

"Do you know any?" I'd asked, rudely.

Of course, she wasn't listening to me. She talked of the Crash that wiped out much of high society and her fear that Hoover eventually leaving the presidency—and the growing rumors that New York Governor Franklin D. Roosevelt might run for the office—would bring doom to the world she cherished.

I'd tried to ignore her, to no avail. On my left was someone I desperately wanted to talk to. An old friend, Sinclair Lewis, whom I'd known since we were both cub reporters in the Midwest. I called him Red and he called me Tillie, inane nicknames that thrilled us as we laughed like fools through our days in the newsroom. He still had that head of swirling auburn curls, and

I supposed I still reminded him of Tillie, the frivolous young girl with the nose for news. I'd been delighted to find myself seated next to him, ready to catch up on old cronies—and his splashy best-selling success with *Babbitt* and *Main Street*—but our reunion was not meant to be: Lady Maud insisted that she tell me what she thought of the desperate landscape that was Manhattan after the Crash.

"After the fall," I finally told her.

"No, Crash," she'd said into my face.

"America knocked out of Eden," I said back to her.

Puzzled, she had no idea what to say to me.

The next day, to my horror, someone slipped me the roto-gravure section of the *Daily News*. An unseen photographer had snapped Lady Maud smiling at me. "Fifth Avenue tycoon's widow chats with close friend, Edna Ferber." Lady Maud was wearing an outlandish hat—white ostrich feathers, blue roses, an embroidered sombrero brim. Obviously, the photographer delighted in the absurdity. George Kaufman talked of nothing else for days.

So I was surprised when I found a note in my mailbox the morning after the debacle at the New Beacon. Quite simply, Lady Maud requested my presence for coffee. I was sitting in my work room, rereading the cursory note and debating what to do about it—"I expect you remember me, dear Miss Ferber, from social occasions"—when my phone rang. Lady Maud's private secretary calling to confirm my visit.

"I don't know…" I began.

She interrupted, "Lady Maud has a busy schedule. She can see you at eleven. Of course, you have the address."

I smiled. It was as though I was the one begging for an interview and the busy woman of affairs would try to accommodate me.

My curiosity piqued, I agreed, though I found myself sitting with the dead phone in my hand, a foolish smile on my face. I considered phoning George Kaufman, my sometime-collaborator on plays, who relished such encounters with privileged society because, in his words, "They are the stuff of my satire, my bread-and-butter on Broadway." But, no, this was to be my own special moment.

The Maddox mansion was a four-story Italian Gothic townhouse that dated back to the last century. A gigantic gargoyle arched over the massive copper-lined Florentine double doors. Floor-to-ceiling leaded-glass windows. Thick draperies drawn against the sunlight. An anachronism, this building, evidenced by the awful shadows of nearby modern skyscrapers inching their way upward. Up and down the avenue the old-money mansions were disappearing as nouveau riche and entrepreneurial contractors demolished the venerable structures of the Vanderbilts and Astors, and replaced them with towering testaments to new money and privilege.

The rich were moving to Park Avenue, living higher and higher, mansions in the clouds, while the upstart couturier Bergdorf Goodman planted its commercial self in the midst of old gentility. Lady Maud may have faced Central Park and gazed up at blue skies from her back veranda, but the awful shadow of the forty-seven-story Ritz Tower spelled doom for her world. As Noel told me, jesting, "The higher the building, the lower the morals."

As I rang the bell, I listened to the *boom boom boom* of a wrecking ball at the end of the block. The wheeze and thud of wood torn asunder, of bricks toppling onto a sidewalk. Lady Maud probably endured countless agonies as she listened to the end of her world. The death knell of aged-in-the-wood money.

A doorman handed me off to a black maid in starched crinoline and lace cap, who in turn ushered me into a small room decorated with a burgundy velvet settee, mahogany tables, and a wall of curios illuminated by hidden light: doubtless Lady Maud's collection of Bohemian art glass, iridescent pinks and sea blues and lavender that came together as a dizzying rainbow. On a teacart rested a tray of cookies and a small coffee urn. The tantalizing aroma of newly made coffee filled the small space.

Lady Maud walked in and held out her hand. "You consented, dear Miss Ferber. A visit." I nodded. "So many people refuse my impromptu invitations to have coffee." She stopped, stared at the urn, and gently touched a bell on the table. In seconds the maid scurried in and poured coffee.

"I see friends in this cozy room." she went on. "So intimate, no?" Her arm flew out, drifted across the wall of art glass. "A collection from my world travels when I was younger. With my late husband. With little Dougie."

"Lovely."

"I wonder if you mean that." She looked away.

That startled me. "Why?"

A thin smile. "People lie to rich women."

"I don't."

She arched her neck and laughed lightly. "Which, my dear, is why you are here." She sipped the coffee, nodded her head as if approving the taste, and nibbled on a cookie. "I should explain." She watched me over the rim of her cup.

"I'm assuming this has to do with Dougie."

For a moment her eyes flickered and her lips were drawn into a tight line. Putting down the coffee cup, she began fingering the sapphire-and-ruby brooch she wore on her lapel.

Lady Maud was a rail-thin woman with her iron-gray hair pulled up in a French twist. Dressed in a snug pale blue satin morning dress with a brocaded filigreed jacket over her shoulders, she seemed a throwback to a Victorian era, tuffs of lace at the wrist, bands of Chantilly lace at the bodice. But the jewels—at this hour of the morning, no less. Yes, that sunburst brooch on her lapel, a spray of glistening, oversized gemstones. Similar rings on her fingers, ostentatious, luminous. Some diamond-studded barrettes tucked into her elaborate hairdo. I imagined an old-fashioned calling card placed on a silver plate by the front entrance: *Lady Maud. At home. Thursdays.* She saw me looking. "Gifts from my dead husband. Henry liked to see me sparkling. 'I want you to compete with the sun,' he said." She laughed to herself.

"I think you won."

She laughed a full, throaty laugh that broke into a cough.

"When Henry died—what? ten years back, I think—I wept and wept. Alone in the world with my only son. Dougie a naïve young man, fresh from Yale, then at the Wharton School. People avoided me, dear Miss Ferber." She looked away, but then shot a look into my face. "You doubtless have heard that behind my back they call me Lady Maudlin."

I nodded. "People are cruel."

An unfunny smile. "What bothered was not *that*. But the 'Lady' part. Of course, I'm not British aristocracy, to be sure"— she actually shivered as if accused of illegitimate birth—"but the implication that I was—snobbish. 'There goes Lady Maudlin.'" She frowned. "Then Dougie started calling me Lady Maud as a joke, savoring it, thinking it funny, and suddenly there I was." She half-bowed. "Lady Maud." She wrinkled her mouth. "The snob."

I counted a heartbeat. "And are you?"

She considered that for a moment, chose not to answer. Instead her fingers played with the gaudy brooch. That, I supposed, was my answer.

Then, suddenly rattling her coffee cup, she raised her voice and pointed at me, "Yes, dear Miss Ferber, you are here because of Dougie."

I sat up, chilled. "I still don't understand."

With a note of exasperation in her tone, she explained. "Of course, he's mentioned you more than once, someone he likes, I know, but I told him I knew you from charity events, shared conversations, intimate almost." She leaned in, confidential. "I am *happy* you have befriended him. A sensible woman, you are, Miss Ferber, a daughter of the Midwest, as myself. I was born in Topeka, the daughter of prosperous grain merchants, solid folks, stalwart, no-nonsense. Others"—she waved her hand toward the window—"others in this city are—you know how a city panders to base emotions. You are the stuff of—your *So Big* told me you value common sense, honesty, tradition, and…"

I broke in. "I'm not following this."

She reached for a cookie but changed her mind. Her gray eyes darkened. "You and Noel Coward were at the theater last night. To see…Belinda Ross."

"Yes, we were. But I don't understand."

She held up her hands, her bony fingers spread out, fanlike, menacing. "Dougie stopped in here late last night, which surprised me. We've been at odds, the boy and me. He was ranting, wild-eyed, furious. A disturber of my peace. Nonsense flowing from his mouth, profane even—never allowed. A Christian upbringing, God's children. I'd been asleep but listened to his ranting, yet gleaned so little that made sense. This—this Belinda seems to have—I don't know *what* she did. But Dougie stormed off, wandered the cold streets like a Hoover hobo, maybe, and then barged in here." She breathed in, a thin rasp from her throat. "Chaos, Miss Ferber. A comfortable world upended, spilled over from the dirty streets of this godforsaken city."

I leaned forward. "I still don't understand."

She lowered her voice, gentle, as if speaking to a slow child. "He mentioned you and—and Noel Coward, witnesses to his running amok."

I pursed my lips, furious. "And you want me to tell you what happened last night?"

She seemed puzzled. "Oh, God no, Miss Ferber. I *know* what happened. I have my spies. I want you to help me *stop* his insanity. Help me to rid him of that gold-digging hussy."

I choked on my sip of coffee. "Lady Maud, if you think I..."

Her voice a screech. "Listen a moment, dear. Let me tell you a story. Dougie is a child, Miss Ferber." She shook her head back and forth. "I know, I know, he's thirty-five. A man. But you know what I mean. An only child, spoiled miserably by an indulgent father. I was born rich, of course, a comfortable life, but a woman who married a man whose family had money dating back to—to the early republic. Tidewater Virginia properties—Washington. George. So the legend goes. Henry's family is railroads, grain, oil, whatever. Old money. We moved into this...this mausoleum, and I made it a home. Dougie, like his father, had a head for figures—for money. For reasonable investment, grounded money, if you know what I mean. His father lived for money—and so did Dougie. To a point." For a second she looked distracted, as though she'd lost her train of thought. "Yes, a chip off the old block. Wharton School, first in his class, he became a partner in Henry's business."

An edge to my voice. "Why are you telling me all this?"

Impatient, a click in her voice. "Let me get there. Dougie was—what word should I use? Myopic. When Henry died of a heart attack"—she pointed—"right outside this door as I laughed with a friend—Dougie and I became very close. A mother-son bond, unbreakable. He was all I had. I was all he had. We didn't need others. He doted on me, favored me. I was on his arm everywhere. Through my long period of grief, unfortunately much of it public—my days as Lady Maudlin, yes—but beyond. He moved money around, clever. The Crash bothered us, but only a little. The world out *there* fell apart. Beggars everywhere. We had friends who jumped from expensive windows, who threw themselves in front of trains. One jumped off the *Twentieth Century* as it chugged into Chicago. Men who left their wives and children, who wept in last year's clothing. But Dougie's steel-eyed authority saved the day."

"Until," I broke in, "he fell in love."

"Love! Really, Miss Ferber. How you talk! That isn't love. That's—here's a man who *never* had need for romance in his life. Until now. Yes, we went to the theater like everyone else did. To the Metropolitan Opera House to hear Verdi. A lunch at Lorber's on Forty-first, just across the street. Mother and son. Companionable. A table there reserved for us. Cozy, pink lamps and satin wallpaper. Elegant. Folks nodded at us. The museums. Teas. Boating at our country place in Connecticut. Of course. But suddenly Dougie is fascinated with Broadway. He *invests*." She spat out the word. "A mistake."

"He invested in *Tommy's Temptations*."

Her words snarled in a biting tone. "Exactly."

"Then the rest of the story is Belinda Ross."

Her voice broke. "Exactly." She waited a moment. "We started to do battle, the two of us. Unthinkable. Words hurled back and forth, horrible, ugly words." Her eyes got moist as she fished in her pocket for a handkerchief and dabbed at her eyes. "And then suddenly he takes rooms at the Stanhope Club—an old Astor carriage house a block from here—starts hanging around with an old Yale chum, this Corey Boynton, a respectable lad, I suppose, yes, though his family is among the questionable rich, but a bachelor on the town. The two of them. His rooms here, of course, intact, but so many nights—there. There. A stone's throw from my door."

"I still don't see…"

"This Corey is a playboy."

"I've met him."

"I know you have. Dougie tells me everything, but I think it's only to hurt me."

I softened my voice. "Lady Maud, it seems to me he still wants you in his life. His visits here…"

She was shaking her head back and forth vigorously. "No, my dear. Gloating, as I see it. 'Look at me.' When he first met this Belinda, he brought her here. His first love—he was a stammering country boy. He expected me to be civil, to celebrate her, this—this Broadway dancer. I asked them to leave. A number of times my doorman calls—warns. It's Dougie downstairs and he's with Belinda. Otherwise he'd use his own key. It's that he needs…approval to bring her into these rooms."

"And you refuse."

"Every time." Her voice was laced with anger.

"Perhaps that's not wise."

"Perhaps I've lost focus, Miss Ferber."

"And that explains my visit here how?" I waited, looking into her strained face.

She laughed. "I've looked into that girl's history. A pretty girl arrived in this city with ambition. That ramshackle theater her brother runs on Eleventh Avenue, a failed enterprise. Brother and sister, schemers, charlatans. Fakirs. There are friends who tell me things."

"Buzzy Collins?" I threw out.

That stopped her. "Whomever." She held my eye. "Yes, Buzzy. Buzzy Collins, an otherwise useless hanger-on in society, a barnacle, tells me the story. An unlikely chance meeting of that old fool, Cyrus Meerdom, Belinda suddenly the darling of the Great White Way, then Tommy Stuyvesant, another fool, but both lacking the riches of the Maddox family. And then there's Dougie, drool seeping out of his lips, drunk with the attention of that *femme fatale*." She stressed her words, deliberate space between them. "Who follows after Dougie, Miss Ferber? Who? After she breaks his dumb heart? The other night he talked of—marriage." She actually shuddered.

"He's a grown man, Lady Maud."

She stammered, "A babe in the woods, my son. You've seen her. A strumpet. Rouged up, half-naked, sparkling with costume jewelry. Dougie demands I *like* her. Impossible."

"At a certain time in a man's life, he can say no to his mother."

Fiercely: "No, he can't." Then, her eyes slits, "There are ways of ruining that harlot's life, Miss Ferber. I am a powerful woman."

Uncomfortable, I rustled in my seat, tugged at the sleeve of my blouse. I was ready to leave. "I still don't understand my visit here."

She waited a moment, then exploded. "I blame Noel Coward, Miss Ferber."

I sat up. "Noel? How?"

She sat back, her voice seething. "He met Dougie at some function, liked him, seems to like all young men, drew him into the world of theater. Actresses, backstage parties. A mistake. Yes, a brilliant raconteur, so they tell me, a playwright with smart and sassy chatter. Unfortunately, I've seen one of his—farces. Dreadful. British, Miss Ferber. An effete dandy, sashaying around in those tweeds and polo shirts and that ivory cigarette holder. I met him once, of course. That clipped voice. Terribly smart. We don't talk like that in America."

I smiled broadly. "*Vanity Fair* termed them Noelisms, you know. Jazzy chatter. I find…"

She would have none of it. "I don't see why you find him so companionable."

"We like each other."

"He called me…darling."

I laughed out loud. "He calls everyone darling."

"It's not funny. I'm nobody's darling."

"I assume that."

"He's taken a liking to my son, advising him, he says. I don't like the British."

"You've already mentioned that." I paused. "Noel is a good friend of mine—and a good friend to Dougie. I think your son needs someone to confide in, to share…"

Again, the raised hand in my face. "Miss Ferber."

"No," I went on forcefully, "there is no way I can help you, Lady Maud."

"Your influence."

Now I raised my voice. "No, this is preposterous."

"I would have thought you'd sympathize."

I bristled. "Then you would have thought incorrectly. You don't know me, madam. I value my friendship with Noel." Blindly, I went to lift my coffee cup, but my hand shook. The cup dropped back into the saucer. The sound of chipped porcelain.

Her eyes on the broken cup. "Dougie is impressionable."

"That may be. Yes, Dougie strikes me as a trifle immature, especially grating in someone who's thirty-five and educated."

She spoke quietly. "The problem, Miss Ferber, is that Dougie is too trusting. A little naïve, despite Horace Mann, and Yale and Wharton and…"

I stood up. "He has to fashion his own life."

She looked up at me. "You're a sensible woman, Miss Ferber."

"That I am, Lady Maud. And my senses tell me this is not a place where I care to be right now."

Her eyes glazed over. "You sound so harsh."

"Good. Then my vocal chords are working as I want them to."

"What does that mean?"

"Good-bye, Lady Maud."

"I've offended you," she whispered, though her tone was not apologetic. If anything, it was—bafflement.

I said nothing but stepped away.

To my back she hissed, "I thought you were a different person."

I swung back to stare into her face. "That news is oddly comforting to me."

"What do you mean?"

"Thank you for coffee, Lady Maud."

As I stepped out of the room, I nearly collided with the maid, standing at attention, listening. She looked afraid. From behind me, Lady Maud yelled, "That Coward man has brainwashed my son. He keeps telling him over and over that he has a right to be"—she paused, seemingly at a loss for words—"interesting. That he's something he's not. Interesting." Wonder in her raspy voice. "Now why would he tell him that?"

Chapter Six

I stood on the icy sidewalk, nodding thanks to Lady Maud's doorman. My mind swam, a kaleidoscope of anger and awe and confusion. What had just happened in there? Why had Lady Maud invited me? To sabotage her son's romance? To get Noel Coward to back off a budding friendship? How did that imperious woman view me—the interloper, the buttinsky, the crusher of someone's dream life?

Belinda Ross and her brother. I flashed to the disturbing image of Jackson Roswell shuffling up the sidewalk last night, hunched against the wind, angry. A schemer? Lady Maud's condemnation: fakirs, both of them. Brother and sister.

Impulsively, I hailed a cab and told the driver to head to Eleventh Avenue. The cabbie was chewing on the stub of a noxious cigar, so I cracked the window. Cold air seeped in, delightful. "Ma'am," he looked back, "it's winter, you know."

"It also reeks of decaying bodies."

He grunted and tightened his grip on the steering wheel.

The cabbie sped through Times Square, past busy movie houses. A lively street, this time of day, crowds gaping at the colored Christmas lights strung in windows, the dim-wattage neon of a bright but freezing afternoon. A large truck, angled into a corner, dispensed sandwiches and coffee to a line of homeless souls. A cheap movie house, the Rivoli, had a line snaking up the block. With their evocative soundtracks—the voice of Greta Garbo wowing the world, echoes in the dark—movies had wooed theatergoers away from live performance, pushed the legit theaters to the side streets. Times Square pulsed and throbbed, the heartbeat of Manhattan, though perhaps that heartbeat missed a few beats.

Color, verve, zing sprang from the splashy billboards with flashing electric lights displaying Planter's Peanuts' golden peanuts showering down from the unseen heavens, a little Eskimo Pie boy bowing from the waist, a huge Camel cigarette with a glowing red tip. A burlesque house that promised leggy showgirls. White-jacketed street sweeps pushed brooms as passersby moved around them. And noise—frenetic din from the blasting radio shops, the music vendors. Chop suey joints, corner candy shops, a dime museum, a tobacco shop with a blue-flame gas jet on the counter for smokers to light their cigars. The Big Stem, the locals called it. Hawkers of jazz journals like the *Daily News*.

Whenever I moved through these streets, I always felt a tick in my chest: alive, alive.

But as the cab veered off Broadway, cruised under the calamitous Ninth Avenue El with its fog of cinders clouding our windshield, and inched its way into Hell's Kitchen, it was as though I'd toppled willy-nilly into the bleak negative of an old daguerreotype. Stolid cold-water tenements and shuttered storefronts, shadowy dullness to the side street, as if a gray shroud settled on the landscape. A grim Hogarth engraving, if you will. A chiaroscuro portrait. As the cab idled at a stoplight, I gazed into a tiny tailor's shop, a slit-eyed old man in a yarmulke hunched over a table under a naked light bulb hanging from the ceiling. He glanced out the window and scratched his beard, then dropped his head back to his work. A junk man whipped a lazy horse that blocked our street. A young bootblack waved at us.

"Here," I told the driver as we turned onto Eleventh Avenue. "The theater."

The Paradise Theater occupied a corner of a weathered four-story brick building. As I stepped out, I looked up the street. A scissors grinder advertised his craft with a handwritten cardboard sign. Next to the theater was a grimy storefront with a makeshift sign over the entrance: Slavonic Fraternal Society. In front, two longshoremen leaned against the plate-glass window, bundled up in burlap coats, cigarettes bobbing in their mouths, slough boy caps pulled tight over foreheads. For a moment they watched me, the tiny lady in the chinchilla coat and ermine muffler, as I paused on the sidewalk, but then, indifferent, they resumed their conversation—a rumble of Slavic tones. Fascinated, I watched, intrusive.

Across the street was a Salvation Army soup kitchen with a line of men spilling out the front door and extending down the block. The worm that walks like a man—that was how Heywood Brown described such sad lines. So stunning, that lamentable sight. A hiss of steam seeped from the sidewalk grate and one of the men stepped over it, rubbed his palms together, yelled something back to the others in line. A burst of rollicking laughter. An old man in a porkpie hat suddenly danced a nervous gig, while another man clapped.

The front doors of the Paradise Theater were wide open, despite the stinging cold. A wooden ladder leaned against the brick façade, and a stumpy man in farmer's dungarees, balancing himself on a top rung, was using a crowbar to twist off the old sign from the marquee, a small wooden sign with peeling gray paint that announced the name of the theater but added: "Nightly Musical Revue!!" Two exclamation points. "All invited." A carnival sideshow, this place.

Resting on the sidewalk was a new metal sign, triple the size, glossy and bright, its borders edged with a string of neon lights: Paradise Theater. No other embellishment, no sideshow barker's entreaty to passing customers. The man on the ladder pulled at the old sign and it creaked, moaned, finally gave way, slipping down. "Watch it, ma'am," he yelled to me.

I slipped into the lobby as the sound of hammering echoed in my ears.

I entered the small space with a phone-booth-sized box-office window that opened into an auditorium of perhaps one hundred seats covered in old crushed burgundy velvet. It reminded me of old-style provincial vaudeville theaters back in Milwaukee or Duluth. Worn, faded, with barely a hint of their splendid history. Flickering gas-lit sconces on the tapestried walls. A surprisingly large stage, the curtain up.

A man stepped from the wings, his arms cradling a wooden box. He jumped when I cleared my throat. "Sorry, ma'am. Didn't see you." He widened his eyes, looking down at me. "Something I can do for you?"

"I'm looking for Jackson Roswell."

Before I could finish, he pointed toward the ceiling but didn't answer me. Silently, still pointing upward, he walked down the stairs and stood a few feet away from me.

"Kent LaSalle here." A quick smile, an exaggerated half-bow. "Ah, Miss Edna Ferber."

Surprised, I smiled back. "You know me?"

"I read *Theater World. Stage.* You—George Kaufman."

"Yes, we're jointed at the hip."

A wide, wonderful smile. "I'd say the funny bone—wherever that part of the anatomy is located. You could be joined with a lot of other lesser forms of mankind."

I raised my eyebrows. "There is that, sir."

He laughed out loud, rocking back and forth, though what I'd said didn't warrant such hilarity. But I'd long learned that folks exaggerated their most basic reactions when dealing with famous people—as myself. The laughter too long and uproarious, the stares too intense, facile agreement with every remark uttered.

He gave me another half-bow accompanied by a hand flourish he'd obviously appropriated from a Valentino movie.

Probably in his late sixties, maybe older, the man seemed an old veteran of the stage, probably a vaudeville trooper who'd played backwater towns like Kalamazoo, Michigan, or Dubuque, Iowa. A circuit I knew—and loved. He was tall, stringy, with a drawn Lincolnesque face, almost a horse face, with skimpy white hair that needed a barber's shears. He wore a cultivated handlebar moustache, the edges tipped up and shellacked. But his eyes caught me, held me: piercing cobalt blue, made more striking in such a withered, pale face. He folded his arms over his chest, showing arthritic hands, fingers twisted.

"Upstairs." He pointed again. "His apartment is a floor above us. Or he's out on an errand. He's never away for very long. His heart ticks in these rooms." He chuckled. "We got a new sign going up."

"So I noticed."

"Depression and Herbert Hoover, be damned."

"Flush times in a time of despair?"

He eyed me curiously. "The second coming of theater on skid-row Eleventh Avenue."

"Mr. Roswell is in the money?"

He didn't answer at first. Then, his arm stretching out over the battered seating. "New seats to be installed. The glorious Roxy will have nothing on us."

"You don't sound happy about it, Mr. LaSalle."

"It don't matter when the house seats stay empty."

"Well, after the Crash, all theaters…"

He cut me off. "Look. I play character parts, Miss Ferber. I deliver a tired Shakespearean soliloquy, rewritten with a comic edge." His voice got stentorian. "Toupee or not toupee." He shuddered. "It would be even sadder if there was someone in the audience to moan at that line. Throw rotten apples." He sneered. "Of course, if someone *had* an apple, they'd eat it."

"And yet you have a new sign, new seats."

He performed a silent drum roll. "Belinda Ross. That's why you're here. Of course." He swung around and pointed up at the stage. "Here is where the darling of the Great White Way began her ascent into the heavens."

"I've seen her onstage, Mr. LaSalle. Exciting. Talented, almost surprisingly so. A sweet voice."

He rushed his response. "And a sweet girl, really. Ambitious as all get out—Lord, you could see the hunger in her eyes—but every two-bit actor that gets off a bus from the provinces is ambitious. You *have* to be to make it here. It's no crime." He shrugged his shoulders. "I was once guilty of such vanity."

I smiled back at him. "I sense a 'but' in your words."

He drew back. "Did you ever read *Frankenstein*?" he asked suddenly.

"Mary Shelley. Of course."

A chuckle. "No one else has, but that's beside the point. Talented girl, yes, and sweet. But cagey, her eye always out that door, her eyes looking eastward to Broadway. Not a crime, as I said. More like the pretty monster forged by the demonic scientist." He contorted his face, deepened his voice. "Ah, Dr. Frankenstein, what have you created?" He waved his hand absently in the air.

"But why Frankenstein? I'm not following this."

He spat out the words. "Jackson Roswell. The doctor of black arts."

"Her brother? Yet you work for him, no?"

He pulled out his pockets, and shrugged. "Pittance in a time of despair, if I can play off your words." A deep sigh. "I shouldn't complain. Her dollar bills and her current paramour Dougie's generous checks—they keep us afloat." A wry smile. "You *did* see that garish sign going up on the marquee?"

Suddenly a side door swung open, a shaft of light illuminated the dark theater, and a woman bustled in. She'd obviously been listening because she was laughing as she spoke to us, though there was nothing funny about that sardonic, cautionary laugh. "Kent, you old coot. Blather and nonsense, really. You know, Miss Ferber, Kent once acted with Edwin Booth. Or was it John Wilkes Booth? Or Benedict Arnold in his younger days? His stories of his triumphs date back to Bunker Hill."

Kent scowled and leaned into me. "Always ready to make a stage entrance, but always to no applause. Miss Ferber, doubtless you don't know Millie Glass, our faded ingénue who still can don a pinafore and talk like an awestruck farm girl gaping at a rainbow and wondering how to buy one."

Millie listened to this run of talk with a bemused eye, then roared in a thick whiskey voice. "At least I have all my teeth, dear Kent. Those wooden ones you stole from George Washington."

He broke her off. "Eavesdropping again, dear Millie?"

She approached us and stuck out her hand. "Miss Ferber, a pleasure."

I nodded back at her. "Longtime friends, the two of you?"

"Kent and I have traveled the boards since creation. We've seen each other without makeup—or without the stage personas we created to keep the world away. Of course, we detest each other. He knows my vices, I barely tolerate his."

Kent was fussing. "Stop performing, Millie."

"What else do I have left?"

A thirtyish woman, slightly plump, but still insisting she look as young as possible. She wore a bobbed Anita Loos haircut, out of fashion but probably hers for life. Tired eyes, grayish. A small mouth, exaggerated now by a smear of dark crimson lipstick. Her hair was dyed platinum blond, but, offstage, was now pulled away from her forehead, bunched in back by a black, oversized ribbon. When she threw back her head, a dramatic gesture she did repeatedly, I saw that she'd once been a beauty—the delicate line of her chin, the soft cheekbones, the almond eyes, pixie ears.

"I'm waiting to see Jackson Roswell," I said into the silence.

A sarcastic hiss. "You mean you're not one of the stage-door Johnnies come to worship at the altar of Belinda's nativity?"

"Not quite."

"Do you know how many such souls we turn away, scatter to the winds?"

"She is the shining light of the moment."

She barked at me, "For the moment."

"I take it you weren't fond of her, Miss Glass?"

She debated what to say, glancing over her shoulder toward the doorway. "I'm not fond of anyone, Miss Ferber, though these days Jackson has discovered *my* charms. I've scraped my way into the bowels of this hole in the wall. Jackson needs me as much as I need him. Together we have plans—his passion, mine. I'm sure you know how acting gets into the bloodstream—the rhythm of the stage." She smiled broadly. "As for Belinda—I knew her as Linda Roswell, fresh in this city—I mentored her."

Kent scoffed, "And you tell everyone how you paid a price for that."

"What price?" I asked disingenuously.

Millie narrowed her eyes. "I actually liked her—fresh, funny, clever really. A real gem of talent, undiscovered. Unlike Jackson who lives and breathes theater but can't say a line that's authentic. He *needs* me. I guess I already said that, right? It needs repeating—especially to him. Anyway, I liked her, taught her makeup, to carry herself in a certain way."

I drummed my finger on my lips. "But success spoiled her?"

She shouted a line. "Unforgiving. Once a student realizes she is brighter, more talented than the instructor, she can go this way or that. One path leads to humility. The other to arrogance."

"And I take it Belinda chose to lord it over you."

She nodded furiously.

Kent spoke up. "You're exaggerating, Millie." He looked at me. "Miss Ferber, Millie—is acting a part here. And not a major role, really. Millie, the walk-on. Belinda is temperamental, yes, but kind…"

"Baloney, you fool. Men get weak around her."

"I liked her."

"Lord, she even betrayed Jackson, who orchestrated her success on Broadway. He called the shots. The girl would betray God if it could get her a starring role in heaven." She looked up to the ceiling. "The two of them living above us, like in the heavens. Brother and sister. The royal couple."

"I sense things changed."

"She's gone, living in the uppity residence hotel for young women. Elite. And Jackson walks around in shiny Norfolk suits, powder blue, black-and-white fancy shoes."

"And jangling coins in his pocket," Kent added.

With a glint in her eyes, she said, "And now I live upstairs with Jackson."

Kent stepped back, a valedictory wave and a half-bow, but Millie, speaking into his face, mumbled, "Have you seen Chauncey? We're supposed to rehearse. Has he disappeared again?"

A low rumble sounded from the back of the theater, a voice shrouded in darkness. "I'm here enjoying the bitchiness of my inferiors."

Millie jumped, squirmed, but immediately swore. "You damn fool, Chauncey."

A shadowy figure rose from the back of the house, stepped into the dim light. "Nothing like a dark theater to remind you that your life has no meaning."

"You're sneaky," Millie said, peeved.

"I was napping until you all began ad-libbing."

Kent, already halfway to the door, turned to me. "Miss Ferber, meet Chauncey White, our juvenile in romantic skits as well as the Italian tenor who sings 'O Sole Mio' while teetering in a gondola."

Chauncey nodded at me but said nothing.

The youngish man of average height, broad-chested, had a square handsome face and a five o'clock shadow, his shock of blue-black hair worn almost in a pompadour. He was wearing a bulky blue sweater that accented his rugged outdoorsy look.

Millie sneered, "Ah, Miss Ferber, here's Belinda's first discarded flame. Her rehearsal lover, or so the rumors suggested."

"Stop that, Millie." Chauncey sucked in his cheeks. "You know that's a lie."

Kent decided to stay. "Chauncey had a crush on Belinda— when she was still Linda Roswell. But of course all red-blooded men did. Bonny Linda. Unrequited love, which is the worst kind. Mooning over an ice maiden."

"Dreamers, the both of you." Chauncey walked near one of the flickering lights, his face in shadows. "Miss Ferber, we did love scenes onstage, anemic as all get out, Southern belle and Yankee intruder, but that's all." His tone reflected bitterness, perhaps. "We *liked* each other."

"Why are you here, Miss Ferber?" Millie asked.

"To see Jackson."

Her voice rose. "Why?"

"Curiosity."

She laughed. "Killed the cat, you know."

Kent interrupted, "Miss Ferber, you must come for one of our performances."

Chauncey murmured, "And sit anywhere."

Kent was amused. "Like third row center. Jackson told us you sat between Dougie and Noel Coward at Belinda's show."

Chauncey spoke in singsong, "Dougie, Dougie, bags of money."

Millie hissed, "We're trying to keep this theater alive, Chauncey. Me and Jackson."

He mimicked her. "'Me and Jackson.' Suddenly it's a joint venture."

Kent, in a stage voice, "Did you hear about the two bankers who jumped off the Ritz Tower holding hands? They had a joint account."

"That's not funny," Millie said.

Chauncey was gathering his coat and heading back toward the doorway. "The truth of the matter is that Belinda was afraid to look any of us in the face—unless Jackson ordered her to. She was always looking for an escape from this hovel."

"Her brother?" I asked.

Chauncey laughed. "Hey, Jackson was the magician charting the course out there—drawing the map. An X marked the treasure trove. Over there." He pointed in the direction of Broadway.

He disappeared out the door, though he stumbled as he came face-to-face with Jackson entering from the lobby. He'd been yelling something to one of the workmen, but stopped when he saw me standing with two of his players. He grumbled to a departing Chauncey, unhappy, "How long has she been here?"

But as he approached me, his face broke into a wide, manufactured grin. He extended his hand. "Miss Ferber, to what do we owe the pleasure?"

"Idle curiosity. Dougie mentioned your theater."

He waved his hands around the dark room. "Humble beginnings."

"We've been spilling the family secrets," Kent told him.

Jackson squinted. "Don't believe a word they've told you."

"And what do you think they told me?"

He laughed, gave a foolish twist of his head. "Unhappy, Kent is, but earning a salary. Everyone I hire thinks they should be starring on Broadway. Or in Hollywood." He said the last word with a snarl. "The new golden land. Star of stage and screen. But we're small-time at the Paradise, Miss Ferber. The ragtag end of vaudeville."

I waited a moment. "So this is a graveyard."

He looked uncomfortable. "Hardly." He offered a sickly smile. "We did produce a Belinda Ross."

"*You* produced a Belinda Ross, as I understand it."

"Look," he said, lowering his voice, "I live for theater. That's all I know. All my life. Back to that small town in Connecticut where we sang and danced in the town hall for the yokels. We dreamed of New York, Belinda and me. You know, our mother was an old vaudeville hoofer back at the turn of the century. She used to tell us she danced with Little Egypt at the World's Fair in Chicago, in fact. In our blood. All of us." His voice rose. "It's in my blood. I'll die in a room like this."

"I agree with you, sir. Theater is in my blood."

He looked over my shoulder toward the stage. "After the Crash it all got harder."

I broke in. "Well, Belinda's newfound success and Dougie's change purse seem to help, no?"

He laughed nervously. "Yes, true. My good fortune. His coins will let me mount a new show, new talent." He glanced at Millie who'd sidled up to him, tucked her arm into his elbow.

"With Millie? The others?"

She answered for him. "We're a team. New lighting. New stage crew. Everything costs money."

Jackson didn't say anything. Kent wore a thin smile on his face.

"Dougie is an interesting man," I began. "I'm afraid his mother, you know, Lady Maud, doesn't favor your sister or this outpost theater."

His face tightened, his voice acid. "You know her?"

"I had coffee with her earlier today. One of the reasons I decided to come here—to see for myself. Her judgment seemed... severe."

His hand flew up to his face, fire in his eyes. "Did she send you?"

That surprised me. "Why would she do that?"

"A spy?"

I breathed in, irritated. "Are you accusing me of being here *because* of her? To do her bidding?"

"Dougie has told me of her—her opposition. Her hatred of Belinda. Her distrust of me."

"Mr. Roswell, I am nobody's spy. I came out of a simple curiosity."

"A word you used before." From Millie, looking up at Jackson's face. "You expect us to believe that?"

I turned away. "I don't care what you believe."

Jackson wasn't through. "She's a vicious, cruel woman." He started to say something else, but stopped and sucked in his breath.

"Yes," I agreed, "a dangerous woman." I waited a heartbeat. "A woman determined to win."

"She wants to destroy Belinda's career." Jackson stared into my face.

I shrugged. "I don't think she cares about Belinda's career, sir. What she cares about is Dougie making a fool of himself."

His eyes swept the theater, panicked. "We've worked too hard for failure."

"We?"

"Yes, Miss Ferber. We. Me and Linda." He caught his breath. "Though these days her dumb passion has made her—distant." He deliberated, his brow furled. "Difficult."

Millie tightened her grip on his sleeve. "Difficult," she echoed. Both remained quiet, watching me.

The two exchanged looks. When Jackson looked back at me, he had a scowl on his face. "Good day."

Unnerved, I swiveled, walked up the aisle, out of the orchestra. In a final triumphant gesture, I pulled at the heavy door, slammed it shut. Nothing, I knew from years in the theater, sounded more thunderous and final than a solid theater door emphatically slammed. Smiling, I headed across the lobby.

On the sidewalk, fuming, I watched the workmen wrestle with the glossy sign, but then turned the corner, headed back to Forty-second Street. A brisk walk, but I didn't want to wait for a taxi to cruise by. Icy wind bit my face, and I turned up the collar of my fur coat.

Chilled, regretting the walk—a gang of shabby youngsters pointed, remarking on my fur coat—I stopped near a small luncheonette, craving a cup of coffee. A five-and-dime eatery, I realized from the scribbled sign over the doorway, filled with poor folks. An egg, baked beans, a bowl of thin soup, a powdered doughnut, a cup of coffee. All for six cents. A line waiting, shabby collars pulled up around necks. As I stared in, a customer walked out, bundled in a pullover cap and scarf. I smelled burnt coffee, cloying, and the raw hint of grease on a grill. I turned away. But the man stopped in front of me and unwrapped the heavy scarf.

"Miss Ferber. We meet again."

Chauncey White wagged a gloved finger at me.

I smiled back at him. "Mr. White, fresh from improvisational drama at the Paradise."

"Answers?" He waited.

I stepped back. "I didn't ask a question."

"Of course you did." He pointed back down the block. "Back there. At the theater." He was enjoying himself.

"And what was my question?"

"You're wondering when—" He stopped and sang in a rumbling baritone, "Here we go round the merry-go-round. All fall down."

"An unhappy ending to this story?"

In a melancholy tone, slow, hesitant, he said, "A late-night jazz tune wailing through the wee hours. Everybody waiting for the ball to fall."

"You're the prophet of doom, Mr. White."

He saluted me, then walked past. "Ma'am, wrap yourself tight in that stunning chinchilla coat. The rest of us are one step away from a small bowl of tomato soup and a chunk of stale bread in that breadline I see every day when I turn onto Eleventh Avenue."

Chapter Seven

After the theater or a movie at the Roxy, anyone flush with cash headed to 21 or El Morocco or the El Fey Club—or, if thirsty, one of the flourishing speakeasies dotting the Manhattan landscape, like Texas Guinan's 300 Club. Some did both, dancing the night away, tipsy and often draped over chromium bars, scotch highballs in hand. I was not one of those people—a dinner with cocktail at Neysa's was one thing, but public tomfoolery, I always insisted, was the stuff of lost souls. Noel and I, leaving the theater after enjoying Clifton Webb in *Flying Colors* and a late-night dinner at the Ritz, careened into Dougie Maddox, lit with whiskey and bumping into parked cars. His face was wreathed in boyish smiles as he spotted the two of us on the sidewalk.

"Christmas," he warbled. "Almost Christmas."

"Not yet," I answered. "Santa's still in his workshop."

"Every day is Christmas when you're in love."

Beside me, Noel groaned and mumbled something about Dougie's having no future as a playwright.

Dougie was walking with Belinda and Corey Boynton and a young girl I'd not met. Dressed against the cold night in Cossack fur hats and woolen mufflers and bulky cashmere coats, the men struck me as North Pole explorers, though Corey sported a dandyish Windsor knot and Dougie a white silk scarf. Not so the women: Belinda wore a Persian lamb coat cut to accentuate her figure, with a mink cap as a stylish accent. The other woman wore fox furs draped over a red velvet coat. As they approached us, the two women were leaning into each other, confiding.

"We had a few belts at Texas Guinan's," Corey told us.

"They asked us to leave," Dougie mumbled, indignant. "Famous people asked to leave."

"We were too loud," Corey added. "Actually this man here—Dougie—was too loud. The rest of us just laughed."

Noel faced Belinda. "You didn't perform tonight? Your show?"

A nervous laugh. "I snuck out after my second number."

Noel frowned. "You skipped curtain call?" He shot a look at me. "That's...forbidden."

Belinda nodded. "I know, I know. Tommy was *furious*." She giggled as Dougie gently poked her. "So unprofessional."

Noel *tsk*ed. "You don't do that, Belinda. The audience expects..."

She stopped moving, her voice sailing over our heads. "You know, I'm tired of people telling me what to do. Tommy's too... possessive." She wrapped her arms around her chest and started to move away.

I caught Noel's eye. Irritation there, but also a little wonder. "Your idea, Dougie?" he said finally.

Dougie stammered, "I—I—it doesn't matter."

"Everything in the theater matters," Noel said flatly, turning away. He wasn't happy. When it came to theater, he played by exacting, inviolable rules.

Dougie tried to look apologetic, but failed, a sloppy grin on his face. Belinda tucked her arm under his elbow, smiled at him, but said to Noel, a rasp in her voice, "I may have made a mistake."

Noel sputtered, his tone very British, "Really?"

"And you are?" I addressed the young woman at Belinda's side, her face frozen in a simpleton's smile.

Corey Boynton answered for her. "My manners, Miss Ferber. This is Kitty Baker. She was in the chorus of *Saturday's Child* at the Corcoran, just closed. She claims she understudied Ruby Keeler in a preview last spring. A new face in Manhattan." With a tickle in his voice, he added, "Or at least that's what she told me. She may be a liar."

Kitty, anxious to talk, spoke over the last of Corey's words. "I am not new in town. I've *been* here." She looked at me, eager. "I have rooms across the hall from Belinda. At the Claremont Residence Hall for Women. When Belinda moved in, we became friends." She threw a glance at Belinda, a look that struck me as unfriendly. That confounded me.

Corey finished, slurring his words, "Then she discovered my charms." He tried to be funny. "I'm still trying to discover *her* charms."

Kitty was short, dark-complexioned, her black hair cascading over her shoulders in marcelled waves, though she topped it with a jaunty veiled pillbox hat, an unsuccessful take on Garbo's movie look. She had a wide face with small pinpoint eyes, a small Cupid's-bow mouth between rouged dimples. In a certain light, I thought cruelly, the girl would be considered attractive—coy, maybe even fetching. Unfortunately, the glare from the streetlight was not one of those forgiving lights. Her red velvet evening coat only exaggerated her desire to stand out. I thought of high-school days—the pretty girl with the frumpy girlfriend. Worse, the plain Jane who wanted to be with the pretty girl, but maybe resented her. A harsh judgment, I admit, but she lacked Belinda's drop-dead come-hither face.

Corey playfully wrapped his arm around her waist, pulled her in to him, a lover's hold, and for a second buried his face in her neck. Though she squealed, she kept her eyes on Belinda. But then—so did Corey.

I nudged Noel. *Let's leave.*

Noel hesitated, his eyes locked on the partying foursome. "Edna, darling, look at these revelers on the ice-cold Manhattan streets." Then, almost wistfully, he pointed at them. "When I first arrived in Manhattan in 1921, these streets took my breath away. The volcanic movement, the thrill of noise and light." He waved his hand over the sidewalk. "To be young in Manhattan!"

I frowned, which everyone ignored. "And that's supposed to interest me—how?"

He smiled at me, but Dougie broke in, his face lively. "Miss Ferber, the night is young. Come with us. We are going to see the Christmas lights. There's a lighted tree at the new Rockefeller Center. It's—glorious at night." He was bubbly. "Then we're going caroling."

Late night, my warm apple-green bed, my wood-burning fireplace, a cup of tea, a book by Pearl Buck, perhaps. Or—the frivolous company of drunken partiers singing "O Holy Night" off-key, lips blue from the cold.

I agreed reluctantly, though I shot Noel a cautionary look. He did his best to ignore my cranky disposition, and reluctantly I found myself returning his engaging smile. He gallantly grasped my elbow as we moved toward Rockefeller Center.

Bizarrely, as we moved, Dougie suddenly seemed out of sorts, dancing around us, a nervous grin appearing then disappearing on his face. Corey watched him closely, puzzled, at one point whispering, "You all right, Dougie?"

Dougie didn't answer. Instead he draped a possessive arm around Belinda's shoulder, nuzzled his face into her neck, and mumbled something I didn't catch. Surprised, she looked into his face, tapped his lips with her fingertip, and gave him a quick peck on the cheek. But the minute she pulled away, gossiping with Kitty, his body got rigid, a melancholic look sweeping his features. A chameleon, I thought—the man whose emotions flashed pell-mell from one unstable extreme to the other. Perhaps sheltered under his mother's forbidding wing, shielded by his dead father's monomaniacal thirst for money, the thirty-five-year-old Dougie, suddenly playing in the quixotic courts of love, had no idea what to do—what not to do. How do you teach a spoiled little boy to play nice?

Midnight—I heard the bells at St. Patrick's toll the hour—and Rockefeller Center hummed and sang. Bundled-up crowds circled the magnificent tree, a wash of brilliant light against a snow-white sky. Snow flurries circled our heads, and the biting wind from the East River stung. Tinny Christmas music wafted from an unseen speaker. Out-of-town tourists—and, I supposed, in-town folks, as well—stood near the tree while others snapped pictures with their boxy Kodaks. Suddenly we were all very happy.

Even dour me, hungry for bed.

Belinda was in a cheerful mood as she linked arms with Dougie, who beamed.

Kitty caught my attention because she stopped walking, her arms thrust out, a mischievous grin on her face.

"What?" I asked.

She sidled up to the couple. "Look." She pointed up at the towering skyscrapers etched against the night sky. The glistening Chrysler Building with its Deco brilliance. The distant top of the Empire State Building. All around us buildings were aiming for the heavens, punching their glass-and-steel way into the starlit night. "Look," she insisted, "isn't that the new Benton skyscraper?"

The wrong thing to say, obviously. Dougie, stepping back, dropped Belinda's arm, glowered. Not at Kitty, who wouldn't stop yammering about city life up in the clouds—but at Belinda.

Corey nudged Kitty, adding, "Lord Almighty, Wallace Benton's white elephant in a time of Depression. Can you believe it? Floor after floor of offices no one will ever rent. Like the Empire State Building. Mostly empty." A mysterious smile. "But a penthouse on the top floor. A lair for mistresses."

Belinda ignored them, waving into the sky. "I think it's magnificent."

"Piles of money," Corey went on. "I can only imagine." His voice got sad. "Not everyone went bust in '29."

"He has more than enough to spare," Belinda added.

"Yeah," Dougie seethed, twisting his head so that his face was inches from hers, "he can send you more flowers."

Belinda sighed but touched his cheek. "Oh, Dougie, it's nothing. A stage-door admirer. I have so many." She stepped back from him.

He spoke through clenched teeth. "And an invitation to supper?"

Her words clipped. "Which I refused."

Dougie stamped his foot. "For now."

"What does that mean?" She glared at him as she took another step away. "Not now, Dougie, okay?" For a second she shut her eyes.

"Money, Belinda."

She whispered, annoyed, "I'm with you, aren't I?" She reached out to touch his cheek but he backed off.

Corey, still a little tipsy, winked playfully. "For now." He danced a two-step, exaggerated. "For now," he repeated, singing out the words, enjoying himself.

"What the hell does that mean?" Dougie flared at his friend.

Corey's eyes popped. He seemed surprised that he'd verbalized his thoughts, stammering, "I only mean—I meant..." He pulled back. "I don't know *what* I mean. Sorry, Dougie."

Kitty had been silent, though she'd kept her eyes on Belinda. Now she said in a cool, even voice, "When you're famous and beautiful, rich men fantasize about you."

She stopped, alarmed at Dougie's face. His lips in a tight line, his eyes darkening, he stared into Belinda's face. "Others?"

Belinda was perplexed at the direction of the squabble. "I don't know what you mean. I don't even *care* to know what everyone's talking about, for God's sake." Hastily, to Kitty she said, "You talk too much."

Kitty, flippant, replied, "Or maybe too little."

Dougie looked into my face, helpless, jaw slack, as though he wanted me to say something.

Cold, I shivered. "What, Dougie?"

But Kitty was in a hurry to say something. "Tell them about Cyrus Meerdom." A purposely explosive sentence. "C'mon, Belinda."

Everyone froze. Belinda's face closed up, and Corey shook his head. "Christ, Kitty. You bring that up?"

"I'm only talking." Kitty's eyes danced.

Jealous, I thought, *this troublemaker.*

Corey hissed at her, "Vengeance is mine, sayeth the broad." He grinned. "Didn't Damon Runyon say that?"

Kitty shot him a venomous look. "I'm just talking, see? Just that we see him around. Me and Belinda. He's—like everywhere. It's unnerving. In that long town car with a driver. Parked in front of the apartment. When I was with Belinda for a dress fitting at Saks. Lord, we're having an egg cream at Rudley's and we turn around and he's *there*. You know how you gotta step down into that restaurant? He *appears*—a table back by the kitchen. Sitting in a corner with a friend…"

"Buzzy Collins," Corey added.

"Whoever." Kitty's voice trembled. "All I know is that he couldn't take his eyes off Belinda." Her voice broke at the end. "It…scared me."

Belinda eyed Kitty, furious. "I told everyone not to mention him. He never said a word to me. Not then—never."

"He didn't have to. That stare."

Dougie shouted, "Weasel!"

"Rich weasel," said Kitty. "But his wasn't the look of—love." She shrugged. "Or maybe it was love turned real bitter." She offered a disingenuous smile. "You don't slap a rich man and live to talk about it."

Belinda yelled out, "I don't want this conversation. Could we go? I'm cold."

I caught Noel's eye. Not happy, if I could judge by his steely look, the pursed lips. He turned his head away from the scene, as if searching for a cab. He flicked his head in my direction, a signal to move.

"You wanted to come along for the party," I told him quietly.

"What?" asked Corey.

"Not a thing," I said.

Kitty went on. "The curse of fame."

I caught her eye and accused. "You make it sound like a blessing, my dear."

"I suppose it is," she agreed with a foolish, self-conscious giggle, then pointed at a quiet Belinda. "All the men will always fall in love with you."

An odd line, I considered—bittersweet, intended as such, but coming off as petty and ugly.

"We poor men, gentlemen rankers off on a spree, damned from here to eternity." Corey bowed.

Impulsively, he saluted Belinda, then grabbed her hand and kissed it. "The continental gesture," he sang out. It seemed a mocking gesture, though perhaps some attempt to lighten the fractious conversation. Belinda laughed out loud. She twisted her head to the side coyly and blew a kiss to Corey. Then, as an afterthought, one to Dougie.

Flustered, Dougie tottered against a streetlight pole, slipped on a patch of ice at the curb, but regained his balance and angrily faced Corey. "What the hell are you doing?"

"Nothing, Dougie." He shrugged his shoulders, dismissing it.

But Dougie, energized, stumbled forward, grasped Corey's sleeve, and pulled at it. Off balance, Corey shuffled his feet, spun away, but looked back. "C'mon, Dougie, we're having fun."

Noel broke in, exasperated. "Dougie, this is nothing. It's…"

What startled me was Belinda's face. The beautiful face was suddenly haggard, worn, her lovely eyes dull and faraway, sadness in them. Trembling, she looked at Dougie. A befuddled look— confusion, yes, but mixed with annoyance. Pain. Hurt. A love sickness, too. Longing. It was an amazing transformation, one I'd not expected, this palette of conflicting emotions, but almost immediately her features hardened as she drew in her breath and mumbled, "You make me so tired, Dougie. Sometimes I just want to fall asleep."

"Nonsense," he yelled back. "Belinda, do you have to have the attention of the whole world?"

Weary, head dipped down, not looking at him, she replied, "That's funny—I thought I only wanted yours."

"Cyrus Meerdom." The man's name, stressed.

"Has nothing to do with me," she said in a dragging voice, barely audible. "A producer."

"I think…"

At that moment Belinda lunged forward and slapped Dougie across the face. "Okay, now everything is even. I slapped Cyrus. I slapped you. Happy?"

No one looked happy. I shifted from one frozen foot to the other. Noel, mouth agape, rolled his eyes.

Dougie looked ready to cry.

"Enough of this," Noel said finally, his voice flat.

Corey had been watching the skirmish with his hands folded over his chest. "Cold." He watched my teeth chatter. "Coffee."

Dougie's body shook.

Watching him closely, Belinda leaned in and grabbed his hand, gave it an affectionate tug. A quick peck on the cheek. "Come on, Dougie. You and me, right? Let's make everything okay. Don't make my days unbearable. This jealousy…this temper."

He managed a weak smile as she touched his lips with her fingertips. "Belinda." Plaintive, drunk with her.

"Quiet," she said gently. "It's almost Christmas. You like Christmas." She spoke as though to an errant child.

Then we all laughed; even Dougie grinned.

"Coffee," Corey said again. "Is anyone listening to me?"

"The automat," Kitty suggested. "Everyone goes there late at night. The swells. Let's all go."

Corey sang out in an exaggerated basso profundo. "Oh, how I love the automat, the place where the food is at!" Grandly, he bowed.

We applauded.

Noel, not to be outdone, sang out, "See Mr. Whitney passing by, munching on Swiss-on-rye. There's Mrs. William Randolph Hearst, saying, 'This is my place! I got here first." He also bowed, adding, "Courtesy of Moss Hart, folks."

Grinning, Dougie nodded at us, and Belinda, watching him closely, took his arm. But the look on her face told me she could no longer abide such childish posturing. My eyes caught hers, and she smiled back at me. *Yes*, I thought—*an ambitious singer, but something else there.* She didn't want to hurt anyone's feelings, even though she knew she might have to. That observation caught me up short—I'd casually dismissed her as one more Broadway darling, but now something struck me as painfully genuine in her, some strain of goodness. I liked her then, the trace of mettle in her blood, and, more importantly, kindness.

Noel and I begged off the automat, a public eatery I'd never visited. I preferred not to obtain my meals from a slot with a glass door. A conveyer belt of indigestible cuisine. Noel hailed a cab and we shuffled into the backseat. The foursome waited on the corner and waved at us. Rather, everyone waved but Dougie. He had both arms wrapped around Belinda, a bear hug that looked awkward—and unwelcome.

"Perhaps your adoring acolyte needs more schooling at the foot of the master," I said to Noel as the cab pulled away from the curb. "A dunce sitting in the corner."

Noel answered me in a strained voice. "I suppose I value the flattery of you Americans too much. I'm intoxicated with Americans. Even those who act like children. You are all like a—a new breed plopped down on virgin soil. Children playing with too much money in a lush flower garden." He grinned. "Perhaps all Americans are children at heart."

"I don't flatter you, Noel dear."

"Of course you do, dear Edna. You hover on the edge of my life like a moth circling a flame."

I laughed. "Yes, that's me, strewing rose petals before each step you take."

His eyes twinkled. "I'm too humble to call myself a genius, so you have to do it for me."

"Are all Brits so drunk with themselves?"

"Only the clever ones. The witty."

I grumbled, "Those who still long for the days when they were angelic child stars. pretty little boys onstage, all London at their feet."

"Yes, the happiest time of my life."

"Until New York began worshiping you."

"Let's see if that's true after I come back from Cleveland."

• • ● • •

In the middle of the night I woke with a start. The telephone jangled, then stopped. Or had I dreamed it? In the dim room I stared at the clock on the nightstand: early morning. Three in the morning. An ungodly hour. I'd been asleep for—what? Barely two hours. Madness, this—dream. I hadn't drawn the curtains and I glimpsed the pale white sky beyond my terrace. A snow sky, I always called it in my days back in Appleton, Wisconsin. The dull, chalky sky that presaged snowfall.

I had trouble falling back to sleep, but in the early morning I roused because the aroma of potent coffee wafted from the kitchen. Rebecca, my indefatigable housekeeper, was whipping up buttery biscuits and frying crisp bacon.

Dragging myself into the kitchen, sloe-eyed, I saw Rebecca shaking her head. "Did I imagine it or was the phone ringing in the middle of the night?"

"So I wasn't dreaming."

"What fool calls then?"

I felt a quickness in my chest as I shook my head. "Rebecca, those calls are doomsday calls."

At that moment the telephone rang, and we both jumped. Rebecca reached for it, but I stopped her. "Let me."

My voice hollow. "Tell me." I waited.

At first silence, then labored breathing. "Edna." One word, ominous.

"What? Tell me."

"It's Noel."

I rushed my words. "I know who you are."

A deep intake of breath, a raspy cough. "Belinda is dead."

I gasped. "Oh, Lord, no."

"Strangled."

"Impossible."

A long heartbeat. "They found her body in a hallway at the back of the automat in Times Square."

My mind went blank. Dizzy, I sank into a chair. "Tell me."

"Well, I don't know anything." His voice broke. "On the radio. No details. I…Last time we…Edna, the automat?"

Quietly, I placed the receiver down and sat with my hands folded in my lap.

Dougie and Corey and Kitty…and Belinda. Coffee? The automat. Last night's squabbles. The tree at Rockefeller Center. Coffee?

Dougie.

A walk. Out of there. I apologized to Rebecca as I got up from the table, quickly dressed, and wrapped myself in my fur coat, adjusted my fur hat. My warm gloves. My scarf. My morning ritual, though different today. Every day a mile walk, even in blazing August heat and fierce Manhattan blizzards. Up Park Avenue, over to Lexington, back downtown. Brisk, my mind swimming with plans for the day. Characters buzzed in my head. A line of dialogue. A facial expression. The Italian butcher on Lexington, blood-stained, a groan as he tacked a sign in his window. Yes—save that image. A short story. Walk, walk, walk.

But not today. The cold numbed, ice bit my face, and I stopped at the corner, turned back. Impossible, this day. Impossible, this awful news.

Dougie.

At a corner news kiosk, the wizened old man I often nodded to was clipping copies of the morning edition of the *Daily News* onto a wire suspended along the top panel. Copy after copy after copy of the flash-fire tabloid, suspended at an angle. A hiccough of sensation. I stood and stared as the old man smiled at me, pointed at the newspapers piled in front of him.

"Such bad news," he said clearly. "And it's almost Christmas."

Almost Christmas.

Dougie.

"You want one?" He picked up a newspaper.

Yes. I fished a nickel out of my pocket. He handed the paper to me, and I stared at the front page. An insert in the upper right-hand corner—a professional headshot of the beautiful Belinda Ross, smiling, glistening, posed coyly. But the entire page displayed a black-and-white grainy shot of Belinda dancing at the Stork Club with Dougie Maddox, identified as the songstress' current beau. "The wealthy scion." Three succinct words. In the background a dazzling crystal chandelier, reflecting mirrors on the side. But what alarmed me was that the photographer had captured the two lovebirds in an infelicitous moment. For some reason Belinda was looking off to her side, her mouth slightly open as though ready to say something to someone out of camera range. But Dougie's face alarmed—he was staring at her profile, his face a scowl. Nothing of the suave good looks now. Nothing of the debonair man-about-town. Certainly nothing of the rich dapper man in the Brooks Brothers suit. No, he simply looked—craven.

No story yet, according to the skimpy copy. Late night news hurried at breakneck speed onto the printing press. Details to follow.

Details.

"The celebrated star of Broadway."

Dougie.

I cringed.

My hands shook as I read the bold-font shouted headline: BROADWAY BEAUTY STRANGLED.

Chapter Eight

Dougie Maddox sat at my Steinway grand piano, one finger pinging middle C, a monotonous punctuation I believed he scarcely knew he was doing—and doing to my nerves. Idly, he gazed out the bank of windows that faced my terrace.

"Stop it, Dougie," Noel said quietly.

"What?"

"Stop or find another key to annoy us with. Middle C is so—the start of a sentence you don't know how to finish."

"What?" he asked again, puzzled.

"Never mind," I said to both men. "Could we be quiet a moment?"

Dougie glanced at me, a sliver of a smile on his face. He stood up and walked to the window, placed his palm on the glass. "I didn't know you lived so high up in the sky, Edna. You can see Grand Central Station. The Chrysler Building. A penthouse, no less. You got a terrace big enough for tennis." He pointed out the window. "All your windows face south. So much sun."

Noel clicked his tongue mischievously. "And we all thought show boats only drifted down rivers."

"What does that mean?" he asked, turning to face Noel.

"Never mind," I repeated.

Silence for a moment, until Dougie spun around, arms flailing, then paced around the room. "I don't know if I should have come here."

"Sit down," I said in my schoolmarm tone, pointing to an armchair. He plopped into it, his body all angles, and immediately began to sob.

I caught Noel's eye—what to do? He shrugged his shoulders and said in a low rumble, "Dougie, tell us what happened."

It was early afternoon, but the sky was already darkening. I'd been on the phone with Noel since early morning. After that first call that sent me prowling the streets, there were other calls, longer and longer, back and forth, none of which garnered either of us any new information. Before noon Noel told me Dougie had reached him—fresh from an agonizing visit to the Forty-seventh Street Precinct—frightened, barely able to talk, stammering about Belinda and dying and cops and pain. More pain. Sobbing. Noel told me Dougie simply dropped the phone, then finally called back, apologizing.

"He begged me to come over. Then he mentioned you."

"Me?" Flabbergasted. "Why me?"

Noel had sounded flustered himself. "You and me—we were with him and the others last night."

"So?"

"So"—Noel had dragged out the word—"so he believes we can vouch for something."

I'd sunk into my seat. "For what? Loutish behavior on everyone's part. Drunken rambles around a Christmas tree? A bunch of dipsomaniacs headed for an ungodly automat at midnight."

Noel had sighed. "Edna, I guess that's the point. You and I can testify that he was in good spirits—not a homicidal maniac ready to strangle his girlfriend in a fit of rage."

"A character witness?"

"This is all madness, Edna. Murder? I'm not—used to it."

The line struck me as bizarre, but I'd answered. "Noel, what do you want to do?"

"He wants to visit us. Talk to us. Do you mind?"

"Of course not. When?" I'd waited a second. "Maybe he has some answers."

Noel appeared at my apartment around one, followed by a skittish Dougie, who immediately grabbed onto Noel, squeezed him—not me, I hasten to add—and sobbed inconsolably. Over his shoulder, Noel caught my eye, and looked uncomfortable.

Dougie looked beaten, the handsome face pale and drawn, deep purplish lines under his eyes, his hair uncombed, his chin unshaven. He was wearing a rumpled double-breasted suit, unbuttoned, a sloppy Windsor knotted tie around his neck. He'd often impressed me as the immaculate dandy on the town, so this disheveled look startled me, though I wasn't surprised— he seemed a man rushed out of his bed, fire alarm clanging, a man hurling himself out the door. At one point Noel pulled at Dougie's lapels, straightening the jacket, buttoning it, tugging at the careless necktie. I smiled at that—Noel, the sartorial master, always groomed as though preparing for a photographer, wearing an expensive Lanvin shirt, gold cuff links, diamond tie clip, the padded shoulders, tucked waist, and billowing trousers. The expensive haircut. A barber's routinely shaved chin. Noel expected people to look at him when he entered a room. They always did.

If Noel ever is charged with a murder—and it wouldn't surprise me, given his intolerance of much of mankind—I fully expect him to appear before an early-morning docket with a Savile Row tailor and a Fleet Street barber at hand. A wash of lilac after-shave lotion permeating the stale air of any courtroom.

Not so, sad Dougie, who curled up in the armchair and looked ready to tuck himself into a fetal position.

"Dougie," Noel began, tenderness in his voice, "you refuse to tell us anything."

Dougie looked up, rubbed his eyes with the back of his hand. "Because I know nothing."

"Frankly," I interrupted, peeved, "you must know *something*. You spent the morning at the police station."

He shuddered. "Have you ever been in a police station, Edna? It's…"

"Filled with criminals," I finished.

"Yes," he stammered. "Yes. People handcuffed, in fact. To chairs."

"I'd rather have them there than on the streets, Dougie."

He whined, "But I'm not one—and they—they think I killed Belinda."

I waited a heartbeat. "Tell us."

Wide-eyed, he sat with his mouth open. Then, swallowing, he said, "Because we had a fight." His voice cracked. "That's why. A lover's quarrel. But we always had spats. Lovers do, right? You don't kill…"

"Some do," I interrupted sharply.

He looked from Noel to me. "I want you both to believe me—I would never kill her. I loved her. She loved me."

He began moving around the room, banging into chairs, pausing by the window and gazing down into the street. "So far down there. I could not live like this—it's too dizzying." He faced us, his face broken. "You know, a man stopped me when I got out of the cab—he asked for a dime. A dime." His voice shook, his face caving in. "Who asks for a dime nowadays?"

I started to upbraid him—Lord, echoes of some anonymous voice on the Zenith singing that redundant "Brother, can you spare a dime?"— but thought better of it. When he sank back into the chair, drawing his knees up to his chest like a little boy, I asked him, "Do you know what happened?"

He spoke to Noel. "I called you the first thing. From the police station. They let me. I couldn't call my mother. So early… She'd—you know Lady Maud."

"So you called me." Noel seemed pleased.

"And me?" I asked. Not pleased.

"I carry your numbers in my wallet. Of course. But I hung up the phone, Edna. Too early. I regretted it—to wake you. I didn't want to scare you."

"Yes," I said slowly. "I feared it was the end of the world."

"You got that right," his voice thundered.

Darkness had fallen now, so I switched on lamps, my room

suffused in lemon-yellow and flame red. His face in shadows, he scratched his head. "I didn't know who to call."

Impatient with his scattered answers, I probed, "What did the police say to you?"

Bluntly, lips quivering, "They asked me if I killed her. They—they pushed me into a chair. No one has ever *pushed* me."

That surprised me. "They came for you in the middle of the night?"

He nodded. "Yes, they woke me up at the Stanhope. How did they know I stayed there? I wondered about that. Maybe a servant at Lady Maud's told them. I don't know. I told them that I'd been at the automat at midnight, with Corey and—that girl Kitty. A little tipsy, all of us. You saw us. We were having a good time. We walked into the automat and sat there laughing like fools. Kitty bought a piece of pie for ten cents. Lemon meringue. I saw that. I had coffee. Corey…"

I interrupted. "But something happened."

He nodded meekly. "Yeah, my fault. Again." He rubbed his chin absently. "I'm such an ass."

"That may be true, Dougie, but what does that have to do with anything?" Noel wasn't happy.

"We were laughing like little kids. I loved it. I really was. You know, I never had friends to—to go to the automat with. To places no one thinks of—even like miniature golf. That kind of thing. There were lots of theatergoers there, whooping it up, some real drunk. I even spotted Buzzy Collins at a table with some friends. He caught my eye but turned away. Corey said, 'Look who's here. The ubiquitous Aleck Woollcott of the society crowd.' We laughed because Buzzy is everywhere—a leech, that man. But when I looked back a few minutes later, he was gone. Vanished."

"He never said anything?"

He shook his head. "Not important, really. But him being there seemed to make Belinda nervous, fidgeting. Somehow, I don't know how I always do it, we got into a little verbal spat, the way we always do—*did*." He hesitated on the word, a sob escaping his throat. For a moment he sat still, his head dipped into his lap.

"And then what happened?"

He stared into my face, hang dog. "I accused her of being unfaithful." He spat out his words. "I know, I know, I can't control myself. Around her. Around Belinda. I am always afraid…"

"Lord, you nail your own coffin," Noel said abruptly.

Dougie squirmed. "Horrible words, Noel."

"I imagine Belinda wasn't happy," I went on.

"She'd *been* happy. Laughing. Free and easy. Then, like a switch turned off, she changed. I mean, she suddenly looked— tired. Like I'd drained every ounce of life from her. Pale. She had nothing left to give me. I mean—she withered in there in front of me. When I saw that, I apologized over and over, but she went away from the table to the powder room."

"What about Corey and Kitty?" I asked.

For a moment he stared off into space. "When Belinda was gone, Corey whispered to me that I was a fool. I guess Belinda had told Kitty—who told Corey who then told me—that she was thinking of leaving me. That news shocked me, stunned me, frankly. When Belinda returned to the table, I cursed at her. My God, she looked so—tired of me. Then she said to leave her alone. All of us. Go on. Get out. She started to cry. In the goddamn automat, sitting at a table and burying her face in her arms. I didn't know what to do. Kitty said—okay, leave her alone. That's what she wants." He shrugged his shoulders. "So we left." Another sob. "Left her alone so someone could kill her."

Restless, moving around my rooms, I switched on the lights that flooded the terrace. A wasteland out there—frozen snow, icicles off the balustrade. Too many shadows in the rooms as the sun set and the sky darkened. I had trouble looking in Dougie's face—such weakness there, emptiness. I fought a horrible image: a rag doll stuffed with straw. Pretty buttons and silk raiment, but—vacuity.

Noel sat back in his chair, arms folded over his chest, and he followed my languid movements. I could read his mind—*You're thinking Dougie is hiding something. True, Edna dear? The way your body stiffens when you walk by him, looking down on his folded-in body, a callow soul slinking from accusation.*

"I don't know what to believe," I said aloud.

Noel's voice rose. "Surely, you believe Dougie, Edna."

I offered a sickly smile, then decided to stop smiling. "Dougie, fill in the pieces. Please."

"I told you—we *left* her." He hesitated. "But I went back."

I sucked in my breath. "And?"

Again, the empty eyes, unfocused. "We walked down the block, crossed the street. On the sidewalk, Corey and Kitty bickered. I said we shouldn't leave Belinda alone in there. It's late, it's—well, late. Kitty wanted to call a taxi, anxious to get home. She was cold, she said. She was angry that we'd made fools of ourselves in the automat, of all places. She wanted to go to bed. Corey wanted to walk. Then I noticed I'd left my silk scarf inside, and I said I was going back for it." He smiled thinly. "An excuse, really. I decided I'd talk to Belinda. Take her home."

A puzzled look on Noel's face. "So you went back alone?"

Dougie stammered, "I know, I know. The police said the same thing—alone? *You?*" he stressed, his voice tinny. "But I did. I left Corey and Kitty and went back."

"For the scarf?"

Dougie read the doubt in my question. His eyes glazed over. "What else could I do? It wasn't there. Neither was Belinda. Gone."

Noel's voice was scarcely audible. "What did you do?"

He gave a helpless shrug. "Well, you know, I figured she left—got a taxi. I dunno. What else? She wasn't there. So I left."

"No scarf?"

"It wasn't there. But I swear I left it there."

"And then?" prompted Noel, who'd stood up, his back to the piano. Inadvertently, his hand struck some keys. A tremendous crescendo exploded, and he jumped. He approached Dougie and touched his shoulder. "This does not look good, Dougie."

Dougie sighed. "God, don't I know it. I rushed back outside, ran down the block. Kitty was gone. I thought I saw Corey down a block or two, but I was too tired to catch up. So I hailed a cab."

He threw his hands into the air. "And home to bed. A few hours later the doorman buzzes my room. 'The cops are here.' A line no one wants to hear. I'm not a common criminal, some homeless beggar stealing from the…grocery." His voice trailed off.

"And what did the cops tell you?"

He seemed not to be listening to me. "You know, I was driving Belinda away, but I couldn't stop myself. I'd step outside myself and say—this isn't good. Be a man. Shut the hell up. You're acting like a baby. No girl wants a jackass who's so…"

"Untrusting," I added when he lapsed into silence.

"Christ, love made me do foolish things."

Noel was impatient. "I still don't know what happened to Belinda, Dougie. The papers had so little information. Too early, the presses. But you must know something, right? She was strangled, but in there? In the automat? How is that possible? All those people there. You didn't see her?"

He shook his head vigorously. "I told you. When I went back in, she wasn't there. I guess she was there, though, in the back hallway. I guess one of the kitchen staff felt the cold air, a draft, figured someone left the door to the outside open—the one at the end of the hallway. Wind through the kitchen doors. When she looked, yes, the back door to the alleyway was wide open. Unlocked. Open. And there on the floor was Belinda, strangled." He buried his face in his chest. "Dead. Christ Almighty. Dead. Belinda."

"No one saw?" I asked.

He banged his fist into his palm. "I don't know. That's all the cops said. At that point I finally called my mother, I had to, waking her up, and then there was a lawyer slinking into the precinct, briefcase and bowler hat, getting them to leave me alone, pushing me into a cab and telling me to shut my mouth."

"But if you have nothing to hide," I began.

"Exactly." Dougie's voice rang out. "That's what I told the lawyer. I didn't do it. I have nothing to hide. I—I loved her."

Noel was irritated. "Stop saying that, Dougie. You're not convincing anyone." Exasperated, he wagged a finger at Dougie.

"People in love kill all the time. Read some Shakespeare, for God's sake." He paused. "I don't know—some verbose and pessimistic American writer. Dreiser, maybe. People drown their lovers in his books."

Dougie frowned. "What are you talking about?"

"Nothing." Noel looked out the window at the black nighttime sky, a faint hint of an unseen moon.

Dougie pleaded, "I'm being honest."

Noel said, "It's discouraging how many people are shocked by honesty and how few by deceit."

Dougie's face showed he didn't like the remark. "You have to believe me, Noel."

I walked to a bookcase, idly ran my fingers across the bindings—the touch of old leather, smooth, comforting. I was thinking of something. "I sense there's another piece to the puzzle you're not sharing, Dougie. Am I right?"

He gave a phony laugh. "Smart lady, dear Edna. There *is*."

Noel actually laughed out loud and pointed at me. "They'd have burned you as a witch in another century."

"This lady's not for burning. Frankly. Some men say smart women are God's Saturday night mistake. Or an accident of fuzzy genetics."

Dougie breathed in loudly. "Yes, Edna, yes." A long pause. "Belinda was strangled with a white scarf. The police found it around her neck."

"Oh, Lord," I said, my temples pounding.

"Yours?" asked Noel.

"My scarves are all monogrammed. DM." He barely got the words out. "It was my scarf. But I insist…"

I held up my hand. "None of this is good, Dougie."

He flared up. "You think I don't know this? That's why I need your help, both of you."

"How?" Noel asked.

"Someone has to believe in me. To talk to people. My friends—who believe me. You're both famous. Famous counts for something in this town. People aren't gonna believe me. The

Daily News. The *Mirror*. Everyone hates the rich. I can't help being rich."

My fingers brushed the leather-bound books. I turned away, unhappy. "Dougie…" I stopped.

"Help me."

He didn't care for the look in my face. He jumped up, sputtered some nonsense, and headed to the foyer where he grabbed his overcoat, threw it over his shoulders. "I need air. I can't breathe in here. We're too far up in the sky, Edna. How can you live like this? There's no air."

He closed the door quietly.

Noel and I stared at each other.

Finally Noel leaned toward me. "Are we gonna help him, Edna?"

"I don't know what to believe, Noel. I just don't."

"None of this looks good." He inserted a cigarette into his holder, struck a match, but then decided against it. He sat back and stared at me, his face pale.

I waited a long time, my eyes staring out into the dark sky. Down in the street blasted a run of blaring horns. Taxis screeched their brakes. High up in the sky, I rarely heard the clatter and hum of the frantic streets below. Down there—murder.

I tried to catch Noel's eye, but he wouldn't look at me. "They also burn murderers in this century," I said.

Noel buried his head in his arms.

Chapter Nine

Corey Boynton was already sitting at a table at Schrafft's when I arrived. As I sat down, he watched me over the rim of his coffee cup, his eyes wary. "I don't know why I'm here." He waved a free hand at me. "What I *should* say is—What are *you* doing here?"

I laughed. "A better question, really."

"How so?"

"Yes, I'd rather be back at my warm apartment pecking out a short story on my Remington."

"If I had the money, I'd be at our winter home in Boca Raton."

"No money?" I arched my eyebrows. "Stranded in the city during a brutal winter? I'm baffled. I thought the Boyntons were rich folk."

He twisted his mouth. "Doubtless you've heard of the Crash, Miss Ferber. My parents are counting pennies these days." He laughed cynically. "Luckily, there are piles of pennies left, so I'm told, but my father prefers bootleg gin mills to his only son working on a creamy tan on a beach, an illegal mint julep at the ready."

I drew in my cheeks. "Sorry for your loss."

"Yeah, right." He glared at me. "This place is for ladies who lunch. Look around, Miss Ferber. Women in mink hats. Women getting ready for a matinee—or a game of bridge." His hand swept across the room, took in the tables of chatting women.

"Yes," I said quietly, "we get our strength from numbers."

"And where do men get their strength?"

"They're still puzzled over that conundrum."

"I've never been in a Schrafft's."

"A treat for you then. I like their ice cream sundaes."

"I'm very careful where I show up."

That line confused me, but I said nothing. We were hardly settled into a den of iniquity. Not with a robust cheesecake staring me in the face.

A young woman walked by and smiled at him. He sat back, ran his palm over his slicked-back hair and smoothed a collar that needed no such attention. "People are looking at me."

"You're a good-looking young man."

He beamed. "Thank you."

"I didn't mean it as a compliment."

He rapped his knuckles on the table, tired of the banter. "This murder, Miss Ferber. Awful. I've talked to the police already. I have nothing to say."

He snapped his fingers and a waitress rushed over. He pointed to his empty cup.

I sat back, signaled the waitress for a coffee. "With whipped cream, not milk."

Corey's eyes flashed, a look that said, *You eccentric meddler.*

I stared into his face, something that bothered him. A sidelong glance at me, then a quick look toward the doorway. He was nervous.

"Dougie implored Noel and me to help him," I told him. "What that means I'm not certain, other than to ask questions. He insists the police will crucify him, given his running in and out of the automat, his decorative scarf found wound around sad Belinda's neck, his…" I stopped. Corey was frowning at me. "What?"

"You're doing the police department's job?"

"Reluctantly, I agreed last night to talk to folks. You, in particular, and Kitty."

He fidgeted in his seat. "She's late." He glanced toward the door. "She's always late. Hey, she saw what I saw, you know. What's more to be said?" He interlaced his fingers and rested them on the table.

"She may have a different perspective. After all…"

He spoke over my words. "I doubt that. She's not overly clever." He dipped his head. "Don't tell her I said that. So… you're attempting to talk to folks."

"Yes, folks."

"And I'm folks?"

"You're at the top of the list."

He started, rattling his coffee cup. "You're joking."

I was making him uncomfortable. "You were there, Corey. At the automat. You're a witness to what came before. If we're to help Dougie, every little detail might matter. Tell me what you remember."

He considered what to say, running his tongue over his lower lip, but always keeping his eyes on me. "I missed the actual murder."

"That's a glib remark," I said sharply.

He didn't seem penitent. "But factual, I'm afraid." He took a sip of coffee and glanced around the restaurant. He nodded at someone sitting at the soda counter but immediately looked perplexed. "God, I thought I recognized—no matter. To answer your question—nothing seemed out of the ordinary. I mean, Dougie and Belinda squabbled, but then they did that a lot. I thought it part of the charm of their love affair. Really. They seemed to enjoy it so much." He hesitated. "No, that's not true. Maybe Dougie did. Belinda seemed resigned—no, that's the wrong word. She seemed—weary."

The waiter placed coffee in front of me, and Corey watched me sample the whipped cream with my fingertip.

"Yet you all left Belinda alone at the automat. I still can't understand that, especially if she was troubled."

A clipped voice. "What choice did we have? She *insisted*. 'Out—get out. All of you.' Very melodramatic. Very Garboesque, I thought. A temperamental star now. The first-rate songstress and third-rate actress playing a part."

"Did Dougie protest?"

"Strangely, no. To tell you the truth, she had a fury I'd not seen before. Almost genuine."

"Another smart-aleck remark."

He was enjoying himself. "So be it. But not her usual stop-stop-stop-it banter. 'Dougie, stop it.' More so—'I'm tired, Dougie, and you're crazy. This night has worn me out. I've had it.' Not exactly those words, but you get my meaning."

I wondered out loud. "How bizarre! Noel and I were with you all a short time before. Yes, the bickering, even the slap that surprised us. But it all seems to go away. Even the slap—game-playing, immediately regretted. Belinda forgave. She even snuggled up to him, showed affection. After all, you were all going to the automat, the place where culinary arts surrender to the power of indigestion."

He laughed a long time. "Miss Ferber, if you must know, I unwittingly suppose I stoked the fires."

"How so?"

"This will not make me look good—what I tell you." But his manner suggested some joy in the telling.

I took a sip of coffee. "I'll be the judge of that."

"A few days back I bumped into Belinda on the street, a little disturbed, anxious, fleeing a disagreeable brunch with Dougie at Lindy's. She left Dougie behind at a table. She was distraught, so I walked her back to her rooms. She rambled, a torrent of clichés—you know, last straw, at wit's end, cross to bear, a string of such nonsense. Although, surprisingly, she kept undermining her anger with apologies—'I do love him, Corey. Of course, I do.' Then, a run of bitterness. Quite compelling, I thought—a woman on the edge. I was the sympathetic ear. She said she was at a crossroads. I took that to mean she was leaving him."

I wasn't happy with him. "A leap for you, no? And something you supported?"

He smirked. "I could care less. Dougie's a friend and all, but a romance with a singer can go nowhere. Lady Maud has to protect her vast monies."

"And you told this to Dougie?"

"Unfortunately, that very night. I mean, Kitty told me something earlier. I guess Belinda complained to her. Still a little tipsy, I leaned in and whispered, 'You've lost that girl, you know. She told me.' I was being very *Broadway* myself."

I sat up. "You were being *cruel*."

He watched me for a long time. "You choose the words you want. Dougie and I come from a different world, Miss Ferber. Different rules."

"So Dougie confronted Belinda?"

He nodded. "I'm afraid so. She didn't react well. Hence the lovebirds' explosion. Hence our hasty departure."

I wagged a finger at him. "You're not his friend, are you, Mr. Boynton?"

He fiddled with his coffee cup. Then, dramatically, he held my eye. "Look, Miss Ferber, I've known Dougie from years back. From New Haven, in fact. Rich boys at school. Yale camaraderie. Rah rah rah. The tables down at Mory's. Families connected through bags of money and blue-green Hampton lawns. That sort of thing. I was Phillips Exeter, he was Horace Mann. But— no, to be truthful. To answer your question. Friendly, maybe. Same fraternity. An in-town pal. But Dougie was unpopular."

"Why was that?"

A hint of self-congratulation crept into his tone. "Christ, Miss Ferber, you've met him. A child. He can add a column of figures lickety-split and slide the extra cash out of a sad widow's meager bank account, but he stares with dumb wonder at a running water faucet."

"Again, cruel."

A slick grin. "Because I'm good at it."

"I'm not so sure of that."

He smiled at me. "You know, I sort of liked him, the way you like a pesky child who annoys his elders. After we bumped into each other in the city, we'd see each other around town, like at the New York Yacht Club on Forty-fourth, at the clubs, and then we ended up having rooms at the Stanhope. He discovered me—assumed I wanted to be with him."

"And you did."

He leaned in, confident. "Dougie has money to spend. I have my father breathing down my neck. I'm used to—" he tugged at the sleeve of his tweed sports coat "—jackets from Donovan's on Fifth. Twelve-dollar white starched dress shirts. Silk socks. I'm a playboy. He's a…boy."

"Do you think he killed Belinda?"

Startled, he waited a moment, his eyes stony, then he burst out laughing. "Of course not. Really, Miss Ferber. Why would he? People in our world don't murder others. We have other ways of destroying their lives." Impatient, he looked toward the door. "Where the hell is that girl?" A sly grin. "I guess we know where our Dougie is today. Hiding in an expensive Park Avenue lawyer's office with his mommy doing all the talking."

"Tell me about Kitty," I said quietly. "What should I know about her?"

He shrugged. "What's to tell? An unemployed chorus girl who trails in Belinda's shadow like a Chinese concubine. Or—*did* trail after her."

"Yet she can afford to live at the Claremont?"

"Daddy sends cash from back home in Grand Rapids. Just enough to keep the wolves from the door. A grain merchant, a squeezed-out living these days after the Crash, so I understand. But daddy is afraid for his little girl in the big, bad city, so the money rolls in. Maybe I should say—dribbles in. Just enough cash to fund the failed ambitions of his daughter."

"I assumed you two were seeing each other."

His laugh went on too long. "How quaint, dear Miss Ferber. Seeing each other. Courting on the veranda on a Sunday afternoon after a heavy pot roast dinner. God, no. I like Kitty. Or at least I think I do. Sometimes I do." Hesitant, his eyes flickering. "She's funny, friendly, someone to squire to a show or Roseland for a dizzy Charleston. But romance? Of course, she may have other ideas, but I can't control that. She's not…pretty. You obviously can see *that*. I know that makes me sound shallow and heartless, but I'm interested in pretty girls. Kitty is…mousy. Not unattractive, true, but too drab. She walks around the city like a Midwest farm girl who didn't read the rule book."

I broke in. "Unlike Belinda."

"True."

"Competition with Belinda?"

"Big time, but we weren't supposed to notice."

I waited a moment. "Did you find Belinda attractive?"

He hated the question, looking away, then darting a glance back at me. His face closed in, his eyes darkening. "Of course, she was stunning. I mean—mesmerizing onstage. In real life—a flawless beauty. It was wonderful to—you know, look at her. So…beautiful." His voice became matter-of-fact. "But Dougie owned that cherished Ming vase. Case closed. Door shut. Gong rung. Finis."

I persisted. "So your relationship with her was strictly friendly?"

His eyes flashed. I'd struck a nerve because he dipped his head into his chest and said nothing. He was debating what to tell me. He pulled his chair back, rocking it, as if ready to stand up, but looked toward the doorway. "Where is that girl? Christ, women who are late are especially unattractive."

"Poor Kitty Baker. I guess the list of her unattractive characteristics keeps growing."

Steely-eyed, unfriendly. "I don't like waiting."

"And men are never late?"

I could see him trying to relax now. "Men have reasons for being late."

"Yes," I countered, "they forget where they're supposed to be. They need women to guide them."

A harsh laugh. "You do not show any mercy, do you, Miss Ferber?"

"Only when warranted." After a pause, I said, "Strangely, Mr. Boynton, you don't seem hurt by Belinda's death."

"Of course I am. But she was Dougie's world, not mine."

Suddenly he reached across the table and grasped my hand, so electric a moment that I pulled back, furious. "Mr. Boynton."

"You don't like me, do you, Miss Ferber?"

But at that moment his eyes flashed to the doorway where a harried Kitty was scurrying in, ignoring the waitress who addressed her, moving through tables and sloughing off her cloth coat. "I'm late," she mumbled. "There are people everywhere. Some sort of protest. A food riot. Grubby people with signs. The cabbie sat in…"

I ignored her babble, speaking to Corey. "One last question for you. When you left the automat, you didn't wait for Dougie?"

His eyes got shadowy as he caught Kitty's stare. "I walked. A long walk. I was still a little tipsy—bootleg gin gives me a headache, I'm afraid—and so I walked. The crisp night air."

"Where to?"

"Does that matter?" His brusque tone made Kitty twist in her seat, her eyes puzzled.

"Probably not. But I'm curious."

He drew his tongue into his cheek but talked to Kitty. "The Spanish Inquisition, dear Kitty. *Show Boat* style."

I grinned. "Thank you."

"I wasn't being kind." He tapped the table with a finger. *Tap tap tap.* Morse code.

"Neither was I."

Kitty's brows twitched as she looked from me to Corey. "What's this all about? I don't know why I was summoned here." She smiled feebly. A blot of red lipstick on a front tooth. She looked—vaguely clownish.

"I'm assuming, perhaps wrongly, that the two of you want to help Dougie. So Noel Coward and I are asking questions, at his bidding, as I told you on the phone. Noel's at an unfortunate rehearsal today for *Design for Living*, so I'm by my lonesome."

Kitty fretted, "I already talked to the police."

"I know, I know," I said hurriedly. "But if we're to help Dougie, we have to examine every minute of that time at the automat. More so, what happened after you left. Some little detail—forgotten. A face remembered. Comments shared. Anecdotes. Little inconsequential moments. Any possible clue. A stranger's passing word." I paused. "Buzzy was there."

She glanced at Corey, waited for him to nod at her. "I gotta tell you, Miss Ferber, I was sick of it all. Dougie snipping at Belinda, Belinda annoyed, even Corey here hissing and leaning in like—like Iago sharing fraternity secrets to the bumpkin Othello."

"Dougie as Othello?" I wondered.

"Ignore her." Corey's words were unfriendly. Then, a sloppy grin, "Kitty disappeared in a taxi."

Kitty was frowning. "You wanted to *walk*. It was freezing out. Sleet was falling, for God's sake. Bums everywhere. I wanted to go to bed."

Nervously, she took a compact from her purse and began checking her makeup, spotted the lipstick on her tooth. She was wearing a red-and-white striped wraparound dress, popular now, calf-length, that hugged her body snugly. A run of Bakelite enamel bracelets on her wrist. She'd painted her face dramatically—rose-tinted rouge, crimson lipstick. Worse—nails lacquered a deep red. I stared—Corey stared, but not favorably. It dawned on me—here was a different Kitty, one who suddenly allowed herself to be—glamorous. I thought, cynically, that she no longer had to compete with Belinda.

She was wearing a French-style blue beret, a Bohemian look that merely suggested affectation—and a huge desire to be looked at. Mousy, Corey had described her. An apt description for a small-boned freckled girl with wide midnight eyes who paled beside the luminous Belinda. Not pretty, again Corey's words. But striking. Corey missed that in her features. There was a curious intelligence in her eyes, something he also neglected to see.

"Did Dougie leave you while you were waiting for a taxi?" I asked her.

She looked at Corey again, but he was ignoring her. She wasn't happy about that.

Finally, she sighed. "Dougie was grumbling about Belinda alone back there, seething, hating him. On and on, intolerable. So I walked away." She held up a finger. "Oh, yes, he mentioned a scarf. 'My scarf, my scarf. A birthday gift from Lady Maud.'" She rolled her eyes. "A talisman from the oracle of Delphi."

I looked at Corey. "You didn't go back with him?"

He jutted out his chin. "I refused to—not that he asked me. They had to play out that scene by themselves. I was witness to too much nonsense. He moved away, so I went walking." Corey's tone had shifted. No longer the glib, abrupt speaker, his tone now struck me as defensive. "Don't look at me. I wanted to get away from it all." He tucked his head into his chest as though waiting for attack. He smirked. "I guess it didn't work because I'm sitting here now with you. Talking about last night."

"And I went home to bed." Kitty threw both hands into the air. "The good girl at midnight."

"Do you think Dougie went back and killed Belinda?" I asked her sharply.

She yelped, covered her mouth with her hand. "Please don't ask me something so absurd."

I leaned toward her. "I think you're going to be asked that question by the police."

"They have already asked me that."

"And you said what?"

"Of course not." She fiddled with a napkin, balling it up, then smoothing it out.

"Was Belinda leaving Dougie?" I asked suddenly.

Her voice got fluttery. She looked to Corey, but he was staring at her, a hint of a smile on his face. "Lord, these questions. I wanted no part of this. This is not why I came to Manhattan."

Corey drummed his fingers on the table. "Miss Ferber likes to play games."

"Only if I get to set the rules," I added.

Kitty sat back, considered my question. "I know that Belinda was unhappy, but she—sort of liked Dougie. That's what I thought. She did hint to me that it might not last." She turned to face Corey. "I told you *that*. Remember? But, to tell you the truth, I often stopped listening to her. She could go on and on about her world, her successful life. She wanted me as a foil. A shadowy mirror she could look into. I was supposed to tell her what she wanted to hear."

"What about what *you* wanted to hear?"

"Meaning?"

"My dear, you seem to crave gossip."

"No, it's just that I had to hear about her rich life now." She flashed her eyes. "Do you know how boring that can become?"

"A life that you coveted, no?"

She looked stunned. "Hey, sister. Just a minute now."

I smiled. "I'm sorry. I'm thinking out loud."

"I'll say. Write your novels, Miss Ferber."

"What about Dougie? He's good-looking, rich…"

She flared up. "Are you calling me jealous?" Then she laughed. "Of course, a little. Who wouldn't be? She had everything. Those looks, that face. Adulation. The toast of Manhattan. A little unnerving for the rest of us peasants. It's hard being in the presence of the noontime sun. You find yourself lost in shadows." A heavy sigh. "She got everything, but that's the way God works, right? There's nothing I could do about it." A fatalistic shrug. "I got my own destiny."

"Which is?"

She said nothing.

Corey cleared his throat and answered for her. "The dreadful life of a gypsy. Broadway cattle calls that lead to a breadline."

She glared at him.

I had something on my mind. "Belinda seems to have confided in both of you, but she never told Dougie she was leaving him?"

Kitty shook her head. "No, not really. I suppose not. I know I heard *him*"—she pointed a finger at Corey—"whispering that to Dougie at the automat."

He yelled at her. "Not exactly."

"Exactly," she yelled back at him. "Do you think I'm deaf?"

"Old friends, chatting."

She made a face. "If that's what you call it." She half-rose from her seat. "I don't want to be here, Miss Ferber. This conversation is unnerving." She looked around the restaurant. "I never liked this place. Look at these women. They sit here laughing at nothing. These women have nothing to do but spend their husbands' money."

Corey snapped. "Then you better get yourself a husband."

A nervous glance at him, a flicker of hope in her eyes. He turned away.

I persisted. "You don't want to help Dougie?"

"I wouldn't know how."

"The truth."

"The one thing that I do know is that she'd had it with her greedy brother, that money-grubbing no-talent."

"Jackson? Tell me."

Kitty twisted in the seat, uncomfortable. "Have you met him? I have." She looked at Corey. "We both have. A failed actor or director or something, he is, but stupidly ambitious. He spouted this blarney about the soul of theater—or something. He saw Belinda as a ticket to his own life on Broadway. Yes, she was ambitious, but I think—you know, once you get to the top you start to wonder if it all was worthwhile. She got—tired. Fed up with it all. I know she sniped at him one time when we stopped in at that scary theater. He actually shoved her. She shoved him back. An ugly scene."

I drank the last of the coffee. "I keep getting this image of Belinda as a pretty gold-digging girl, talented, but hungry for money. Cyrus Meerdom, then Tommy Stuyvesant, then Dougie. Maybe I'm working with a cardboard caricature. Am I wrong? Actors at the theater thought her—kind." Out loud I wondered, "Who was this woman?"

Suddenly, her eyes flashing, Kitty confided in a low voice. "She was seeing someone else."

Corey made a *tsk*ing sound. "For Christ's sake, Kitty. You do run off at the mouth."

She ignored that. "No, no, I mean it. She hinted it to me once. I don't know for *sure*. A little drunk, maybe. But she said someone else..." She stopped. "I don't know why I'm telling you this."

Watching her mask-like face, I believed she was making up a story. She had the look of a schoolyard girl tattling on a friend. But why lie now? "Back to Cyrus?"

She shivered. "God, no, though he seemed to be everywhere she was. Obsessed, that old fool. Smitten, drunk with her. He couldn't get her out of his head. I wouldn't put it past him if…" She shook her head. "Enough talk." She gathered her gloves. "Dougie was all right, Miss Ferber—he's a lapdog, yes, but harmless." She looked at Corey, her expression flat. "You men are blinded by beauty. It makes you all walk into walls."

"But could he kill for beauty?" I asked hurriedly.

She was standing up but dropped back into the seat. She looked frightened, as if I'd touched on an explosive topic. "She left a trail of broken hearts behind her, Miss Ferber. Let me put it this way—she was always thinking of tomorrow's lover. What can I say?"

Corey snapped at her. "That's cruel, Kitty."

"Yeah, so what? What can I say?"

"I don't think you liked her," I concluded. "Either of you. Frankly." Then I added, "And you don't like Dougie."

I stared at both of them as they shot glances at each other.

Corey snarled, "Christ's sake, Miss Ferber, you don't really get it, do you?" He exchanged a conspiratorial look with Kitty that unfortunately included me as well. "When you're rich, you can't afford to like anyone."

Chapter Ten

"Midnight in Manhattan." Noel's buttery words drifted through the telephone lines. A light chuckle as he went on. "Edna, the two of us, a walk on the wild side. The mysterious automat calls us to its doors."

"Yes, the wild side. A bite of a pastrami on rye that's lingered untouched in a glass cubicle for a good part of a bad day. Too Wild West for me, dear Noel."

Immediately he got serious. "Edna, it's time we asked a few questions. Dougie is becoming more and more morose, hidden now in his mother's unforgiving lair. He walks the streets like a Bedouin nomad. You and me, the approximate time of the murder. Midnight. The folks there might remember something."

I sat back in my chair, sipped the cup of tea at my elbow. "According to the papers, the police thoroughly questioned the workers there. What makes you think…?"

He didn't wait until I finished. "You know, Edna, we're not the police. We have our own questions. They have an obsession with facts. You and me—we're writers. We have an obsession with lying."

"True. That's one way to describe my life's work—I make my living lying."

"Then you're the perfect sleuth. You can spot when others are making things up."

I drew my tongue into my cheek. "Liars. Lord, Noel, especially Corey and Kitty, two people easy to dislike. But these

days I'm also wondering if our boy Dougie is telling the truth."
I closed my eyes. "Is he one more liar?"

I could hear Noel dragging on his cigarette. "He lied?"

"Not so much lied, but cheap with the truth. He seems to
skirt around it, trusting we won't notice."

A long silence. "Yes, I sense that."

"What secrets is that man hiding?"

"I'll pick you up in a cab after eleven, Edna. Bring coins for
the machines. I've never been in an automat. Even the name is
absurd, no? But so American. It'll be...mad."

"I suppose I'll be ready."

I could hear him laughing. "You're too puritanical to ever be
late for anything, Edna."

"Said by a libertine wastrel."

"And yet we adore each other."

I clicked my tongue, though I smiled. "Sometimes I'm not
so sure, Noel."

A high-pitched laugh. "One insurmountable difference
between us, dearest Ferber, is that you write stories about folks
who flatten their consonants, like Midwestern farmers and
riverboat captains. I write plays about folks who elongate their
vowels as if they are in pain." A considered pause. "Daaarling."

Smiling, I hung up the phone.

The automat was a place I'd never considered frequently. Of
course not. Yet everyone I knew relished dropping in, inserting
their nickels or dimes, then raving about the futuristic slice of
apple pie that appeared magically before them. Science fiction
coming to life in a heavenly glass-fronted kitchen.

"Americans want as little contact with other people as
possible," he told me in the cab ride over. "Machine-age food
production." His voice rose. "I envision a day in America when
robotic arms will be all the rage in loving embraces."

"Noel, you're not making much sense."

Ever since Irving Berlin's musical revue *Face the Music* became a smash hit, the crowds at the automat in Times Square had mushroomed—with self-proclaimed swells sailing in dressed in formal evening attire. In that stage production the rich who'd lost their fortunes after the Crash and could no longer get a table at the Ritz found themselves hobnobbing with other gentry at the pedestrian automat. Society dames in elbow-length silk gloves and diamond necklaces yelled across the room to others dressed in outdated Parisian finery. And everyone gleefully sang, "Let's Have Another Cup of Coffee," a song you heard incessantly on the Zenith in the family parlor. A delightful romp, the revue featured a big-boned battle-ax of a matron named Mrs. Martin Van Buren Meshbesher, a woman "lousy with money," so bejeweled that on a clear day "you could see me in Yonkers."

The Hart & Hardart Automat on Broadway in the middle of Times Square was an architectural wonder. No simple eatery, this place, like prosaic Child's, where you could stand on the sidewalk and watch a pimply boy flip pancakes in the window. No, the automat had a dazzling brownstone façade with intricate terra cotta inlaid panels, magnificent acorn-shaped ornaments speckling the friezes over the entrance—with a spectacular illuminated marquee dominating the whole affair. The word AUTOMAT was spelled out in swirling Art Nouveau lettering against a stained-glass backdrop. The splendor of it all. The food gods, celebrated. An orgy of conveyer belt cuisine.

"A cathedral," Noel quipped. "To commerce."

"To culinary catastrophe."

Noel squeaked at me. "Snob."

"You bet."

Outside, huddled in shadows, a few shivering men and a woman watched us walking in. A young boy, maybe fourteen or fifteen, bone thin, started to say something, but the woman's arm reached out, touched his shoulder. He drew back into the shadows. When I glanced back at the shabby loiterers, they turned their heads away.

Walking through the massive revolving door, I was overwhelmed by the vast, high-vaulted interior: a magical kingdom of glittery, colorful lights, a rainbow of sunshine yellow and orange and forest green. A towering ceiling grandly painted with gaudy flora—lush tropical rain-forest blooms twisted gracefully down the white marble pillars. Tiny gargoyle-like figures perched high on pillars, gazing down at us. Bacchanalia, I thought—a hymn to dime-store gluttony and the awesome power of macaroni and cheese.

Noel, dizzy from arching his neck to take in the "divine show, really," immediately inserted a nickel into a slot and proudly held up a powdered doughnut the size of one of the lesser states, holding it aloft as though it were the lost ark of the covenant.

"Noel," I said softly, "it's a doughnut."

"No, it isn't. It's—America."

I surveyed the walls of glass compartments. A nickel for a ham sandwich. Fish croquettes, slices of roast turkey, baked mac and cheese, mashed potatoes. Pecan pie á la mode. Banana cream pie. Gigantic silver spouts shaped like leaping dolphins dispensed hot coffee.

At midnight the tables were jam-packed. I sized up the crowd, immediately creating lives for them: backstreet vaudevillians, gypsy dancers, dungaree-clad dock workers, zoot-suited connivers and hucksters, a street walker with a Lucite box purse, a dime-a-dance girl from the Orpheum, women in furs and Empire Eugenie felt hats, feathered—a Garboesque affectation. Jean Harlow platinum blondes. George Raft gigolos. Speakeasy bouncers. Overweight drummers from Newark.

I turned to face a fussy-looking man in a baggy gray flannel suit, the jacket one size too large. His sliver of a moustache twitched as he smiled at us. A nametag on his lapel: Josiah Farnum, Night Manager. He rocked back and forth on his heels, though his sudden salaam was overly dramatic.

"Celebrities," he intoned, running his tongue over his teeth. "Noel Coward and Edna Ferber."

"Yes," Noel said, "we know who we are."

"An honor. We…"

I broke in. "Mr.—"I leaned in, squinted at the tag to get the name right. "Mr. Farnum, a favor, please. We're friends of Dougie Maddox, the man who…"

He held up his arm, actually putting his palm close to my face. He whispered, "Awful. Just awful." As he spoke, his head surveyed the packed room.

Noel said, "Sir, if you would allow it, we'd like to talk to any of your staff who worked here that night. Curiosity—his family wonders."

Mr. Farnum made a grumbling sound. "I was off that night." He lowered his voice. "Unfortunately. I missed the…horror of it all." Then he thought better of his word choice. "I mean, the whole thing was…unfortunate."

I raised my voice. "Dougie Maddox is a suspect, as you know."

His head shifted, again checking out the crowded room. "They're saying he's the murderer." He shivered. "Back there." He pointed behind a closed door.

"Who says that?" I said hotly.

He backed up, startled by the force of my words. "The police have been in more times than I can count. I mean, they've swarmed all over the place. And the crowds. Look at this room. Packed. We're not usually so—so busy at this hour. Why is it a murder makes average folks want to stand in the same spot? Crowded tables, wanderers back to the hallway. Lord, enough with the *Daily News* and their flash-bulb Leicas. Intrusive." He sounded indignant. "We are *not* the circus."

Noel was impatient. "Nevertheless, if you could help us."

His eyes glistened. "How can I deny Noel Coward and Edna Ferber?"

"Good point." I said. "Sensible man. Now…"

He snapped his fingers and a young woman hurried over. "Could you call Thelma from the kitchen?" He turned to face me. "The cops took the names of the dozen or so people here that night. I mean, customers."

He waited until a woman approached us, and he whispered something in her ear. "Thelma Mickles," he told me. Then he pointed to an empty back table.

Thelma Mickles wore a look of utter fear in her face as she sat down at the table. I smiled at her and Noel half-bowed, reaching over to shake her hand. Neither gesture allowed her to relax.

"A few questions, my dear," Noel told her, and her lips trembled.

"I ain't know nothing but what I told the cops." A thick Irish brogue, a singing voice that enchanted me.

"Ireland?" I asked.

She looked at Noel. "England?"

He nodded.

"I don't know you two," she said flatly. "Him"—indicating the manager who was standing ten feet away, making believe he was inspecting a line of ketchup bottles—"whispered that you are famous. The both of you."

"That's not why we're here," I said. "We're friends of the young man the police think killed Belinda Ross."

Matter of-factly, "Oh, the murderer?"

I started. "Well, we want to prove him innocent."

She scoffed. "Well, good luck with that one, honey."

"And why is that?"

She counted the reasons with her calloused fingers. "One, you got you a body with a scarf tight around her neck, and two, you got his name all over the piece."

"Still and all," I went on, heated.

Noel held up his hand. "You wouldn't want an innocent man convicted, would you, darling?"

Her eyebrows rose. A grunt. "Happens all the time in this country."

I ignored that. "Anyway."

"Don't mean to offend nobody." She offered a girlish smile.

Thelma leaned back, draped one arm over the back of her chair. The chubby big-boned woman had wide footballer shoulders. Her gray curls were partially hidden under a net cap, though a few vagrant strands drifted down her forehead. Her fingers were short and stubby, the nails bitten to the quick. When she smiled, her face became warm, inviting, her small eyes lost in the folds of her flesh. A dimpled face, though that charming feature was nearly hidden by rolls of chapped, blotchy skin. Her dumpy faded blue uniform, bunched at the waist with a frayed belt, sported a large reddish stain on her chest.

Noel pointed to it. "You look like you've been shot in the heart."

"Many times," she laughed out loud. "Married three times. Men never miss the heart when they aim." She caught my eye. "Of course, you knows they miss everything else they're supposed to hit."

Noel pulled out a folded sheet from his breast pocket. The front page of the *Daily News*, Dougie's sour face and Belinda's scattered expression. "Did you see this man in here?"

She shook her head vigorously. "No, sir. I work back in the kitchen. Almost never come into this here room." She looked around the restaurant. She grinned. "Not dressed for company." She seemed to be seeing the crowd for the first time. "It's a circus in here tonight."

"But you saw *her*?" I indicated Belinda.

She bit her lip. "Only when that poor girl was dead in a heap on the floor, that infernal scarf tight around that pretty neck. I swear to heaven, I crossed myself and called out to blessed Jesus. I nearly fainted. Nobody gets kilt in this place." A sly grin. "And don't make no cracks about the food."

Noel was munching on the doughnut, a smear of white powdered sugar covering his pale chin. "I wouldn't think of it."

"Can you help us in any way?" I asked.

She made a face. "I don't know how, seeing as I don't know nothing." She breathed in. "But, okay, here's the story like I told it to the cops over and over. 'What was that again?' they keep asking. Deaf cops. No wonder the city is falling apart. That, and Herbert Hoover, him looking like an undertaker at a wedding." She glanced at the manager who was holding a fork up to the light, a frown on his face. "I think she was crying earlier. I mean,

I walked into the hallway earlier, maybe four or five minutes before, and I heard someone crying real loud in the ladies room. That stopped me cold. Yeah, folks get into fights here—crying, this and that. But this was—real sad. I go to open the door but she pushed against it. 'Go away.' Sweetest voice, I thought. Okay, somebody warring with an ass of a boyfriend. Happens all the time." She closed her eyes for a second. "Now I think it was her."

"How can you be sure?" I asked.

"I can't, but, you know, I got a gut feeling. The cops said the same thing."

"Then what happened?" asked Noel.

"So I'm back in the kitchen and all of a sudden I feel a cold draft on my feet. Right through the closed door. Getting colder and colder. What in heaven's name? Bad enough I got no heat in my cold-water flat out in Queens. So I swung open the door and there she is, heaped up, twisted, arms bent under her body. Her eyes open like she seen the face of the devil—like surprise in them. I swear to God." She crossed herself again.

"The outside door was wide open? To the alley?"

"Yeah. And I'm thinking the murderer run out that door."

"Could he have come in by that door?" I asked. "Not through the front door?"

The question alarmed her. "Well, yeah. It ain't locked. Marvin over there"—she pointed to a wiry Negro sweeping the floor around some empty tables—"he got to bring out the trash every hour or so."

The manager made a harrumph sound, clicked his heels like a Prussian soldier, and Thelma stood up, though slowly, stretched out her arms. "I gotta get back to cooking. I bring home the only cash in the house." A mischievous grin. "Husband number four is curled up by the old Motorola listening to Jack Benny and laughing hisself silly."

Nodding at us, she walked away.

Mr. Farnum snapped his fingers and a young man clearing some tables and running a wet rag over them stopped what he was doing. He ambled toward us, nodding to the manager.

Blinking wildly, he stammered his name. "J-j-j-ohnny Hicks, my name." He waited. The manager yelled to us. "Johnny was working the tables that night."

"Please sit, Mr. Hicks."

"Johnny," he said. "Nobody calls me Mr. Hicks." Glancing at the manager, he insisted, "I'll stand, if it's okay with you. Gotta keep my eyes on my tables."

"You saw the girl who was murdered? The others with her?"

He was nodding quickly, eager to talk. His moist tongue kept rolling out over his lips, like a swamp frog anticipating a treat. "I was finishing up, stayed past my hours. I gots me a long train ride deep into Brooklyn. Two hours. Maybe more when she breaks down in the tunnel. So I was rushing. But I seen them four."

Perhaps in his late twenties, Johnny was a short skinny man, with a long bony face with a faint beard stubble. His watery blue eyes under bushy eyebrows kept blinking, staring away from us.

"What can you tell us?" Noel said.

Johnny had rehearsed his story, the words tripping out in measured, emphatic sentences. "They were arguing. Or at least two of them was. The real pretty girl. Someone told me she was a famous singer on Broadway, but I ain't never been on Broadway. But an eye-catcher, she was. At least I couldn't take my eyes off of her. Anyway, I overheard them. She goes off, comes back. She looked—tired."

"Did you hear what they were saying? Arguing about?" I asked.

"Dunno. Just bickering like." He grinned. "Like I do with my girlfriend. Squawking ain't nothing but people learning to be together."

"What about the other two? The man and the woman."

"They said nothing, so far's I could tell, though the other guy was mumbling something at one point."

"Then she was alone?" I asked.

He nodded quickly. "Strangest thing, though. I mean, she flares up—I was just coming out of the kitchen and I seen it—and tells them all to get lost. Real loud, but teary, you know. The murder guy"—suddenly he pointed to Dougie's face in the front page article, spread out on the table—"him, the murderer, he looked furious. His buddy nudges him. Like—let's get the hell outta here. This bomb is gonna explode. So they go, and she sits there. Like alone as can be. Just staring into space. That pretty girl."

"Then?" I prompted.

He lowered his voice. "You know, I kinda felt sorry for her, real bad. I walk up and whisper, 'Get you a free cup of java, Miss?' I ain't supposed to do that but what the hell. She looked—real sad. But she shook her head and said no. But real sweet. Her voice was like—kind. She looked up into my face like seeing me for the first time, and she smiled. God, it made my heart jump. No girl smiles like that, folks. Even though she was crying to beat the band."

"Did you see her go back into the hallway?"

"Naw. I was cleaning some tables by the window and when I turned back, her table is empty."

"But Dougie"—I tapped his face in the article—"he came back?"

"Yep. I mean, he stands there looking around, puzzled like."

"Did he look for his scarf?"

"Ain't seen no scarf, ma'am. Yeah, the cops asked me the same thing. Could have been there. But I seen him starting to leave, or at least it looks like that, headed to the front door. Maybe not. I go into the kitchen, and when I come back, he ain't there."

"Thelma…"

He interrupted. "Christ, the screams that come from that woman."

"How much later?" Noel asked.

"A few minutes, maybe. Five. Couldn't tell you."

He stood up, gave us a deferential wave and grin, and noticed that a table near us had the remains of someone's dinner: a half-eaten piece of pumpkin pie, a bit of chicken pot pie, a small chunk of dark pumpernickel bread. "Lord," he muttered, and then looked back at us, a feeble smile on his face. "People leave food all the time. Excuse me." While we watched, he gathered the food and I expected him to dump it into a waste bin. Instead, nodding to himself, he placed the food at a table positioned near the front door, and walked away. He lingered at our table and whispered, "No one's supposed to notice."

But I did. Quietly, a woman and her young son slowly slinked into the room and sat at the table, facing the sidewalk, their backs to us. My heart jumped, touched, saddened.

Johnny leaned into us. "The manager—he's is a real tyrant sometimes but, you know, look at him now." We did. "He stares at the wall like there is something there he had to see."

He left us, saluting us again as he walked away.

Mr. Farnum approached us. "So that's it." Finality to his tone. "The witnesses saw nothing that can help the police."

I pointed to the Negro sweeping the floor. "Was that man here that night?"

He furrowed his brows. "Marvin?" I nodded. "Well, yes, but I don't think he has anything to say about it. He sweeps the floor."

"Nevertheless," I insisted. "A minute with him. Please."

He wasn't happy but motioned to Marvin, who seemed surprised. "Marvin Peeples," Mr. Farnum said in a clipped voice before stepping away.

The black man watched us closely, his fingers interlocked and cradling his potbelly. An old man with murky white shorn hair, a pale chalky face, pocked, bearing a scar at the corner of his upper lip.

"Have a seat, Mr. Peeples." I pointed to a chair.

"Thank you, ma'am. No thanks. I'll stand, if you don't mind." He glanced toward Farnum who was scratching his chin, his eyes focused on us.

"All right," I said. "A moment of your time, sir. The night of the murder..."

His dark eyes got wide. "I seen them all," he said slowly. "I seen them fussing and going on about things, but then leaving. The girl sits there, right there"—he pointed to a table near us, so quick a gesture that I jumped—"then goes in back."

"Did you see the white scarf the man left behind?"

"Dunno. Might have been there."

"Did you see this man return?" Again, I pointed to the picture.

He nodded. "Yeah, I seen him back at the table. Standing there—like confused."

"Did he have a white scarf with him?" Noel asked.

"The police asks me the same thing. Funny thing is, I could of sworn he was wearing a white scarf. Could be wrong—maybe I'm thinking when he walked in because they were a noisy bunch of folks walking in—but I thought I seen him wrapping it around his neck."

I shot a look at Noel. "Not good."

I thought of something. "Had you ever seen him before in here?" I tapped the news photograph.

He shook his head. "No, ma'am. Not him. I remember folks. I keep an eye on everybody. People tickle me, you know. Always up to something."

"What do you mean 'not him'?" I asked.

"Well, I seen *her* before. The pretty girl what got strangled."

"Belinda? In here?"

"Yes, ma'am. She was with that other guy, you know."

"What other guy?" I asked quickly. I caught Noel's eye. My heart raced.

"The other guy at the table. Like a week before, maybe. Late afternoon, maybe. I seen her sitting with that guy."

"Corey?" I said to Noel.

"Are you sure?" asked Noel.

The man nodded, a hint of a smile on his face. "Yes, can't forget that face, ma'am. He warn't nice, that man, excuse me if I say so. Yes, like he was patting the pretty girl's hand, like comforting her. She looked all sad and weepy."

"Corey." I spoke to myself.

"Yeah, ma'am, he was the man. I remember 'cause he yelled at me when I bumped into a table next to them. He jumped up, spilt his coffee on his gray flannel pants. He yelled at me, 'Can't you see we need a little privacy? Go sweep some other place, boy.'"

Chapter Eleven

In the darkened theater someone was singing onstage. Midday, the doors of the Paradise were unlocked, with no one in the lobby. Passing under that glittery new marquee sign, Noel and I had strolled in, our footsteps echoey on the old boards. We paused at the back of the orchestra, looking around. A faint light switched on in the wings made the stage shadowy. Another light from the lobby illuminated the rear seats, though barely. I stumbled, bumped into Noel, who grabbed my elbow.

"Walk much, Ferber darling?" he said, a nervous grin.

"Why are we here?"

"I told you. A cryptic call from Jackson Roswell," Noel grumbled. "He woke me up. I regret giving the man my number."

I stared up into his shadowy face. "And he made no sense?"

"He may have made sense—there's a chance he was amazingly articulate, in fact—but at dawn my eyes were shut to the world, my head sunk into plump silk pillows, so the insanely rapid speech of the wide-awake American is Greek to me."

I laughed. "So you interpreted his Gatling-gun spiel to mean he wanted an audience with us?"

"A loose translation, my dear. As I told you in the cab—he ended by saying he wanted answers. Or—I had answers. Or, maybe, he had answers. Do you have any answers, Edna?"

I walked down the aisle. "No, but I have lots of questions, Noel."

He made a ta-da sound, danced a two-step. "And that's why we are here today."

It was at that moment, the two of us speaking in subdued voices for no apparent reason, we heard muted singing on the stage. I could barely make out a figure perched on a stool in the corner of the dark stage. A throaty baritone, thick and mournful. The song rang out in the dark theater, covered us. For a moment the singer hesitated as we approached, perhaps conscious of our being there, but then, his voice louder, he sang out:

Who dat a knockin' at the door below,
Who dat a shivrin' in the hail and snow,
I can hear you grumblin' Mister Rufus Brown,
Just keep on a knockin' babe, I won't come down,
I wants to tell you that you can't get in,
Have you been a gamblin'
Honey, did you win?
What's that you tell me,
Coon you lost your breath?
I hopes you freezes to death.

A slight pause as he stood up and finished:

"What you gonna do when the rent comes 'round?"

It was an old ragtime song from back before the Great War, a staple of provincial minstrel shows, featuring disheveled hoofers in garish black face exaggerating the Southern dialect. But this version was slowed down, a mournful dirge.

Suddenly the front-house lights snapped on, and a voice snarled, "Kent, I told you to cut out that crap. You hear me? You're making us all crazy."

Jackson Roswell rushed onto the stage from the wings, swung his fists in Kent LaSalle's face. But the old actor, watching his boss strut around him, simply sat on the stool, arms folded on his chest. With the lights on I could distinguish his face: a bemused look, taunting. Finally the old actor stood up, smiled broadly, and pointed to Noel and me as we stood in the darkened aisles. "Ah, Mr. Interlocutor."

Jackson muttered, "Goddamn it all to hell."

"Mr. Roswell," Noel began.

"Why is everything a surprise to me?"

That remark baffled us, and Noel strode forward, raising his hand in greeting.

"But you called me, sir."

Jackson seemed flustered now, whispering to Kent, "Just go. I don't want to hear that coon song anymore."

"From my glory days in vaudeville," Kent said, smug.

Jackson smirked. "Yeah, and look where it got you, you damn fool. A broken-down actor at the end of his days warbling in a..."

Kent finished, "In a broken down theater."

Jackson's hand pushed against the small of Kent's back.

Bowing to the two of us, Kent shuffled off the stage as Jackson walked down to greet us. He looked over his shoulder at the departed Kent. "He's losing his mind, frankly. Too much hooch at the gin mill a block over. Every day I walk in and he's doing one-man shows in a mad house."

"He sounded very good to me," Noel offered. "A rich baritone."

"Yeah, so what?" Jackson pointed to some seats, so we sat down.

"You called?" Noel said again. "I didn't quite follow your early morning summons."

A sickly smile, vaguely apologetic. "Yeah, sorry about that. I can't sleep since...since the murder. Belinda. Jesus Christ. Murdered. I walk these hallways like a ghost." He closed his eyes for a second. "I keep hearing her singing on that stage." He looked back to the empty stage. "Our early days in Manhattan. Starting out." He breathed in and then looked away. "Somebody took that all away."

"Of course you have our deepest sympathy," I began, but he suddenly stood and turned his back to us. A big hulk of a man dressed in an old flannel shirt, untucked, he bent over, his tremendous shoulders shaking.

Then, facing us, he said in a firm voice, "I called you, Noel, because Dougie said you were his closest friend. When Dougie introduced you to me—I can't remember where we were—I felt you were on his side. On Belinda's side."

That news startled Noel, who flicked his eyes. "Yes, I suppose so."

"And I'm troubled by...Dougie." Jackson paused, as though he'd explained his problem sufficiently.

"Just what do you wonder about, Mr. Roswell?" I asked.

He sat back down in a row in front of us, his body turned at angles to ours. "Is he the murderer? Dougie?" His voice echoed across the theater. "The police think so. Everybody thinks so. The scarf. The fights they had. But he walks in here and takes me by surprise. I don't know what to make of it."

"Dougie comes here?" I asked, surprised. "After Belinda's death?"

He puffed out his cheeks. "God, yes. More than once. For Christ's sake, folks. I turn around and he's *standing* there." He pointed. "Or there. Everywhere. Just standing here. Or he drops into a seat like—like waiting for a show to begin. It gives me—it gives everyone—the willies."

"What does he say?" From Noel.

He scratched his chin. "Most times nothing. This—like a haunted look on his face. Christ, a ghost. We're rehearsing a skit—we got a show scheduled—we need the money." He seemed apologetic. "We were closed a couple days after the—the murder. But we got to make a living."

Noel told him, "I hear Tommy Stuyvesant is planning a memorial at the New Beacon."

"I know." A flash of fire. "That's *my* job, no? My job. Anyway, Dougie...I said to him, 'Dougie, what are you doing here?' He doesn't answer at first. I don't want to go near him. I'm thinking—this is the man who killed poor Belinda. My sister. Linda. He strangled that beautiful girl. A murderer." His voice broke. "And he's sitting here. Staring, just staring."

"Did he say what he wants?" I asked.

Jackson looked over the empty seats. "'I just wanna be here.' That's what he tells me in this tiny voice, like a little boy who lost a toy. 'I wanna sit here. I don't wanna be any place else.'"

"My God," I said, shivering, "he's hurting."

"I know, I know. But it's eerie, sickening."

Noel held up his hand. "But understandable, isn't it? He loved her."

Jackson's face contorted. "But he killed her."

Silence, Noel and I making eye contact. I went on, "Mr. Roswell, I know you're grieving, but don't rush to judgment. You do know that Dougie maintains his innocence."

Bitter, eyes piercing mine. "I know you two *think* that. His friends." He tapped his heart. "But my heart knows what's what."

Again, I waited a moment. "What do you want from us?"

"Tell him to—to…" A helpless shrug. "I don't know." A nervous tick in his voice. "I don't want to make him angry, you know. I'm in a bind. We got no money here. Piddling audiences. We're hanging on by a thread. This is my lifeblood. The stage is my…my life. My *only* life. Belinda was helping out, you know, but she was just starting out. Just making bucks. But Dougie…"

Suddenly I understood his dilemma. "But Dougie was helping out more. His cash—his unwanted presence. A conundrum, sir?"

He watched me closely. "I know I sound real shallow and mercenary, but these are bad times. If I alienate him—or, I don't know, make him forget that we're here, that wouldn't be good for us."

"'What you gonna do when the rent comes 'round?'" Noel sang out the line, unfortunately in a feeble Uncle Remus inflection.

Jackson frowned. "That's real cruel, Mr. Coward."

"Mr. Roswell, you seem to be in a hard place. One hand held up against the face of a man you insist is the murderer of your sister. The other hand is conveniently in his pocket."

Standing up, he stepped into the aisle, his head turned toward the stage. "Oh, my God. What kind of man do you think I am?"

"You're not that difficult to read," I insisted.

Noel touched the sleeve of my coat. "He *is* grieving, Edna."

Jackson smiled at Noel, a thank-you nod at someone he believed was his advocate. Jittery, beads of sweat on his brow, his upper lip twitched.

"Yes, I am."

"So am I," I insisted. "I'm saddened by the loss of that young life. A girl just starting out. So unfair."

"Then you understand. Then…"

"Then," I went on, "you have a wrinkle, sir. You're going to have to make your own decision. Not me—not Noel."

Jackson spoke in a small voice. "Every Thursday a check was messengered to my office."

"Yesterday? So…"

"A day late," Noel noted.

He nodded.

I said sharply, "Maybe he's preoccupied. He is trying to save his own life from the electric chair."

Jackson shuddered. "How you put things, Miss Ferber."

"And we're"—I pointed to Noel—"we're hell-bent on helping him escape that fate."

For a second his eyes flamed, a burst of anger. "You got a hard road to travel then, the two of you. Good luck." But then, dropping his voice, he squirmed. "I was hoping you'd talk to him. A few words from friends could…" His voice trailed off.

"Never." My voice echoed off the ceiling.

He stiffened, his arms folding over his chest. Color rose in his cheeks.

"You know, you're the only ones who think he's innocent. Maybe you two got cloudy vision."

Incensed, Noel stood, backed away. "You're not a nice man, Jackson Roswell."

He swiveled on his heels. His shoulders hunched, he barreled past us, disappearing into the lobby. A door opened and slammed shut—Jackson headed upstairs to his apartment.

"That went well, Miss F," Noel said.

I gripped the back of a theater seat. "Something else is going on here," I told him. "This is not the whole story."

He looked into my face. "Like what?"

"For starters, I don't trust this man." My eyes went to the empty doorway. "He has a secret he's afraid will get out."

"How in the world do you know that?"

I pointed to my chest. "Gut instinct."

"Infallible?"

"Always."

"Do you think he killed his own sister, Edna? Unlikely, no? She had the golden touch. Miss Midas with a paramour sitting on tons of cash. Why strangle the golden goose?"

"There may be more to the story."

"I think with Jackson everything always comes back to— money." He touched my elbow. "Let's get out of this rat trap."

An angry voice erupted from behind us. "You ain't being fair to him."

Millie Glass rushed up the aisle from the lobby. The actress planted herself feet from us, her jaw set, one fist pummeling the air. "The man is hurting real bad." Her rough, brassy voice flattened. "Damn you all. Goddamn you all to hell. I mean it—goddamn you all."

"For God's sake," I said to her, "calm down, Miss Glass. He was the one who asked us to come here."

She glanced back to the lobby, and snarled, "I told him it was a mistake. Busybodies, the two of you. Famous, yes—but Dougie'll never listen to you. A mistake."

"And why is that?"

"And frankly, Miss Ferber, he asked *him*." She pointed to Noel. "Why are *you* here?"

Noel found his voice. "And you are?"

"Millie Glass," I answered for her. "One of the featured players. We were introduced last time."

"Hah!" she yelled out. "Featured player, my ass."

Noel's eyes widened, delighted. "We haven't had the pleasure. Pleased to meet you, Miss Glass."

Millie was having none of it. "You're here to bring down these walls."

"What?" I asked, startled.

"This theater got one feeble breath left in it, and that's Jackson. He loves…"

I broke in. "Yes, we heard from him—his love of theater, the stage in his soul, the classic muse of theater whispers." I sighed. "The litany that's repeated in this place more than Hamlet's soliloquy, I imagine."

"Don't mock me."

"I'm simply being descriptive."

She stared at us. "Dougie killed Belinda, and that's the end of the final act. The curtain can come down now." She stamped her foot. "Jackson and me—we now gotta keep this place afloat. I'm telling you the truth—I got tired of blinking my eyes like a lapdog at that rich fool. Jackson devoted every ounce of his blood to Belinda's career. He *made* her."

"And he won."

"Did he? I suppose so, but not so's you'd notice."

"What?"

"Belinda got greedy."

"How so?" I asked.

For a moment she looked away, a nervous catch in her throat. "Simple. Not greedy for money. For—for attention. The adulation of rich men. A string of them. The small-town girl with a history of mindless infidelities, according to her brother. And he should know. This heart broken, that one. She wouldn't listen to Jackson when he cautioned her. Instead, she ignored us—she even refused his calls."

Her mouth twisted. Without stage makeup, her face was drab, flat with a wide mouth under a pixie nose, and hazel eyes that someone probably told her were her best feature. Last time, meeting her, she glittered with rouge and lipstick, a line of kohl under her eyes so that she look vampish. Theda Bara from a silent era. The It Girl.

A decade too late.

"So you think Dougie killed her because she was unfaithful to him."

"What else?" She laughed harshly. "We heard she found a richer man."

"But who?"

"Dunno. Rumor only tells you so much. Jackson even heard it from her chatty girlfriend—whatever her name is—and he pushed Belinda but she played coy. 'I only love little Dougie.' Some prattle like that. 'You don't understand. I'm *not* that girl.' But Jackson warned her—stop these idle flirtations. You're a star now.'"

"And she was a star," I told her. "She did the impossible—made it big on Broadway. The start of riches, fame. A lifetime of..."

She jumped in. "What are you saying? I'm *not* a star?" A pause as she clapped her hands together. "I had to take a backseat while she strutted and preened and bowed."

"Millie, we're not talking about you."

Her voice broke. "God spreads talent around, you know."

Noel quipped, "But some players always drift at the end of the line."

She eyed him, her lips twitching. "I'm doing okay. You hear me?" She stepped away. "All right. Enough. Just leave Jackson alone. Leave *us* alone. Call off Dougie. He's giving everyone nightmares. We're rehearsing and he's—there. In back. Watching. Just watching. This—one time there was like this high-pitched keening coming from his throat. Lord, it's like Banquo's ghost visited on us." She shook her head back and forth. "I hid in the dressing room. Jackson don't want to shut the doors of this theater for good."

"But will he have to?" I asked.

"You'll have to ask him."

I looked toward the wings. "Where is Chauncey Waters today?" I turned to Noel. "You met Kent, or, at least, *heard* him. But last time there was another featured player. A young man who had a lot to say."

"None of it good," Millie said.

"Is he around? Perhaps a few words with him…"

"Gone."

"He left?"

She shared the news. "The day after Belinda was killed, he comes in and says, 'I have to leave you all now.' Like that. Like a line he rehearsed. Said in his phony stage voice, the fool. Probably grieving for his lost moment with the available-for-parties Belinda."

"No reason given?"

"I told you. Gone." She snapped her fingers and laughed. "Pouf. Like that. Oh, yeah, his parting shot at Jackson: 'This place is a tomb. I don't wanna be buried alive.' Imagine that? A freak of nature, he is." She smirked. "Don't know which way to shoot his arrows, if you know what I mean."

Noel grumbled, "You do have a way with words, dear Miss Glass."

"Sorry, I never liked the guy."

Noel turned away, his voice filled with sarcasm. "We'll give Dougie your best."

Her voice rose. "You just tell him to stop these scary visits." She thought a second. "Lord, a day ago I walk onstage, getting ready to rehearse my silly monologue about a dumb blonde in a typing pool who dreams of a dance marathon—stolen from Damon Runyon's *Guys and Dolls* or somebody like that—and there he was. Standing in the middle of the aisles. Like where we are."

"We know," I said, impatient. "You've already told us."

"No, no. But that ain't the crazy part. What makes it nuts was that suddenly I spot that old fool, Cyrus Meerdom, you know, the coot she left for Tommy Stuyvesant—the one she ditched for Dougie Maddox. I mean, the old fool mooning after her. Everybody talks about it—like…following her, that sad sack face of his. There *he* is, sitting in the back row. And there's Dougie right about here. I actually cried out—so scared I was."

My heart raced. "What happened?"

"Well, nothing. Dougie spots him, panics, and rushes out. I'll tell you—the look on Cyrus' face was something else. Murderous, I'll say. Even from the stage I could see the hatred there. Lord, folks. Belinda is dead—yet her lovers still haunt this damn theater."

Noel was anxious to leave, tugging at my sleeve, making mouth noises that sounded vaguely digestive. Millie rolled her eyes.

Suddenly Kent LaSalle's deep baritone sounded from offstage.

"According to Saint Sullivan, the world's greatest magazine writer, a psalm for all of us:

Hoover is my Shepherd, I am in want.
He maketh me to lie down on park benches,
He leadeth me by the still factories,
He restoreth my doubt in the Republican Party,
He guides me in the path of the Unemployed for his party's sake,
Yes, though I walk through the alley of soup kitchens,
I am hungry."

We waited, looking at each other, nervous.

Then, a sad, sad line: "Out, out, brief candle." Then, in an arch, mocking falsetto he mimicked Jenny Lind's annoying treble. He sang out: "She was only a bird in a gilded cage."

The front house lights suddenly shut down. Then the stage lights. The theater was plunged into darkness.

Chapter Twelve

James, the doorman at my building, opened the front door, a deferential bow, but paused, uncertain. He quietly greeted me but nodded over my shoulder. I was tempted to ignore him, tired from my morning stroll up Park Avenue and down Lexington, but something in his expression gave me pause.

"Miss Ferber, a visitor."

I turned to face Chauncey Waters rushing toward me from a few doors away, maneuvering between two parked cars, his breath bursts of icy clouds as he hurried. "I've been waiting and...I couldn't wait inside."

"It's not a hotel," I smiled at him. "And James is very protective of the expensive residents who hide from the world."

That stopped him, but he laughed out loud. "Are you hiding from the world, Miss Ferber?"

"No, I hope not." I waited a moment. "But I am an expensive resident. How might I help you, Mr. Waters? Do you often lurk on sidewalks, ready to assail folks doing their morning constitutional?"

We both glanced at the sidewalk where a white-gloved houseman was walking two miniature poodles, maneuvering around the two of us.

He looked back at me. "I was hoping to have a few words with you. I mean, I knew where you lived. Everyone read that article in *Stage* about your life in this building. Your grand piano.

The thick-pile carpet. Pictures of your terrace, your apple-green walls, your favorite pewter candlesticks, even…"

I laughed out loud. "I knew I shouldn't have been interviewed by that pesky reporter. I'm one who values my privacy."

"Then you shouldn't let photographers click through your rooms."

"I agree, but too late now." I smiled thinly. "You're here."

He drew in his breath. "But I mean you no harm. I talked to the doorman who turned me away."

"I'm tempted to do the same thing, Mr. Waters. I haven't had my coffee yet, so chances are I'm not a good conversationalist."

He eyed me, grimly. "I'll do all the talking, ma'am."

• • ● • •

We found a Child's coffee shop on Lexington and sat in a booth by the front door. Seated, he lost the cockiness of the street encounter, his fingers drumming the table, one leg going up and down like a mechanical hammer. Under the overhead light, his clothes looked frayed, shabby. An average-Joe eatery, this familiar coffee shop, but filled now with businessmen in double-breasted dignity and feathered fedoras, glowing cigars held between manicured fingers. Women chatted in fur caps and two strands of cultured pearls.

"All right, Mr. Waters. Why this early morning intervention?"

He squirmed in his seat, his eyes perusing the menu. "Miss Ferber, I have to tell you." An embarrassed smile. "I'm broke—Jackson stiffed us all—so I can't…" He tapped the menu.

"Mr. Waters, I invited you." I smiled at him. "Actually, *you* invited me, but don't worry about it. Order, please."

And he did—toothsome buttermilk pancakes with Vermont syrup, a side of crisp bacon, steaming coffee. I did the same, though I insisted my coffee be served with real whipped cream. "A bad habit I acquired in Vienna," I told him.

"Miss Ferber, I'm leaving Manhattan at noon today. I walked away from that failed theater, as you know, and I can't afford to stay in the city. A friend got an old Ford jalopy, a million miles on it, enough money for gas to Erie, Pennsylvania. His uncle got a truck farm outside the city, promises work when spring comes. Grubbing work, backbreaking. But it's better than standing in a breadline on Eleventh. Or living under a Hoover blanket in Central Park. A whole lot of folks there at night. Cold. Scary."

"A Hoover blanket?" I was confused.

He laughed. "Cardboard." He twisted in his seat and pulled out the lining of his pockets. "Hoover flags."

"Good Lord."

"Hoover leather."

"Let me guess—cardboard in your shoes."

"The current style, ma'am." An infectious smile, charming.

"No more acting?"

He shook his head. "In a time of despair and want?"

"I'm sorry to hear that."

"I was never any good, anyway. Jackson paid us pennies—told us to eat at soup kitchens. He told us we had no talent." He paused. "But I thought I'd take a chance—to see you. Maybe. Talk to you."

"And here we are." I looked into his face. "What is so important, Mr. Waters?"

He locked eyes with mine. "Because when you were at the theater, they...lied to you. They're afraid of something, afraid you might stumble onto something they're hiding. I mean, this was before poor Belinda's murder." He sucked in his breath. "And last night I stopped at the speakeasy over on the docks on Hudson, a grimy hole in the wall, and there was Kent, who almost lives there, drunk as a skunk on that rotgut swill they serve. But then he usually is."

"Yes, we saw him at the theater. He seemed...overly dramatic. He spouted a parody of the Twenty-third Psalm."

"Yeah, he loves that bit, but drink has withered him, ma'am. That, and age and want and a dreaminess about a life he believes he once had."

"And he told you about Noel and my visit to the theater?"

He nodded, took a sip of coffee. "Yeah, he mentioned how you asked about me. I liked that—you remembered me."

"He eavesdropped?"

"Yeah, he doesn't miss anything."

"And then he plunged the theater into darkness."

"What?"

"No matter. Talk to me."

He swallowed a forkful of pancakes, a contented look on his face. "I never trusted Jackson, ma'am. Even from the beginning, before everything bad happened, I always felt he was harboring some secret—a big secret." He looked into my face. "No one has ever allowed you a true picture of who Belinda was."

That line startled. "I'm not following you."

He gulped down hot coffee. "The fact of the matter is that Belinda had changed lately, and Jackson didn't like it one bit. Schemers, the two of them, yeah, but I always felt Belinda was more an unwilling creation of Jackson's plans. Here you got this real talented girl, beautiful, a singer, dancer, God's blessed one, and Jackson knew it—figured she was the key to paradise. His gold-plated meal ticket. And she was. At first. I think she went along with his plans."

"Which were?" I interrupted.

"Come to the city, showcase her wonderful talent, get her to Broadway—and that's the way it's supposed to be, actors, that persistent dreaming—but he wanted money. *Craved* money. Greedy, that man. For himself, really. I heard them whispering all the time—hook her to some rich boy's rising star."

I sat back. "Dougie."

"Or someone else. Tommy, Cyrus, you name it."

"And it worked."

He bit his tongue. "It didn't really."

"Why not?"

He sat back. "That's my point. Because Belinda changed. That's what they didn't talk to you about. That's the lie—at least one of them. You see, she had a falling out with her brother. Real violent, the two of them in the dressing room behind closed doors. Then she wouldn't even go back there after a while—ever. Even a knock-down-drag-out fight with Millie Glass. Belinda wasn't planting her feet in the spots they drew for her."

"They?"

"Millie Glass looms large in this story." He smiled dreamily as he forked a slice of bacon.

"She struck me as someone jealous of Belinda."

"Wow, yeah, to put it mildly, Miss Ferber. She ran to Jackson with all sorts of stories, most, I figured, she'd just made up moments before. She knows stagehands at *Tommy's Temptations*, and so gleans bits and pieces of information—all negative, of course. She bad-mouthed Belinda while telling the world that she trained the young girl, readied her for stardom. Baloney!"

"When did she get involved romantically with Jackson?"

He waited a while, considering what to say. "The day Belinda moved to the Claremont, Millie moved her things into the apartment. What was hidden before suddenly became open. A rotten shame, I figure."

"Why? Jackson has a right to his own life, no?"

"When his sister was living in the apartment, they kept apart. We suspected something was going on, but…tensions between Belinda and Millie…"

"I see." I drummed my fingers on the table. "But I still don't see why we're sitting here."

"Secrets, Miss Ferber. Belinda was pulling away from her brother, ignoring him, refusing his visits, going through some changes that made him furious. The times he did see her were screaming matches. He'd go the New Beacon, but she wouldn't let him backstage into her dressing room. 'You're not doing what I told you to do.' A favorite line. 'Do you want to jeopardize everything we've worked for?' Or: 'You owe me.'"

I looked into his face. "You never liked Jackson?"

His voice thick with anger. "A man impossible to like. He barely paid us decent wages. He ran the theater like a fiefdom. He ridiculed us. Stagehands quit. The crew hates him. He always thought he was one step ahead of the world. 'People in this miserable city think they can pull a fast one on me. Nobody tricks this savvy city boy.' Dumb lines like that thrown in our faces. And he'd beat his chest like that ape in that O'Neill play. 'I was an acrobat in vaudeville. I balanced a dozen plates on poles.' Big deal! He got obsessed with his own success but knew he had little talent, something that made him bitter." A weary smile. "Money filled the cracks. But lately he got afraid—he was like looking over his shoulder."

"What was he afraid of?"

"Belinda turned her back on him—his theater. She stopped playing his game. He got panicky. The well was drying up. Being with Dougie changed her. Jackson got nuts. You own the golden goose—you expect the gold coins to keep flowing out, right?"

"I can see Jackson like that, but you're suggesting Belinda was like him—craven. Calculated."

"That's my point. Yes, at first. Then—no. Again—Dougie was the reason. People change, Miss Ferber."

"Do they? That's not been my experience."

He pointed a finger at me. "Of course, they do."

"Tell me something. Was Belinda going to leave Dougie?"

He waited a while, concentrated on his syrupy pancakes, carefully cutting wedges and popping them into his mouth. "Yeah, according to Millie. A rumor she spread. Overheard conversations at the New Beacon. Backstage. Another love interest looming. Frankly, I never believed it."

"Why not?"

"It was just that—talk. Dumb talk. People never got to see what Belinda was really like. I watched her with Dougie—one time. Walking arm in arm. It was—*real* for her. " He looked into my face. "You know, I liked her—most of the time. Not when she was hell-bent on Broadway—ambitious. But the quiet times."

"Tell me, Mr. Waters, what was she like? I saw so little of who she was. It was easy for me to dismiss her as…a gold-digger. Millie suggested you had an affair with her. Maybe."

Chauncey laughed a long time. "Yeah, I heard that. You know, Millie flirted with me, and I turned my back on her. Then she found Jackson. Or they found each other. No, Belinda sought me out in that den of madness. Coffee up the street—like what you and I are doing right now."

"No romance?"

"Not with her." A sloppy grin.

"So Belinda changed."

"The last times she visited she flared up, battling with Jackson. She crossed Millie, and that wasn't pretty. She was depressed. Real sad, hurt, loving Dougie but tired of him. He's so—babyish. His behavior gave her—heartache. Jackson didn't help, getting snotty with her, warning her. One time, the last time we saw each other, she said to me, 'Sometimes I want to go back to Sayville, Connecticut, that dying little town. Everyone is dead there now. Everybody but me.'"

"Did Jackson know about that?"

He shook his head. "The times Belinda got sentimental about her childhood, Jackson stormed around, got mad. 'Shut up about it.' His favorite line. 'That dump.' It was like he wanted to forget the past. She wanted to embrace it. Like I told you—I always felt there were secrets, things unsaid."

"Mr. Waters, you quit the place."

"You know why? The day after Belinda was murdered—Lord, what a horrible day that was, all the crying, Jackson hidden in his upstairs rooms all morning, sobbing—the whispering began. Millie and Jackson. It stopped when I walked in. Or Kent. The stage crew. It was like they were afraid of something coming out. I could tell that. When I said something, Jackson snapped at me. 'Mind your own business. You ask too many questions.' But I never asked any questions. I kept my mouth shut. But I watched."

"Maybe somebody was afraid you'd get some answers."

He looked over my shoulder. "They're running scared."

"Why are you telling me all this, Mr. Waters?"

"Because I caught Millie and Jackson whispering about you. I heard Millie say, 'She's a snoop. If she finds out…' Then she stopped. Jackson never liked Mr. Coward—even back when

Dougie first introduced them. But now, after you've been coming around, they're afraid."

That intrigued me. "But why?"

"Because you care what happened. Because you want to *know* what happened. Kent told me that. And because you gotta know that Belinda's murder started in that theater."

I jumped. "I…"

"Jackson created a life for her and then she refused to live it."

"Mr. Waters, your words alarm me."

A thin smile. "They should." He stood up. "Good-bye, Miss Ferber." He pointed to his empty plate. "And thank you. This wasn't the day I was supposed to eat." He nodded sheepishly.

"Thank you," I told him. "Good luck." As he walked away, I stayed in the seat, watching. I called after him, "Mr. Waters, will you ever go back to acting?"

A wan, hesitant smile. "What do you think I've been doing this last hour with you."

● ● ● ● ●

Lady Maud insisted I visit her without Noel, whom she'd met once before, a meeting that left her disillusioned and unhappy. I insisted she meet him again. She balked. We compromised— Noel locked arms with me as we stepped into the foyer of her mansion on Fifth Avenue. We were shown into a fifth floor solarium that faced the East River, and we sat on creamy white wicker chairs. Lush, deep green potted plants, cascading ferns, teak wood tables and wall shelves lined with exotic orchids, deepest purple, pinks, salmons, bridal white. A wash of utter tropical color. But intoxicating, the scent of those blooms, a heavy sweetness covered the room, musky, so powerful I caught my breath. An opium den, I imagined, some forbidden narcotic bliss, this overheated room with the floor-to-ceiling glass panels facing a canopied terrace. While we waited, I caught strains of a radio playing "Stardust" in a nearby room.

"Act two," I mumbled to Noel. "I barely survived act one in these rooms."

"She plans to drug us into submission. The perfume of these lethal plants. Her slaves for life," Noel whispered.

I surveyed the room. "I died for beauty."

Noel hummed in a singsong voice, "Her blood is royal blue, not red." Then, surprisingly nervous, "What shall we talk about?"

At that moment Lady Maud sailed in, apologizing, though her icy glare belied her words. Dressed in a deep burgundy tea gown, cut amethysts circling her neck, she seemed herself a hothouse plant. She slipped quietly into a chair, observed us without speaking, and then she snapped her fingers. Immediately the maid entered and placed a Japanese tea service on the table, hummingbirds flitting across pale green reeds. She watched as the young woman poured tea, a sour look on her face. The servant never looked up at her—or us.

When we were alone, she began, her voice thick with fury. "The reason I called you here today, Miss Ferber." An arctic glance at Noel, who was smiling at her. "And Mr. Coward."

"The reason?" I asked. "I expected to see Dougie here."

She spoke over my words. "Whenever that boy is in town, he's in trouble. I sent him with our driver to Albany for the day. Family business needing attending, which he seems loathe to do these days." She sighed heavily. "It's best he not be here."

"And why is that?" Noel asked.

Silence, Lady Maud staring at the tea set, the filled cups no one dared touch. Arsenic, I mused, served with flowers for my funeral.

She spoke through clenched teeth, yet purposely ignored Noel, her body slightly turned away. "Miss Ferber, the last time we sat in these rooms I told you of the pernicious nature of theater—how Dougie's entry, his business investments there, but worse, his aimless loitering in Schubert Alley with actresses"— she paused as though she'd lost her train of thought—"would come to no good. Mark my words. I'm sure you thought me an old fool, prejudiced against *that* world." A ragged cry escaped her throat. "A possible murder charge. Do you hear me? A young man who is in danger of losing everything he—or we, my dead husband, me—planned and built and dreamed of. Gone." She waved a hand in the air. "Stupidly gone."

"We believe Dougie is innocent," Noel volunteered.

She fairly sneered. "Of course he is. Don't be ridiculous."

"Then why…?" I began.

"He told me that the two of you are investigating, asking questions, visiting that dreadful theater in Hell's Kitchen." She shuddered. "Appropriate name, wouldn't you say? Satan's realm, the last stop on the journey to punishment—where that evil girl hatched her plans with that no-good brother of hers. He told me he considers you—friends. He asked if you could help him." Again, her hand flew out in the air.

"Is there a problem with that?" I asked.

She pursed her lips, the dedicated schoolmarm who has failed with the class simpleton. "Frankly, yes. I asked you here today, Miss Ferber, to tell you to—stop. Stop this running around. Do you know how much attention there is on my family now? You'll only bring more unwanted attention to the awful incident."

Noel burst out, "It's more than an awful incident, Lady Maud. It's…murder."

She cringed, tapped her heart. "And sleepless nights for me. My Dougie hauled off to a grimy police station like a street pickpocket or—or a shiftless ne'er-do-well. One of those…those shabby hobos selling chestnuts over a barrel up the block—chased away by the cops but back within minutes. You've seen them. You two are celebrated names in this ugly town. Famous, as it were. Very famous. Talked of people in the press. We are already being hounded, and I don't mean by the police—luckily there are lawyers who can stay that chaos. I'm talking about the pesky photographers who hover outside on my sidewalk, snap photos as we leave. Lord, flash bulbs crunch underfoot as we rush to the car."

"They're just doing their job."

She snapped at me. "Are you that naïve, Miss Ferber? They persecute. A rich man, a murderer. Playboy, late nights at El Morocco, hotsy-totsy girl singer. It's tabloid heaven. No Maddox has ever been on the cover of the *Daily News*. The *Daily Mirror*. That guttersnipe Walter Winchell.

"No one is following us," Noel insisted. "We ask questions. We talk to theater people. Harmless, but maybe productive. Someone might tell us something they won't tell to the police. A bit of information they don't deem important, but…"

Her hand held up in his face. "Stop. Do you really believe what comes out of your mouth, sir?" Noel's jaw dropped. "I warned him if he got involved with theater folk"—she glared at Noel, no doubt the culprit of Dougie's lapses and transgressions—"there'd be hell to pay. Yes, of course, his name must be cleared. All scandal minimized. Life must get back to normal. His fling on Broadway forgotten."

"I still don't understand."

Her words were clipped, fierce. "I've hired my own private detective, one who works with families such as ours—who need discretion. Recommended by a business associate of my late husband's. A Vanderbilt, if you must know. Discreet, confidential, professional, he will find that murderer. We will end this nonsense, but quietly."

"Dougie approves of this?" asked Noel.

She stared into his face, her dislike so apparent. "Dougie has no say in the matter. I hope he's stuck in an upstate blizzard as we speak. Let him meditate on his errant behavior."

I smiled. "So we're to back off?"

"Exactly." She tugged at the sleeve of her gown. "So thank you." She looked toward the door. "Marlene will show you out." She stood up.

We didn't move, which baffled her. She sank back into the cushions. "Have I not made myself clear?"

"I'm curious," I began. "What has the detective found out so far?"

She seemed ready to chastise me, but decided against it. "If you must know, enough to convince me that my son was cruelly victimized by avaricious schemers. A pattern of greed and sneaky trickery. That girl's past suggests a slew of other men anxious to kill her."

I caught my breath. "Like?"

"He reported a remarkable conversation with Tommy Stuyvesant, for one—or, I should say, an *attempt* at conversation. One of her victims. Who, surprisingly, finally refused to talk to the detective, stopped the conversation dead in its tracks. And Cyrus Meerdom, whom I know socially, but never liked. A fawning profligate who abandoned a wife to weep over a pretty girl. He *followed* her, dumbstruck by her beauty. Everyone talked about it. One night the entire ballroom at the Waldorf-Astoria gossiped of nothing else but his…his dogged devotion to that awful girl. We all expressed sorrow for his poor wife, in fact. Others, probably."

I turned to Noel. "I'm surprised Tommy wouldn't want to help the investigation."

Lady Maud ran her tongue into the corner of her mouth. "Not if he's the real murderer. She did give him a hard time."

"Do you really believe that?"

"What I have learned," she went on, "is that she and her brother got off a bus from Connecticut, some hick town of grubbing farms."

"That's not a secret, Lady Maud."

She snapped, "I'm not finished. They set up shop on that derelict avenue of beggars and malcontents, and set their sights on Broadway—and Fifth Avenue." A confidential, smug tone. "He learned that Belinda—then a prosaic Linda Roswell—was a wild girl in that cow town. Wanton, in fact. She actually ran off with some man, eloping, only to have her father find her and drag her home. What does that tell you?"

"She was married?" I sat up, startled. "That *is* news."

"A high-school girl. Imagine. I gather her father dashed that foolhardy plan." She stood again. "Enough. I know you think ill of me, but I don't care. I tell you frankly—I'm glad that girl is dead. She did nothing but wreak havoc on a stable family. She…she broke everything up into pieces."

"She was horribly murdered." My icy voice cut the air.

Her look was glacial. "But not by my son."

Noel was frowning. "You've assembled a contingent of high-priced lawyers keeping him from prison bars, no?"

Her eyes hard, dark. "You're a naïve man, Mr. Coward. I don't know how things are in your country, but in America the rich are vulnerable. The *hoi polloi*, especially in these days of want, cry blood, want blood. Demand blood." She glared. "I will not have my son's blood spilt because rabble are in arms."

"Cocoon," I mumbled, remembering Moss Hart's words after Noel's birthday party.

She wasn't listening. "The rich go to jail, Mr. Coward. That news might surprise you. A few years back that awful Bobby Frank case in Chicago. Leopold and Loeb, rich boys on a foolish lark, a mindless stunt, a stupid murder, and all that family money—Lord, even Clarence Darrow at his most eloquent—could not keep them from jail, where they now sit. Seconds away from the electric chair." Her eyes got moist. "Not my Dougie." She hissed a final line. "Good-bye. You'll stop your snooping around."

"I don't think so." Noel half-bowed to her.

She glared at him.

"Maybe we'll find out the true story," I added.

She opened her mouth but nothing came out. She blanched, grabbed at the amethyst necklace so tightly that I thought she'd rip the beads from her neck.

Chapter Thirteen

Christmas Eve: the city glowed and glistened. As I headed back to my apartment at twilight, the streets were already taking on that quiet rhythm I loved about the holiday—excited voices muffled by the bitter cold, distant strains of caroling from a church I passed, a string of multicolored lights strung over the doorway of a bakery on Lexington, a young father and his little boy dragging a bulky green fir tree down the sidewalk. But as I stepped into the foyer of my building, I glanced back at the street: depression still soured the Manhattan days. Steps from my home was a makeshift Hooverville planted in Central Park, homeless souls huddled under cardboard and burlap and corrugated tin in the cold night. The birth of Jesus celebrated in a minor chord this year.

I'd begged off parties, though Moss Hart called twice, lying to me: "Edna, Christmas without you is empty. Who is going to help me find the star in the East?"

I'd smiled. "Yes, dear Mossie, my acerbic commentary which no one welcomes."

"I do," he'd insisted.

Every party I was invited to was hosted by someone Jewish. That fact tickled me. But in Manhattan Christmas often had little to do with religion—it was the welcome spirit that covered you like an old familiar blanket. My housekeeper Rebecca had prepared a cold dinner, left covered on my kitchen counter, as she hurried off to spend the holiday with her family in Jersey. I'd get into my favorite silk robe, prop a tray on my lap in my bed, tune the Philco to a station playing uptown jazz or maybe Paul Whitman's Christmas music, and read a new novel by old friend Louis Bromfield. Perfect. All is calm, if not bright.

It was not meant to be, I soon discovered. Dougie Maddox phoned minutes after I arrived home. At first, listening, I had no idea who it was because his voice was so scratchy, low, spaced with silences. Finally, a throat cleared, and Dougie mumbled, "I wanted to say hello." A line barely articulated, stretched out, crackling.

"What's the matter?" I asked, alarmed.

Silence, then: "I'm back from Albany. From one exile to another."

"Where are you?"

"At Lady Maud's. Solitary confinement."

I hesitated. "Dougie, are you all right?"

A phony laugh. "Lady Maud is filling up the house with people. A Christmas Eve party. Can you believe it? Like…like she's making believe the world is all right, that her only son is not under a cloud of suspicion. Unbelievable! There's silver tinsel hanging everywhere, so many poinsettias I feel I'm at a Mexican funeral. A decorated tree that belongs at Rockefeller Center. A piano player is tuning up as I speak. Good God, Edna, he's got sheet music for, I swear, 'There's No Depression in Love.' Yet piles of food everywhere. Depression? It's insane." Another stiff laugh. "No irony, Edna. Why is it there's no irony in this house?"

I interrupted. "Catch a cab and come here."

A deep sigh, almost a rattle. "Good, I was hoping you'd say that."

But he didn't arrive, and I thought he'd changed his mind. When Noel called to say hello and wish me well, I told him a miserable Dougie was wending his lonesome Christmas way to my apartment. "I guess there definitely is room at this particular inn."

Noel mentioned Moss Hart's soiree, his destination that evening, then said, "I'll stop in, Edna. All right?"

"Of course." I smiled. "I was hoping you'd say that. Somehow, facing Dougie tonight alone is…daunting."

The minutes passed. No Dougie. I worried, but thought he was hiding in his room, shutting the door to keep Lady Maud and the world away. When Noel arrived, he asked, "Where is he?"

"Perhaps he changed his mind. He sounded—hollow, lost."

Noel was drumming his fingers on his chin, his gaze faraway. "We need to talk to him."

"Tonight?"

"As good a night as any." He looked around my apartment, a clownish grin on his face. "I hope he's not distracted by your gaudy Christmas tree over there and the excessive red-and-green garlands festooning your draperies. The partridge in the pear tree. The lords a-leaping. The star of Bethlehem on your terrace. The sudden appearance of the Magi *sans* camels, I trust."

I laughed. "I figured you'd arrive with an appropriate wreath around your neck."

"Father Christmas with an ivory cigarette holder and a terribly British public-school ascot. My impression of Oscar Wilde singing 'Deck the Halls.'"

"With boughs of...folly."

"You know, dear Edna, I've always thought 'The First Noel' was written about me. A birthday song to cheer a lonely boy."

"That doesn't surprise me."

When Dougie did arrive, apologizing and saying that he had to sneak away from Lady Maud's persistent control and some drunken souls arriving to celebrate the birth of Christ—"The help have the dual role of keeping the whiskey flowing but also guarding the murder suspect so he doesn't venture astray"—he was overjoyed to see Noel sitting in the wing chair, his head lost in a cloud of smoke. Immediately Dougie settled on the piano bench, leaned into it, and hit a few notes. I groaned—not a pathetic reprise of his last visit, the Johnny-one-note mournful display he'd shared with us.

Noel told him to close the keyboard. "We're not taking requests quite yet, Dougie."

Dougie sat across from me on the divan. "Thank you." For some reason he was dressed in formal wear, an elegant dinner jacket and nattily knotted black tie, yet his shoes were scuffed. The creases in his trousers so sharp they could be knife blade. The debonair man-about-town, to be sure, but something had shifted, and when I caught Noel's eye, I was certain he noticed what I did.

Gone was the boyishly handsome face, that wide-eyed babyish innocence, that boys'-choir openness. What had appealed about him had always been that inviting face—not a grown man's rugged look, perhaps weathered skin and pronounced jawline, a hint of five-o'clock beard stubble. No. Dougie appealed because of the huckleberry boy in the man. A mischievous Tom Sawyer, grown now but still brandishing a whitewash brush. Peck's Bad Boy chomping on a piece of Spearmint. The boy next door, trusted, welcome to marry your daughter. A Congregational Church boy, sort of.

But Dougie had undergone a startling transformation, the charming face now haggard, his eyes cloudy. Dark blotches under those haunted eyes, a web of wrinkles radiating from his mouth. Pale lips, chapped even, a spot of dried blood on one corner of his lower lip. An uneven toilet, minuscule tuffs of missed hair at the jawline. He looked—beaten. The Hoover hobo dressed up for the cotillion and then refused at the door.

Under his breath Noel mumbled one word in my direction. "Wounded."

We sat at my mahogany dining room table, the three of us bunched at one end, and I served the dinner Rebecca left me: marinated cold chicken, a German potato salad, a loaf of rye bread Rebecca had picked up at Katz's Delicatessen on First Avenue, sour cream cauliflower. Picnic in Central Park food, though I lit two candles and dimmed the lights. Dougie absently nibbled on a chicken leg and with his fork pushed away the cauliflower, though he squinted at it, as if trying to identify it as flora or fauna. He did sip the tumbler of whiskey I provided, a generous Christmas gift from Neysa McMein, who insisted the coming end of Prohibition meant she'd have to invent new Christmas gift ideas in future years. "Damn that Roosevelt." Her favorite curse these days. Dougie idly poured himself a second glass, though I considered stopping him. I didn't.

"Talk to us," Noel began.

Dougie waved his hands in the air aimlessly. "I don't know what to say."

"Start," I jumped in, irritated, "with why you are back at your mother's."

He sighed. "I never really left. After our problems, those arguments, I did stay mostly at the Stanhope."

"So you've given up your rooms there?" From Noel.

He nodded. "Yeah, I *had* to. Everyone looks at me. Everyone accuses with their eyes."

"That's to be expected."

A flash of anger. "You'd think people would be better behaved. Especially at a place like—the club."

"Rich people aren't excluded from incivility." Noel said. "Usually they perfect the art."

"Whatever that means," Dougie grumbled. "It's just that people avoid me. You know, I never really had close friends— somehow my parents didn't allow it—and no one from school. Lord, even at my mother's the staff turns away from me. They hide away from me, they whisper, they approach me as if I'm a leper." His voice got raspy. "I *am* a leper." He twisted around. "I have trouble looking in a mirror."

"For now," I said, comforting. "This will end. When…" My words trailed off.

"Will it?" Another flash of anger. "For God's sake, this will be the story of my life forever more."

I finished my sentence. "When they find the murderer, Dougie. That's what has to happen."

"How? How?" His voice broke.

A moment of silence, Noel gazing out the dark window and me—I stared into Dougie's shaking face and didn't know what I hoped to see. Noel was obviously troubled—puzzled. You could see it in his eyes. I had a harder edge, I realized—I was bothered by Dougie's anger, his weakness. Maybe I sensed that he was callow. And yet—and yet there was that soft spot in me that wanted to hug him. An amazing man, I thought—he elicited such a welter of conflicting emotions in me. I found myself looking away, like Noel who was gazing toward the window at the black night.

"What about your buddy, Corey?" I asked. "You mention having no friends, but Corey…" I stopped as I recalled Corey's own dismissive remarks about any friendship with Dougie.

His laugh was mocking. "Fair weather friend, Edna. You've met him. I mean, at the Stanhope I saw him all the time—that's really how we reconnected after all these years. We'd always nodded at each other at clubs. We'd even talked. We made up memories from our days at New Haven. There—back then he *snubbed* me. His folks summered near us, but he ran with a livelier crowd. Jazz babies. In the city he sought me out." A harsh laugh. "He's really broke—sort of. My dollar bills fueled his attention to me. We went to places."

"That night at the automat he was with you and Belinda and even Kitty. When we met on that sidewalk. You all seemed— longtime friends then."

He scoffed. "Yeah, but when he left the automat, he took that long walk down Broadway and disappeared from my life."

"Not really," I insisted.

"Might as well be. You know, I call him up and he's distant. I can tell by the tone of his voice that he wants to get off the phone. It's like he believes I'm—I'm a murderer. That scares me. I asked him to leave the city for a few days, the two of us, maybe skiing in Vermont, a long weekend at our lodge, but he didn't even answer." A sliver of a smile. "Yeah, I know the cops told me to stay in the city, but…" He shrugged his shoulders.

"Dougie, granted you two were never close, but lately you did spend a lot of time together."

He looked perplexed. "You know, I thought I could tell him anything."

I counted a heartbeat. "And did you?" My tone sharp.

He watched me carefully. "There was nothing to tell."

"What are you getting at, Edna?" Noel asked. He rested his fork on his plate and dropped his hands into his lap.

I hedged a bit. "Corey struck me as a little bit of a trouble-maker, no? He passes on gossip—rumors. He seemed to enjoy telling tales of Belinda's behavior. That idea rankles me a bit. "

Dougie's voice got heated. "That's what frat buddies do, Edna. Would you have me stumble around in the dark? A fool. A laughing stock. A...a cuckold of sorts."

"That's a little extreme, no?"

He sighed heavily. "I never questioned it."

"Maybe you should have," I said, but regretted my harsh-ness. He looked at me with sad, questioning eyes. I attempted a feeble, reassuring smile—but failed. I dabbed at my lips with my napkin.

He sat back, eyes wide. "What I do know is that the police are breathing down my neck." A slight smile. "My lawyers' necks. I know that because Lady Maud's voice gets shrill —maybe shriller is the word—when she talks to them on the phone. The police have no other suspects. They aren't even *looking* for other sus-pects." His voice trembled. "It's—me! I don't want to go to jail." His eyes got moist. "Or—the chair. The electric chair. My God."

Exasperated, rushing my words, "You must have thought about that night, Dougie. Who would have killed Belinda?"

He threw back his head and groaned. "I don't know. I can't sleep at night. In the morning I'm so tangled in my blankets that I feel roped in. Belinda...Belinda spoke her mind, yes, and there are always folks who resent other people's success, rising in the world. Especially theater. Jealous. Anger. Pettiness. Right, Noel?"

Noel pursed his lips together. "Yes, I still resent that pedestrian George Bernard Shaw's inglorious rise to fame."

Dougie simmered. "Christ, no, I'm serious. Listen to me. Belinda didn't step *on* people to get ahead. She just kept...step-ping. Moving." He reflected, "Though her brother cajoled...pres-sured maybe..." He shook his head. "No, that's what people do."

"She had to have enemies, no?" I insisted.

"Everybody's got enemies."

"That's a glib answer," I told him, my voice stern. "The people she worked with at the Paradise. Millie Glass. Kent LaSalle. Chauncey White. Others. Tommy Stuyvesant. Cyrus Meerdom." I narrowed my eyes. "The men she saw before—you."

He fumed. "Not that again. C'mon, Edna. Please. A laundry list of make-believe suitors. Yeah, I've heard it all before. I've seen it. Remember that—slap at your party?" He looked at Noel. "She only saw—me."

"Yes," Noel said quietly. "The bell that was rung to tell everyone that it was time to stop having fun."

For a while we watched one another, silent. Noel reached into his pocket for a cigarette. Dougie nodded at him and Noel handed him one. When Noel looked at me, a cigarette extended, I shook my head. No thanks. Dougie waited for Noel to light him, and for a second his eyes got dreamy as he drew in the smoke. Fascinated, I watched the two men watching each other smoke. The narcotic walls they built around themselves. Boys' club, I thought.

"You know," I said, "your mother told me she wanted us to stop helping you."

He put his cigarette out in an ashtray. "I know. She told me. She said a photographer staking out the Paradise spotted the two of you going in and snapped your picture. I guess Winchell made a snide comment in his column in the *Mirror*." He smiled. "'Paradise lost,' he wrote."

I grumbled, "Walter Winchell thrives on innuendo and malice."

"What else did he say?" Noel asked. "I missed that."

"He said, 'Ferber and Coward are asking the questions we all know the answer to. Who's the coward here?'"

Noel grinned. "That gnarly boy sure do know how to turn a phrase. I bet his mamma is plum proud of her little boy Wally," he said with a peach-blossom Southern accent.

My mind was racing. "Okay, Dougie, think. You must have ideas about that night at the automat. Who else was there? Someone must have followed you all there. How else to know Belinda was there? Or spotted her there? Who? I know that Buzzy

Collins supposedly was there earlier but left with his party. The police, I know, talked to him—he was with the same people he left with. Long after midnight. Could he have called someone?"

Dougie's lips twitched. "You mean like Cyrus Meerdom?"

"For one." I sighed. "A man who couldn't let go of Belinda's attention."

"But," Noel added, "even if Buzzy called Cyrus to come and strangle Belinda, there's the time factor. Cyrus, probably across town, an old man readying for bed, scurrying to the automat?"

"Impossible," I said. "What? Sneaking into the back door, waiting for Belinda. What are the odds?"

"Nil," Noel said.

"Unless," I mused, "Cyrus was hovering around the neighborhood, following in that town car."

"Edna, Edna," Noel laughed, "you do paint an improbable scenario. Rudolph Valentino slinking around the oasis looking for Theda Bara."

Dougie hadn't said anything while Noel and I ran on with our impossible speculation. Suddenly, his features contorting, he stood up. At the sideboard he poured himself some whiskey, drank it down in one gulp. "Lady Maud said Tommy refused to talk to the detective she hired."

"I know. Your mother told me. Why? That struck me as strange," I admitted. "Perhaps your mother's detective is not the right person for the job."

Noel smiled. "Maybe Edna Allan Poe knows best the means of ratiocination."

Pushing my plate away, I stood up, signaled to the two men as I blew out the candles and moved from the table into the living room. They followed me, Dougie avoiding the piano bench—my baleful eye guaranteed that—and choosing the wing chair he'd sat in earlier. Surprisingly, Noel dragged a chair close to Dougie, facing him, a few feet apart. A curious tableau, I thought: Aristotle contemplating the bust of Homer. Well, not quite.

"Help us," Noel said, looking into his face.

Dougie looked stunned, sputtering, "I don't know how."

"We're stumbling in the dark." I threw my hands in the air.

"I know." A whine to his voice, unattractive.

Watching that mobile face, so hangdog now, I realized at that moment how easy it would be to dislike the young man. Yes, I'd found him appealing in a fresh, engaging way, the new kid in my town—my small circle of acquaintances—who looked with wonder at everything. But more so—I admitted to being flattered by his servile attention to me, his delight when I approached him. It baffled me because young men ran from me—I had little patience with their posturing and vainglorious love of themselves. Cruelly, I called them all one derisive word—Bub. But now, suddenly, I wondered about Dougie offering his devotion to me. That annoying whine that sometimes laced his words, his noisome passivity, his—avoidance. Here was a man who had stepped outside of heaven and wondered how to get back in.

Road maps to paradise were not available in my living room.

"Tell me," I began, another attempt to get some answers. "Any idea who this new person was that Belinda was supposedly leaving you for? The rumored interest?" Blunt lines, said purposely, and Dougie stared, mouth agape. Even Noel arched his eyebrows, though his eyes twinkled.

"Belinda's infidelities." Noel's coda to my harsh words.

Dougie floundered, uncomfortable. He wrapped his arms around his knees, leaning forward, the little boy in the principal's office, squirming.

"No," he said finally. "Just the stories told to me."

Another blunt line. "I know you worried about Wallace Benton. Richer than any of us. That new skyscraper. The invitation to dinner. The roses sent to her dressing room."

He bunched up his face. "Which I stupidly smashed to the ground."

"He was wooing her?" asked Noel.

"Him—or someone else." Frustrated, swinging his arms around. "I don't know. But I know it drove me crazy. I was afraid Belinda had her eye on the horizon."

"We all do," I insisted. "What else is there to do?"

"That's not what I mean, Edna. I think her louse of a brother programmed her like that Czech robot to do his bidding."

Frustrated, I challenged him. "So she had no say at all in her own destiny?"

"A little extreme, no?" From Noel.

"But she did love you," I added. "And you loved her."

For a moment Dougie's eyes got moist, glassy. "God, yes. We did love each other."

"But you fought tooth and nail," I went on.

His fist pounded his knee. "My damned fault. I know that now. You know *she* didn't fight me. She *answered* me. She resisted. She rejected what I said. 'Only you, Dougie, you.' A litany for her. 'You!' And I still didn't listen." His eyes got wide now. "I ruined everything because I didn't trust any more. Every rumor I ran with—brought it to her doorstep like a cat dragging a mouse to its owner. Look! Look! Answer me. I—I tired her out. She had no energy left. It was all my fault."

"No matter, really, if, indeed, she was stepping out on you."

"I *hate* that," he thundered. "Even if I *knew* it, I hated the idea of it. You know, I'd go to the Paradise, stop into see her brother early on, and the way he acted got me nervous."

Noel spoke up. "The time we all had lunch—you, me, Belinda and Jackson—the let's-introduce-Noel tour, he bothered me. 'I have ideas for plays. We need to talk.' No, we didn't have that need. I found him unpleasant. Those eyes."

Dougie was anxious to talk. "I didn't trust him—ever. I mean, I'd go with Belinda and he was all fussy and nice, but I knew he was a weasel. Money-grubbing. Hands out. Alms for the poor theater player. But when I was out of earshot, I'd hear him whisper to Belinda. Things like—'What the hell you think you're doing? Behave yourself. You think I don't hear the stories? He's gonna hear, too.' The "he," I knew, was me. When I got near, he was all smiles. But Belinda was grim-faced, sober."

"So Jackson must have heard about her new interests," I said.

"The way you talk. 'Her new interests.' A nice way to put it."

"That's what it was," I said grimly.

"I know. But"—a faraway look came into his eyes—"when I went back to the theater after Belinda died, Jackson didn't know how to deal with me."

"Understandable," I said. "The police…"

He spoke quickly, his hands waving in the air. "When Jackson was out of the room, that Millie Glass hugged me. Said how sorry she was. 'Oh, what a loss!' Then, batting her eyes, she said that if I ever wanted to talk, she was there."

Noel stormed, "She flirted with you?"

"She always flirted with me. I paid no attention."

"Did Jackson know?"

"Not on your life."

I clicked my tongue. "It seems the women around Belinda wanted what she had."

Dougie's voice dragged. "You know, I spotted Kitty on the street the other day. Another one who avoids me. She actually ducked into a green-grocer when she saw me on the sidewalk. I followed her, tried to get her to talk to me. Like Corey, she sees me as a murderer."

"You don't know that for sure," Noel interrupted.

"You know, I never trusted her either." A crooked smile. "I guess I don't trust a lot of people. But there's something petty about her. A schemer in her own right. Those eyes always on me. No—worse, those eyes on Belinda. I never thought she was good for Belinda."

"Why?" From Noel.

"I think Kitty saw herself as one of the…as a darker planet hidden behind the sun, and she resented it. She tried to get close to Belinda. Yeah, the four of us went out together all the time. She flirted with Corey, yes, and he flirted back. But Corey told me he wanted his own sun—his own Belinda."

"Maybe he wanted Belinda," Noel remarked suddenly.

Dougie snapped, "He knew better." He paused. "Kitty was no friend of mine. She poisoned the well. She was afraid Belinda might abandon her. If Belinda rose in the world, maybe Kitty could rise, too. More than once she asked Belinda to help her get back onstage. A chorus part. Anything."

"And what did Belinda say?"

"She never answered." He leaned forward. "Belinda told me Kitty was a drone. Never the queen bee. Worse, a drone that had outsized dreams."

"Could Kitty have killed Belinda?" I asked. "Yes, she caught a taxi, but she could have circled back, gone in by way of the alley."

He cut me off. "No."

"You seem so sure."

A helpless gesture. "I don't know what to believe anymore." A deep sigh.

"What about Jackson and Millie?"

"I assumed they were lovers," Dougie said. "In fact, I mentioned that to Belinda once and she flew into a rage. That led to another argument."

"Why would that bother her?" I asked.

He shrugged. "She didn't like Millie Glass."

"And she liked her brother?" I asked.

He waited a heartbeat. "That's another thing. Recently it was clear that she disliked him, wanted him away from her. She didn't want to talk about him. I guess they—fought. I mean, even physical."

Noel wondered out loud, "That's the wrinkle here, no?"

"They'd struggled to find a life in theater in this city," Dougie said. "They clung to each other—shared a dream. They managed to get out of that small village in…"

"In Connecticut," I finished. "Sayville. Outside Bridgeport. I've seen the signs on the New York New Haven line."

"That's another thing," Dougie added. "I wanted to go back there with her. To visit. She said their farm had been sold. Her family died. I said, so what? A day's car ride. 'I want to see where you were born.' She refused. 'That's a world that's over and done with.' Her words. 'A graveyard.'"

"Sometimes we have bad childhood memories. I cringe at the idea of Ottumwa, Iowa, a backwater village that treated my family horribly. Dirty boys in knickers trailing after me and shouting, 'Sheeny, sheeny, kike, kike.'"

"Good God." From Noel, furrowing his brow.

"Nightmares for me."

Noel was tapping his finger on his knee. "Maybe her life in that village holds some answer."

"Maybe her brother is her killer," I said, again emphatically.

Dougie twitched. "God, Edna, you do it again."

"Possible."

"No." Dougie looked into my face. "No." He shuddered. "When I went there, he looked at me like *I* was a killer. I felt like an alien. Out of place. Yet I can't stop going there. It's like— Belinda calls me there. Back to days when everything was *good* for us. Beautiful. The laughter. The joy."

"Are you still sending him money?" I asked.

Dougie looked puzzled, "You know, I haven't thought about it. But, no, how can I pay someone who accuses me of murder?"

The evening was coming to an end. Dougie started moving around the apartment, picking up a jade figurine, leafing through a copy of *Vanity Fair*, staring at the small Chagall lithograph over the fireplace. He wanted to leave but didn't know how to do so. Watching him, I experienced a welter of conflicting emotions. A wave of sympathy, yes, and compassion. Concern. But also wariness, a sudden need to distance myself.

Despite the cold night, I left the two men and strolled out onto my terrace, stepping on the ice-crusted snow. From my lofty penthouse, my rarefied aerie up in the sky, I gazed down at the street below. Quiet now, a few cars passing. A few stragglers, pinpoints from outer space. A hum of distant noise. A horn wailed. In the inky blackness strands of purple and blue—specks of gold as cars inched along.

The door opened, and Noel joined me.

"You'll freeze to death."

"I need some cold air."

"What to make of that man." He pointed back at Dougie who was leaning against the piano, watching us, his eyes hooded.

Noel took out his long cigarette holder and inserted a cigarette, struck a match. I nodded toward the pack in his breast pocket. Surprised, he offered me one, and lit it.

"A cigarette a month," I told him. "At moments like this."

We both watched the trail of gray-white smoke curl and drift into the night sky.

From across the way a hint of music. "Another party I was invited to," I told him.

My neighbor across the terrace was Richard Rodgers, and through the lighted windows I could see his holiday guests moving, dancing, laughing. Richard was playing carols on his piano, and his guests sang along. Robust snatches of "Twelve Days of Christmas" drifted out onto the terrace.

Noel grinned. "My true love sent to me…" He waited. "Finish the line, Edna."

"Okay. Sent to me…the four horsemen of the Apocalypse."

His hand swept the city beyond my terrace. He sang another line. "For purple mountain majesties."

"No fruited plains here."

He pointed to the rising skyscrapers, some soaring higher than my penthouse refuge. The dark canyons far below. The low-lying clouds. A few lights switched on in nearby buildings. A hazy skyline, mauve-tinted, speckled white.

"Somewhere out there," he whispered, "is a murderer we can't identify. Somewhere celebrating Christmas Eve maybe. Or wandering the streets, tormented. Or glad. Triumphant. Somewhere, Edna, out there."

"Or," I whispered back, "or he's leaning on a grand piano and watching us freeze to death."

We both turned to face Dougie who was still watching us.

Chapter Fourteen

Early on Christmas morning Noel and I headed into Connecticut for a holiday breakfast with actor Clifton Webb, who lived with his mother Mabelle in an over-heated Colonial in High Acres, Greenwich. Flush from cash from his widely popular Broadway smashes like *Flying Colors* and *Three's a Crowd*, Webb had moved with his imperious mother into the gigantic house. A precious man I'd never taken to, Clifton was Noel's good comrade, which explained our two-hour trek into Connecticut. Earlier that spring, with Aleck Woollcott, the trio had sailed to England. Noel confided that Aleck spent much of his time complaining about me—and Clifton kept *tsk*ing, agreeing that I could be difficult.

"I defended you," Noel insisted.

"I can just imagine. The three of you—Macbeth's sinister witches jabbering on webbed deck chairs."

Noel had rubbed his hands together maliciously. "The cauldron boils over."

I expected to be annoyed in Connecticut—I was, of course. Not so much by the theatrical guests at the gathering, many of them my friends from the city, but by the posturing and saloon performance of Webb's starstruck mother. Her first comment to me on entering: "Oh, good, you're both properly dressed."

As she glared at me, I told her, "I assumed it was hobo outfits optional."

Her son spent most of the time drifting around his mother like a feather duster looking for a dust mote.

The first hour was passable, with Neysa's husband, Handsome Jack, ribbing a bashful Irving Berlin. Jack sat on the piano bench and delighted everyone with a mildly ribald parody of Irving's hit song "Always." In an affected squeaky falsetto he sang out:

Not in rumble seats,
Not in taxi cabs
Not in telephone booths
But hallways.

Laughing so hard, Mabelle slipped off her chair, complained that the schoolmarm bun atop her gray head was askew, and downed the tumbler of potent whiskey in one gulp. After eggs Benedict and Monte Christo cigars and too much badinage, the maid cleared the table for backgammon and Russian banque. A young man in a tight-waisted sports jacket started to sing off-key while a slender platinum-blonde showgirl hiccoughed. The chauffeur drove the Berlins to the train depot, and I nudged Noel, who was having a good time.

"I have a plan," I whispered.

A knowing nod. "Your plan is to escape folks you can barely tolerate."

I smiled. "That, true, but another plan."

"Darling, you're driving."

And I was, in the long black Packard I'd commandeered from the doorman, secured with a generous tip. Noel had dressed for the motor ride—sleek sealskin jacket, a jazzy bowtie, and a plaid driving cap. A raspberry-colored scarf, very Isadora Duncan. We said our goodbyes, but as we were pulling out of the driveway, a local cab drove up. A blasé Tallulah Bankhead sauntered from the rear seat, her face nearly disguised under a gigantic Tyrolean mountaineer's snow hat. Noel wanted to socialize but I pressed the accelerator, the car lurching, sliding against a frozen snow bank.

"Really, Edna," he said, "you insist on making our adventures together the stuff of Buster Keaton slapstick."

I nudged him. "Take the map out of the glove compartment, Noel."

He was grinning. "Edna, I can read your mind. I knew your nefarious intent when you insisted on driving into Connecticut hinterlands, refusing a perfectly good ride with Cole Porter's crowd." A phony, shocked expression covered his face. "And I thought you were more mysterious."

He wrestled with the road map, but shortly his fingertip tapped a dot. "This what you're looking for, darling?"

Sayville, Connecticut. A minuscule dot next to Bridgeport.

I headed in that direction, Noel sputtering out directions.

"It looks like snow, Edna. Are you sure…" He peered out the window. "And it's Christmas day."

"Perfect. It's Connecticut. You've seen the movies, no? We'll be driving into one of those evocative Christmas cards you see everywhere—rolling snow-covered hills splashed with shiny glitter that you can't get off your clothing, wisps of black smoke from the blazing fire of a saltbox farmhouse. Children sledding down those hills. A sleigh. Santa maybe. The horse knows the way…"

"Santa's stuck in a chimney in Bridgeport. The stockings are filled with coal. Merry Christmas afternoon to all, and to all a…"

"There." I jumped. "A sign for Bridgeport."

After the heated opulence of Webb's home, nestled as it was on a street of expensive if cookie-cutter Colonials—all that chalky white clapboard and forest green shutter and wrought-iron lamppost—Bridgeport stunned: weathered steel or iron mills in the hardscrabble city cast deadened shadows on the landscape. Boarded-up factories. Deserted storefronts.

When we crossed the line into Sayville, a farm town of perhaps a hundred homes, maybe less, I maneuvered the Packard down a tight lane of small, green-asphalt-covered bungalows, most likely homes for workers, some with sagging porches and dipped roofs. Packed snow everywhere, gray and dim.

But Sayville had the feel of a Western ghost town, a farming village that once sent its sons into the nearby factories and mills of Bridgeport. One house had an abandoned jalopy in the front yard, a rusting dump truck tipping on flattened tires. The house had a boarded-up front door, its windows smashed in. A faded For Sale sign nailed to the front door. Next door another bungalow with a foreclosure sign tucked into a cloudy front window.

"How do we find the Roswell farm?" Noel wondered out loud.

Baffled, I pulled the car to the side of the road, staring up and down the quiet street. No life—stolid, unassuming homes dotting the landscape. Silence, deadly.

"There." I pointed to a small town green up ahead where a tiny Congregational Church sat on a rise of land. Garlands of green pine were strung over the ancient windows. As we idled in front, someone stepped quickly from the entrance, headed to the rectory next door. I leaned on the horn.

"Really, Edna." Noel shook his head. "It's Christmas."

"I know what day it is, Noel. Horns work on Christmas."

The old man stopped, squinted at us through the wisps of falling snow, and then approached the car. A shabby overcoat, unbuttoned, a pastor's white collar. He smiled at us. "Lost?"

"Yes, quite," Noel told him. "We're looking for the Roswell farm."

He shook his head. "Nobody lives there now. Empty."

"Still and all," I insisted, "we'd like to see…"

A sudden blast of cold air rocked the car. The pastor shivered and rocked backward. He tugged at the overcoat, wrapping it tightly around his skinny body. In a hurried voice, though still with that polite smile on his face, he said, "At the end of this road, a sharp left, then down a mile or so into farm country. You'll see a cluster of hemlocks to the right. A dirt road afterward. A mile or so down there. Can't go any farther. A gray farmhouse with a fallen-down red barn to the right of it. Roof mostly caved in. Can't miss it." He backed up. "You'll miss it if you wait for dark, coming soon." He waved. "Merry Christmas."

"Merry Christmas," I told him, then added, "Happy New Year."

"Yes, Edna," Noel mumbled as I sped away, "it is Christmas, and here we are on this wild good chase."

I ignored him.

The pastor was right, of course: deserted, that house, weathered, boarded up. A ripped foreclosure sign in the window. As we walked onto the rotting porch, a field mouse squealed and disappeared into a crevice. Looking in the windows, I saw a few pieces of furniture: a broken Windsor chair by the fireplace, an enamel table on its side, one leg missing, even a scattered stack of old *Everybody's* magazines piled by some broken crockery.

Noel groaned, "Any other ideas, Miss F?"

"I don't know what I was hoping for."

Nervous, Noel looked back to the road. "Let's go. If darkness falls and the snow picks up and we have to sleep here, I'll never forgive you for my early death."

"The world will miss your tremendous ego."

Disheartened, but perhaps not surprised, I drove away. What had I expected to find? A craggy old uncle, sequestered among the decaying rafters, mad as a barnyard hen, ready to blather hideous family secrets? Rochester's maddened wife cowering in the attic?

Cruising through the center of town, eyeing the shuttered businesses—an Esso filling station with two bubblehead pumps, a feed and grain store, a mom-and-pop luncheonette, a lawyer's office with the shingle flapping in the wind and loosened from its pole. Dead: Christmas day. Families celebrating. At the end of the lane was the Sayville General Store. Est'd 1891—according to the sign on a front post.

"Getting dark, Edna," Noel muttered. "I understand darkness only when surrounded by city cabs and subway entrances."

"Look."

In front of the general store someone was shoveling the snow off the landing with an old coal shovel. Bent against the wind, hunched over, stabbing at the snow, chipping ice at the corners. When the figure turned to face us, I could see it was an old woman dressed in a man's long overcoat, her head swathed in a scarf and a man's bulky hunting cap. She paused as I pulled the car over. Leaning on the shovel, breathing hard, she tucked her head into her chest like a curious bird.

"Help you?"

"We were visiting the Roswell farm…"

She chuckled. "The squirrels and you have a conversation?"

"We used to know a girl who lived there."

"Yeah, that Linda Roswell. Her, I suppose you mean."

"We knew her as Belinda Ross."

"So the papers say. Got herself kilt."

"We were hoping to find family."

"Hope is a worthless occupation sometimes. Like this trek you two took upon yourselves today. No one left, so far as I know."

"Nothing is open today." I motioned back toward the closed shops.

"It's Christmas." A twinkle in her eye. "You got Christmas in the city?"

"You know we're from the city?"

"Don't take no Sherlock Holmes. From the looks of you. Expensive furs and that man"—she pointed an accusing finger at Noel—"with the fancy-schmancy cigarette holder like he's the king of England. And that hat that makes him look like one of the Wright brothers."

Noel started to say something but sputtered to a stop.

"I'm Edna Ferber and this is Noel Coward."

She had no idea who we were. An expression that said: Good for you.

"I'm Angela D'Angelo. Owner, proprietress of this here general store. Closed today. Christmas, as I say. You two heathens?"

"Yes, and proudly," Noel said.

She tapped on the car door. "You, ma'am, is shivering from the cold."

"That I am. The window is down and…"

She looked up and down the deserted road and scratched her neck. Stepping back, she grasped the back of the shovel she'd stuck in the snow. She was watching us closely, head tilted to the side, a quizzical smile on her face. "Time for my Christmas dinner." She looked into my face. "You two look like harmless folks. Not your usual ax murderers and holy-roller born-again crusaders. Perhaps you'd like a bite to eat. As I said, it's Christmas." A sly grin. "Even for heathens from the big city."

I looked at Noel as he shot a glance back at me, puzzled. I shrugged. "A pleasure."

"Edna," Noel admonished, "do you think…?"

Angela D'Angelo said, "If he ain't comfortable with an old lady what's a good cook, maybe he can stay in the car. We can bring him treats like he's an old ornery dog."

Noel burst out laughing. "Dinner is served."

"You bet it is."

We followed her through the aisles of the general store, headed to a back stairwell. Uneven floorboards, old-fashioned pegged wood, creaky, spongy, the feel of an old barn, musty. Starved shelves, I noticed: wooden racks with scattered canned goods, bolts of fabric, hardware tools, sets of crockery. A cracker barrel nearly empty of flour. A molasses jar. For a moment I was taken back to my father's failed general store in Appleton, Wisconsin. My Store, his quaint name for the emporium that struggled to find customers. So much like this meager emporium with its mishmash of sundry goods for sale. A momentary tug at my heart as I remembered the lonely aisles and my father sitting in front, quietly waiting for business.

She caught my eye. "Folks ain't got much money to spend, especially when you got nothing to sell them."

At the top landing, unlit and cluttered with old wooden crates, Angela opened the door a sliver, peeped in, then smiled back at us. "Make sure the dog ain't gonna run down the stairs."

Little chance of that, I figured, as I spotted the ancient orange dog lazily watching us, rheum-eyed and indolent, from a corner of a sofa. For a second an ancient tail wagged, but then stopped, the dog yawning, closing its eyes.

"Better hang that coat on a high hook." Angela indicated my chinchilla. "Leroy might think it's one of his long-lost relatives come to visit, and try to greet it warmly."

I stepped into the warm room, breathed in, and smiled. On the cast-iron kitchen stove a covered pot of simmering sauce, pungent, spicy. On the linoleum counter loaves of fresh bread wrapped in bleached-white dishtowels. Water at a low boil in a huge cast-iron pot. Intoxicating, all of it, mouth-watering.

"Sit yourselves down at the table," she directed. "I made a heap of food, always do, bad habit in such times, but I was hoping my daughter and grandkids could make the trek from Worchester. But no bus money this year. But I was hoping. You never know." A smile, infectious. "A Christmas miracle in a time when there ain't no miracles."

Noel was eyeing the steaming loaves of bread. He whispered to me. "Once again the Bible had it all wrong. There is actually room at the inn."

Angela fussed around, banging pots, pulling china from a Hoosier cabinet, setting dishes on the kitchen table. "You like grappa," she asked, but didn't wait for an answer. She poured the blood-red liquid into tall glass tumblers and watched as we took tentative sips. Potent, hair-chilling, wholly satisfying. "There's dandelion wine if this ain't your cup of tea."

"No," Noel told her, "this tea is just what the doctor ordered."

She watched him closely. "Call the cops." She chuckled at her own joke. "Prohibition and my dead husband taught me how to break the law."

We ate quietly, both of us ravenous, our heads bent over the plates while Angela picked at her own plate, her curious eyes on us. Piles of thick spaghetti, homemade, she told us, glistening yellow strands buried under a robust tomato sauce spiced with basil, oregano, garlic, and God-knows-what other mysterious and tantalizing spices. Meatballs the size of tennis balls, lopsided and flaky, sprigs of parsley peaking out of the meat. That Italian bread, crusty and golden on the outside, warm and chewy inside, slathered in home-churned butter.

We were drunk with it all, Noel and I, barbarians at the Roman feast.

We ravished and celebrated that simple meal, unabashedly, maddingly. Rail-thin Noel, as finicky an eater as God put on this earth, a man who cut the edges off his toast and insisted food was a delaying extravagance before an evening of wit and charm, transformed himself into a giddy glutton. He smacked his lips, which surprised even him. His eyes danced. When he caught my eye, he laughed out loud. "Lord, Edna, I'm acting like an American."

Angela sat back, thrilled, eyes bright, her hands folded in her lap, watching.

You saw a heavy-set woman whose generous bosom strained the old housedress she wore, a seam spilt at the side revealing a white cotton slip beneath. Chubby arms with stubby fingers, her nails blackened, chipped. A round, pancake face with tiny mouse eyes over a stub nose. Her hair, freed from that snowcap, was a Minerva tangle of iron-gray curls, uncombed. Bushy gray-ish eyebrows, wild like the eyes of old potatoes in the winter bin. A plain face, enlivened by those small marble blue eyes. Parchment skin, chapped from the wind and snow perhaps, but a light crimson flush in her cheeks. The bright overhead light gave her a girlish look. Majestic, I thought, and wonder-ful—Neysa McMein needed to paint her. The hell with those insipid, cherry-cheeked all-American girls.

"All right," she announced as she placed an old blue enamel coffee pot onto the stove, "time to answer questions you got and are bursting to ask me."

"Thank you," I said.

"Talking to people is my Christmas treat, I have to tell you."

"No," Noel told her, "sitting in this room is our treat."

"Then we're even. Okay, now we're done telling one another how blessed we are." She chuckled for a while. Then, abruptly, she said, "The Roswells. Everybody talked about that family."

"Why?" I sat up.

"Because they sort of wanted you to talk about them. This here is a tiny town, everybody knows everybody else. Folks go to the Congregational Church or to St. Peter's Catholic over to Bridgeport. That family went nowhere."

"That's why folks talked about them?" I asked.

"Naw," she said. "Maybe a little. Peoples' religion is their own business. God don't care what pew you sit in. But you see, the old man bought that decrepit farm, and he don't know nothing about truck farming. Tomatoes withered on the vine, cucumbers looked like twigs. Green peppers like a schoolboy's marbles. You get the picture? He worked in a factory over to Bridgeport. But his wife was an old vaudeville performer—or circus. Never knew what it was actually. Sort of high-strung, the woman. She's the one who pushed her kids to perform. And perform, they did. School chorales, glee clubs, 4-H meetings, community theater, sing-alongs if you looked twice in their direction. Dancing fools, all of them."

"Any good?"

"Yeah, I guess. But the girl…she was talked of. Sweetest voice. I heard her once at a Grange Hall potluck dinner one year. Like an angel, gave you chills. She sang 'Jesus Met the Woman at the Well.' Chills, I say. And gorgeous. A curse, of course."

"Why a curse?"

Angela poured us coffee. A kick to it, and I winced. She brought out a pitcher of heavy cream from the refrigerator, "Sun-dried chicory," she told me. "From my backyard. It gives coffee a life of its own." She took out an old Schrafft's tin box from the cupboard and emptied the chocolate cookies onto a platter. "Fresh-made. Chewy." She sat back down. "A curse because the boys chased her. Old men chased her. Lord, the village idiot would have chased her if he had any sense of direction. Now her daddy was a tyrant, a mean old fussbudget, unhappy. Beat those kids. Beat his wife. Can't tell you how many times the sheriff knocked on that door. No neighbors to speak of, down at that end of town, but you'll see the kids in town all banged up, black and blue."

"Yet they sang," Noel commented.

"Like chickadees." She sipped her coffee slowly. "Now Linda hooks up with this older boy in some church chorale group, seventeen she is, and he's considerable older, maybe in his twenties, and she runs off to get married. Some say she actually got married—lied on the documents. Two smitten fools running amuck. Her daddy chased them over to Hartford, supposedly stopped the marriage, took a pitchfork to that cad so as he was never seen coming round their porch again. I heard the sheriff had a long talk with his family. Read the riot act to that fool."

I looked at Noel. "Just what Lady Maud told me—Belinda had been married." I bit into a cookie, then greedily reached for another: crisp, tangy, a hint of sweet mint.

"Maybe." Angela stressed the word. "Maybe. Anyway it didn't take. Short time afterwards her father died of a stroke, no loss to humanity, God forgive me for saying that." She crossed herself. "But God sometimes makes copies that got blemishes in the finish."

"What happened to their mother?"

She nodded at the coffee pot, and I nodded back. She poured me another cup. "Times got bad and then worse. No money. The town sheriff foreclosed. But you know how it is—folks resent the government taking homes from decent folks. On the auction day the locals bid like pennies on everything, shut out the scavengers with rifles and cautioning looks, if you know what I mean. So the bank give the house back to the mother. But she don't last long. I mean, a beaten woman, she was. She'd wander in here for something, looking lost. She'd forget what she come for. I give her a piece of fudge, and the old lady teared up. Pitiful. I think a few too many blows to her head by that crazy man. So the farm went under again."

"And the children?" I asked, eagerly.

"They talked a lot about New York City." Angela purposely spaced the name out: New…York…City. Each syllable stressed. "About performing there. Getting rich. Making it big. Money to burn. So one day you turn around, they're gone. Lock stock and barrel. Somebody said they seen them with cardboard suitcases headed to the depot in Bridgeport. On foot. Didn't have no car. Next thing I know, a few months later, the mother dies." She sat back. "And the place goes to the rats and squirrels and wandering bums who lost their way."

"My Lord," Noel muttered.

"But you heard about Linda…Belinda's success?"

"Rumor, much later. Someone comes in and says, 'Remember that pretty girl with the voice of an angel? That Roswell girl? Well, she reinvented herself on Broadway. Belinda Ross. Go figure."

"Go figure," I echoed. Noel smiled.

"By that time their ma was long buried in a pauper's grave over to Ridgefield. Forgotten. They never looked back."

"Linda and her brother."

Angela eyed me. "Brothers, dear. Brothers."

I sat up. "There was more than one?"

"Of course. Two brothers. All performers like their mama. Linda was close to one of them, but he was sickly, consumptive, always coughing in your face like he was sent by Satan to infect the world. Handsome lad, though. Like that Valentino actor. The other was a lot older, I remember. He didn't get along with the others. Took after his papa maybe. Always had a scowl on his face, wouldn't give you the time of day. Linda hated him, so I was told."

"Two brothers," I repeated, shocked.

"Yeah, Linda and Jack headed to the city to seek their fortune. The other went to Chicago, I was told. He worked in some theater there."

"Two brothers," I said foolishly, and Noel rolled his eyes.

"You hard of hearing, Miss Ferber?" Angela grinned.

"It's just that—I only know of one brother."

"It don't make no difference anyhow. All three of them ske-daddled out of town and nobody ever looked back." She clicked her tongue. "And now one of them got herself murdered."

Chapter Fifteen

The other brother. The one who went to Chicago.

I woke the next morning thinking of the unmentioned brother.

I had no idea why the idea of that other brother lingered with me. Yet Angela D'Angelo's harsh comment on the older brother the others did not get along with—a brother as mean as the dead father—intrigued me. Of course, there was no reason Belinda or Jackson had to mention him, but…somehow the idea of the miserable family dynamic back in that niggling Sayville village gave an edge to my morning.

Brother and sister, two schemers afoot in Manhattan with plans for wealth and fame. Maybe fame. Wealth, definitely. Jackson the maniacal force behind his sister's rise to glory. Rags to riches. An Horatio Alger school primer. Yet at the back of my mind the nagging image of that sad, struggling theater warred with images of the brother who went far away.

Nonsense, but my gut propelled me back to Hell's Kitchen. There was a story not being told. Belinda's murder—if not Dougie, then who? The creaky walls of that old theater held secrets, echoes of Chauncey Waters whispering in my ear. Secrets there. The walls talking.

They're afraid of you and Mr. Coward.

The taxi dropped me off in front of the theater just after noon. The line for the soup kitchen stretched down the block.

Breadlines opened at six in the morning, I knew. At four the men began lining up. For a moment, watching the numb, quiet line inching along, I felt a wave of dizziness, tottering against the brick wall. A passing stranger reached out to steady me, gripping my elbow. As I thanked him, he shrugged it off, but tipped his battered railroad cap and gave me a bittersweet smile. I watched as he joined the snaking line, and felt a tug at my heart. A desolate street, this Eleventh Avenue, a wasteland of gaunt faces, bent bodies. Across the street a mattress-spring discarded in an alley, a packing crate upturned. A family sifted through a pile of garbage, their bodies moving in slow motion.

The doors of the theater were locked, which surprised. Overhead was the brand-new, glossy marquee, but no announcements of upcoming revues. I peered through the dusty glass windows and saw nothing, a lobby shrouded in darkness.

I stepped away, flummoxed—I had no plan B—but noticed an entrance at the side of the building that doubtless led to the upstairs apartment. An old-fashioned bell with a typed nametag inserted in a metal strip: Roswell, J. I pressed the bell and waited.

From above me came the grating sound of an old window being raised. "Yes?"

I stepped back onto the sidewalk and looked up. "Mr. Roswell?"

"Miss Ferber? What?" He sounded groggy, roused from a nap.

"A few words with you, sir?"

He debated that, his head disappearing for a second, then reappearing. "The door's open. Walk up."

An unlit stairwell, a wobbly banister that did nothing to help me maneuver the worn steps in the murky dark. Suddenly a door at the landing flew open, a wash of feeble light illuminating the top stairs.

"Sorry." Jackson watched me. "The landlord doesn't believe in lighting your way."

Nearing him, I smiled. "A stairwell out of Dickens."

"Yeah, the ghost of Christmas present in little old New York."

He stood aside as I walked into his rooms. His breath was a cigarette smoker's raw, hot scent. Stale body odor, foul. Small, messy rooms, a table sagging under piles of sheet music and newspapers. Clutter everywhere, clothing draped over chairs. A makeshift clothesline with drying shirts extended from the clanging cast-iron radiator by the front window back to a doorjamb.

He saw me looking around.

"I would apologize for the disarray," he began, "but I'm not much into apologies to people who surprise me in my own house."

Idly, he scratched an armpit, then wrapped his arms around his chest. An old dress shirt, collarless, pulled out of his trousers. Loose suspenders draped over his hips.

I laughed. "And a warm welcome too." But I got serious. "My apologies, then."

He yawned. "It's all right. I wasn't going anywhere."

He rustled about, clearing a chair and sweeping old copies of magazines off the sofa onto the floor. A copy of *Collier's* slipped onto the floor near me, the frayed cover stained with coffee rings. A stack of the *New York World* scattered across the floor. I stepped over the mess and sat down, sank into broken cushions. A wire cut into my lower back, and I shifted my body.

"We never have guests," he said, eyeing me.

"Again, my apologies."

He held up his hand and repeated, "It's all right." His face tightened. "Has something happened? The murder?"

I shook my head. "Sorry, no. That's not why I'm here. I have no idea what the police are doing."

He scoffed at that. "Nothing. At least so far as anyone tells me. I stopped calling the precinct. Family counts for nothing in this godforsaken city. Belinda murdered like that, and the curtain comes down. Finis."

"Dougie no longer stops in?"

"No, thank God. Another ghost of the past haunting these rooms downstairs." He waited a second. "Not even Cyrus, the headless horseman."

"Your theater is closed?"

He nodded. "For a while. We'll stage a production after the first of the year. We lost Chauncey Waters." He made a face. "No loss there. A whiner and malcontent. Untrustworthy. Limited talent."

"And Kent LaSalle?"

He gave a sardonic laugh and looked around, reached for a pack of cigarettes on a side table, and lit one, dragging on it, expelling smoke, a contented look on his face.

"Another failure, but more dramatic. Disappeared into the cheap gin mills over by the docks. A drunk, big-time, you know. Just walked away. Folks tended to like him—so much the veteran that he'd put to memory dozens of lines. He could spout soliloquies from Shakespeare, Christopher Marlowe. Christ, even the Bible. Lately he mouths an irritating 1932 Psalm, as he calls it, stolen from a newspaper column."

"Yes, I heard it. Chilling."

He frowned. "Unnerving, to say the least. I don't need a reminder that we're in a Depression. As a young actor he must have been something. But now…" His hand waved in the air.

"Now," I finished, "he's an old drunk."

"You said it. And gone."

"What will you do?"

He breathed in. "As I said, after the holidays. What choice do I have? Find some new actors and stagehands who'll work dirt cheap. Real cheap." He grinned. "I may have to hire the Swiss Bell Ringers. Whatever." His hand stretched out toward his derelict furniture. "We had hopes of moving out of this dump. Money coming in."

"Belinda's?"

"Yeah, but no more. You may have noticed that she no longer is a star."

"I'm so sorry."

"Yeah, well, we're all sorry. Poor Linda. Christ." He puffed up his cheeks. "In my blood, you know. Theater. I can't stop now. No audience, so be it. No money for rent, so be it. We get by.

Sooner or later this Depression gotta end. People want theater."
He half-bowed. "I'm waiting in the wings."

"But you need money…" I began, thinking of Chauncey's
words—Jackson and Belinda, schemers after gold.

He shrugged his shoulders. "I can always sell apples on the
corner."

"You already have competition out there. The *Times* reports
that there are over six-thousand men already selling apples…"
I pointed out the front window. A visible rooftop across the
street, a shabby wooden water tower, an old billboard nailed to
the shingles. D'Arcy's Dime Museum. Oddities and Curiosities.
All Welcome.

A wide smile. "I'm charming. An actor at heart."

"Are you acting now?"

He didn't answer. Then, slowly, "We'll probably have to move
out of here."

"No stipend from Dougie?"

He set his mouth in a grim line. "I told you—he's disappeared."
He grumbled. "Everybody's disappearing, especially Dougie."

A voice from the hallway startled me, high-pitched laughter,
but dark, cynical. Millie Glass walked into the room. "I'm sure
he's been sent to the Caribbean for the winter. Isn't that what
rich people do when their sons commit murder?"

Jackson wasn't happy. "Christ, Millie, a little insensitive."

She glared at me. "What do you want me to say? He plays
at dalliance, then moves on."

"Maybe he's innocent." I stared into her face.

She arched her eyebrows and looked at Jackson. "I *told* you—
don't let her upstairs. Accusation."

"I'm not accusing anyone."

Jackson played peacemaker. "Millie's a little angry because
we may have to give up these rooms."

Sarcastic, a titter. "Yeah, when you get used to such luxury…"

"Sort of cozy." I looked around. "A lived-in feel. I like rooms
with magazines, lots of books." I looked at the overloaded side
table. "Piles of sheet music."

Jackson couldn't read my expression but decided to be friendly. "Coffee, Miss Ferber. I was waking up from a nap, and just brewed…" He pointed to the kitchen.

Millie was tapping her foot. "Really, Jackson."

I watched her closely. "Belinda lived in these rooms with you before her success."

For some reason an explosive line because Millie muttered something under her breath, and Jackson frowned at her. A look came into his eyes—Be careful, Millie. Careful.

When he looked back at me, his eyes were cloudy. "Yes, of course. She was happy here, Miss Ferber. *We* were happy here, starting out, dreaming, acting. A cold, harsh city, a brother to protect her."

Millie squirmed, uncomfortable. "Yeah, hours spent embroidering 'Home, Sweet Home' to hang over the holes the rats burrow through."

"For Christ's sake, Millie." Jackson wagged a finger at her. "We got Edna Ferber in our house. *Show Boat*. Can you at least…?" His voice trailed off, then, louder, "Coffee? Do you want any?"

I shook my head. "Thank you, no. I really can't stay."

"Then why are you here?" Millie took a step closer to me.

Jackson shot her a look that said: Shut up. I told you—shut the hell up. His eyes blazed.

"A question I have, that's all. I am curious about family."

"What?" A nervous edge to his voice.

"I was in Connecticut for Christmas," I began slowly. I watched his head jerk forward, eyes narrowing. "Greenwich, then Bridgeport. Then, because we were near, Noel and I drove into Sayville. A pinched little village, stung by…"

He tossed a look at Millie, then at me. "What?"

"I was in the neighborhood."

His voice quaked with anger. "There's nobody there any more."

"So I learned. We cruised by your old farmhouse."

Twisting around, catching Millie's eye, Jackson sputtered, "A little intrusive, no?"

"Curiosity."

Millie hissed, "Killed the…" She stopped, flustered.

Jackson's face was dark. "Millie, leave this to me."

"Yeah, you're doing a good job of it."

He turned to me, all the friendliness now gone, his voice a squeak. "And what did you discover about our past?"

I waited a heartbeat. "I learned that Belinda—then Linda—ran off to get married. To some man she met in chorale."

He chuckled. "That old story? Christ, Miss Ferber. Small-town gossip. Our father made short shift of that nonsense. Who tattled that silly tale to you?"

"No matter, but…"

"If you must know, Linda—Belinda was headstrong, foolish, easily falling in love with any of the hundreds of boys who gushed around her. She was convinced she *had* to be married—eternal love, stars shining bright, moonlit honeymoon in Niagara Falls." He cleared his throat. "Whatever scenario she read in some sensational, claptrap romance."

"But it did happen, yes?"

He hesitated, trying to read my expression. "Yes, it happened. For a moment. Then she got dragged back home crying and cursing."

"What did you do?"

Again the hesitation. "Me? Simple. I told her that her future was in this city. Broadway. Her looks, her voice. The whole package. I'd take care of it. I was the shining star she'd best hitch her wagon to, if you know what I mean. I had the brains. When our father died, we headed out."

Millie had been listening, but was anxious to say something.

"Yes?" I turned to her.

"She was lucky there was someone to save her from herself."

Jackson pointed a shaking finger at me. "Why is this so important to you, Miss Ferber? Our past." He sucked in his breath. "Are you stupidly going to try to pin poor Belinda's murder on somebody in my theater? On me?" He laughed a phony laugh. "The man who lost everything when she was murdered."

"True," I agreed.

"Then what is it you want from me?"

I counted another heartbeat. "I also learned that you have another brother."

Jackson blanched. "Christ Almighty. Nothing is sacred. The ghost of good old Russell, the brother nobody liked."

"I gather he went to Chicago."

He broke in, agitated. "Yes, and was never heard from again. Good riddance. We don't talk about Russell. Rusty, he was called, a name that described his soul. My father's dark shadow. What's he got to do with anything? Really, Miss Ferber—nosiness is…"

"Even when Belinda became famous? He didn't try to contact you?"

"He better not. Frankly, I know nothing about him, Miss Ferber. He knows nothing about us. We parted on real ugly terms. Blood threats. Even a fistfight that wasn't pretty. There's a reason he went to Chicago. Here's a man who snuck out in the night with what little money we'd stashed in a coffee can in the cupboard. The family savings. All of it. Every measly dime. He may not even be there now. A wanderer. A…"

"A schemer?"

That didn't make him happy. "I don't care about him at all."

He wasn't looking into my face, and I felt to my marrow that he was lying about something.

Millie was watching him closely, puzzled, unhappy. "You never mentioned Russell. A brother."

He snarled, "No need to."

"Belinda never mentioned him."

Sharply, cutting. "No reason to. Enough. All of this. Stop this craziness." He yelled out, "Miss Ferber, you are up to something. You're trying to put a noose around our necks." That fake laugh again. "Myths and legends. What's the truth?"

"I wonder about that myself."

Jackson stormed to the door and threw it open. "Again, thank you for your visit." A sneer in his voice. "I'm assuming Dougie's many lawyers put you up to this. If not, then what? Maybe you should mind your own damn business, Miss Ferber."

I stepped out onto the landing. When I glanced back, Millie rushed toward the door and slammed it so hard that flecks of old plaster crumbled off the wall and landed at my feet.

Chapter Sixteen

"I had a disturbing call from Dougie," Noel began as we sat having lunch at Sardi's two days after my unsettling visit to Jackson Roswell's apartment. "This morning. Early. I'd asked him how he spent his Christmas day. After all, Christmas Eve at your place was so—well, disturbing."

"Is he at Lady Maud's? I've been wondering why we haven't heard from him."

Noel shook his head. "On Depression Street, he told me. That's the name he gave me. That's what he said, and I drew a blank. But he spent the day in Central Park—in Hooverville. That tumble-up village. Have you heard of that, Edna?" A quirky smile. "Tarpaper shacks and oil drum stoves under your expensive window?"

I pushed my plate away. "It's not funny, Noel. In the shadow of all those wealthy apartments, deep in Central Park. Twenty or so ramshackle homes, spaced out, filled with homeless families. Small children even. Arrested, dragged to court—then back again. A city drained the reservoir there, planning to build a wonderful blue-green summer lawn, but ran out of money. Now desperate folks are building makeshift homes out of corrugated tin, cardboard sheets, old bricks, scrap metal, wood, even grease barrels—anything for shelter from the winter. You know, I watched it grow during the summer when I took my walks through the park. Depressing, though the residents have a sense of humor. I mean—that sign that announces: Depression

Street. Black paint slapped onto an old pine board. But I've seen the emptiness of those folks' faces, Noel. Haunted faces standing in shabby doorways against pinewood slabs of rotting timber." I shuddered. "Such sadness there."

"The city allows it?"

"Most cops and judges turn a blind eye. The cops move in, forced to—complaints from citizens, I'm afraid—arrests for vagrancy, but no one condemns. After all, that beefy Irish cop fears he may be a next-door neighbor as the economy plummets even more." I paused. "What was Dougie doing there?"

"A wanderer, he said. He walked through one morning and met a man named Sam who once worked as a houseman for Lady Maud, fired by her for some trivial act. Dougie, bothered, sat all day long in Sam's hovel, a wood shanty warmed by a makeshift wood stove that makes the interior feverishly hot, he said—all day, drowsy, sad, talking to Sam, going out to buy food for his family. For others. There's even a young homeless boy named Josiah Smith who gives tours to folks who want to see the shantytown, nickels in his pocket from the gapers. Dougie drifted the whole day there, so he said, and then he went home to Lady Maud."

"Okay, a little disturbing I admit, but what bothered you?"

He waited a while. "Dougie talked a little crazy, Edna. I fear he'll be speaking in tongues shortly. Messianic folderol. He rambled on about Belinda and his hope that the world was coming to an end."

"Good grief."

"Exactly. And I thought the British were inhabitants of the dark side of the moon."

"What did you tell him?"

"What he told *me*. He told me that Manhattan is a city of ghosts."

"What?"

"'Everywhere you look there are ghosts. Deep in the subway— ghosts.' Then: 'I am one of the ghosts. You can see right through me.' That scared me, Edna. What's he saying?"

I considered Noel's words. "The fact that he's having this...this epiphany in a Hoover Valley hovel bothers me."

"Social awareness arrives in our Dougie?"

I shook my head. "That would be welcome, I admit—yes. But no. I think Dougie feels he's walking among the dead."

Noel shivered. "Lord, dear Edna, chills up my spine."

"Meeting this Sam—someone tossed willy-nilly out of a comfortable world, forced to survive—got to him. Everyday—what to eat. Where to sleep. What to do about his family. Dougie never *thought* about poor people. It jarred him. Dougie sees them as the dead."

"And now he sees himself as one of them?"

"I'm afraid so."

Noel fiddled with his napkin, dabbed at this lips. "I remember something else, Edna. He said, 'Once you realize that you are one of the ghosts of Manhattan, you have the power to fly.'"

The hair on the back of my neck stood up. "Noel, we need to talk to him. I'm not happy hearing this. This all scares me."

"The funny thing is that Dougie seemed so happy. You know how lately he's so sad, even distraught. When he was telling all this to me, there was laughter in his voice. It was almost as though he was at peace."

"I want to see him."

Noel sat back, a smile on his face. "I'm one step ahead of you, darling. I was worried, too. Of course, I was. So I got him to promise to go out to dinner tonight. You're invited. The three of us. Chambord's under the Third Avenue El. Very nice. I've been there. Duck a l'orange. Mouth-watering. Their Alsatian chef Pierre is...anyway, eight o'clock reservations. Meet at my doorstep around six for drinks and...Sorry, darling, you will be forced to hear me recite some newly-crafted lines from *Design for Living*. An evening of hilarity and foolishness."

I frowned. "Bad timing, Noel."

"The only timing we got."

I twisted my head to the side. "Let's see if he shows up at your place."

"He will. I *warned* him." Noel shifted the subject, a smile on his face. "Now, Edna, tell me about this mysterious Roswell brother. I know you're driven to learn his story. Tell me, did you learn anything?" A bemused look on his face. "I don't understand your fascination with this elusive brother. This...this Russell Roswell hunkered down in the Windy City." Then, looking into my face, a twinkle in his eye. "Your monomaniacal obsession these past two days."

I smiled back at him. "I have a reporter's heart and soul— and doggedness. Jackson's panic at the mention of his brother's name...frankly, that set off alarms in my *Appleton Crescent* cub reporter brain."

He laughed out loud. "Jackson is a soul completely unspoiled by...failure. Okay, tell me. You were successful?"

I hesitated. "Of sorts. I don't know if any of this relates to Belinda's death, but I always like to flesh out the people in the stories in my head. Paper-thin people don't tell me about their souls."

His eyes got wide. "And you learned about this character's soul?"

I laughed out loud. "Not his soul, really. But I learned that something fishy happened on the way out of boondocks Sayville by those three children."

"I'm listening." He leaned forward.

"First off, I needed to trade in a few favors back in my old Chicago stomping ground. My family still there, in fact. My mother spends a good part of each year staying with relatives on Calumet Avenue."

"So you can catch your breath in New York?"

"Unfortunately *her* breath is often stronger than the breezes off the lake. She gossips about how I fail her as a daughter and the telephone lines start ringing in Manhattan." I waved my hand, dismissing the thought. "No matter, that unhealthy bond of mother and daughter. I have friends at the *Chicago Tribune*, a paper that once refused to hire me. Something I'll never forgive."

"Another digression, Edna." He was grinning widely at me.

"Be that as it may, dear Noel. A few phone calls, and the machinery got moving. But the name Russell Roswell meant nothing to any of my friends in theater. In old-time vaudeville. Nothing in the newsrooms. "

He drummed his fingers on the table. "And yet you persisted."

"There is no other way." I stabbed a pickle in my dish, watched it slide away. "The business directory lists a 'Roswell, R.' as the owner of a local movie house. One of dozens, I gather, opened after talkies made America delirious. A few calls and I found myself on the line with Russell Roswell, who was at first startled, then curious, but finally very, very annoyed."

Noel was enjoying this. "But he did talk?"

"Of course. My old-style news wiles, painfully honed on the dusty streets of Appleton, Wisconsin. It also was in my favor that he knew who I was. After those pleasantries were done with, I mentioned the murder of Belinda Ross."

"His reaction?"

"None. Silence, then, 'I don't know a Belinda Ross.' Of course, that floored me until I realized that Belinda's fame was newfound. A contemporary Broadway sensation."

"But he never made the connection? Articles in the press?"

"No reason to, I gather. Not in Chicago. His sister was Linda Roswell. 'She got herself killed?' he asked, almost matter-of-factly, like a passing comment on the weather. More silence. Then, 'Why are you calling me? I didn't do it.' He made a point of saying he has no interest in Broadway theater, despises Manhattan, indeed, most of the East Coast, and spends his time organizing the accounting books of a movie house that is floundering under economic depression. A five-minute harangue about Hoover that segued into a harangue about Roosevelt."

"Doesn't he watch the Movietone newsreels his movie house shows?"

"I think he sits in his counting house, bent over like disgruntled Uriah Heap sifting through his pennies." I sat back in my seat. "But I did learn some things about the Roswell family. Yes, he was the oldest, probably the meanest. 'Those two were wild, out-of-control brats.' His words. 'Spoiled up-to-no-good brats. Linda moody, impossible some days.' I asked him why he said that, but he didn't answer. Finally he wanted to know my interest, and I told him a friend of mine was suspected of strangling his sister."

Noel's eyes got wide. "He didn't slam down the phone?"

"To the contrary. He said, 'Is he being rewarded by the city?'"

"They said he was cruel."

"Yes, but—my God, heartless has a new name in Chicago."

"When was the last time he saw them?"

"His story is different from theirs. He claims *they* left first. They were the ones who robbed the family treasury and beat it out of town. He was left with a dying mother. Penniless. A mortgage they couldn't afford. So he left."

"Each one blames the other." Noel was nodding to himself.

"He was surprised at something else. About Jackson, a despised brother who was always sickly. Consumptive, most likely, a boy who spent his winters under covers in the farmhouse. 'I'm surprised he's still alive,' he said. 'But then, orneriness can make a person live forever.'"

"I like that," Noel broke in. "You and I, I suppose, will live forever then."

"And then probably occupy the same room in hell."

Noel held my eye. "I get to pick the furnishings, dear Edna. Your taste is so…"

"Sensible?"

"You need more gossamer in your life, Edna."

I pursed my lips. "You need more—burlap." I glanced around the restaurant. "He did make an interesting observation about his sister. It seems Jackson bears most of his wrath—a petty schemer, liar, brute. But Linda, he said, was soft. That was his word. And, he added, gullible. He thought her a little simple-minded. He finished by saying she was Trilby to her brother's Svengali. In fact, Russell did show a modicum of concern for the dead beautiful sister."

"What did he say?"

"He said Linda's tragic flaw was that she sometimes betrayed kindness."

"Good God," Noel said, "hang the woman!"

"Not a likable man, this Russell."

"So he had no interest in her murder? Or who did it?"

I shook my head. "He was in a hurry to get off the phone, kept cutting off my sentences. I started to say something about keeping in touch because…I never got any further. He put his mouth close to the receiver and seethed, 'Don't call me again, Miss Ferber. That chapter of my life is over. For good.' He slammed down the phone."

Noel chuckled softly. "And none of this has to do with the murderer."

I shrugged. "Maybe not."

He tapped my wrist. "Poor Edna, a wasted chat with a lout."

"I'm sure it won't be the last time I find myself confronting a lout."

He looked at his watch. "Things to do, Edna, before our little Dougie taxies down to Beekman Place."

We walked out of the restaurant and headed back to my apartment.

"There," I pointed. "Look, Noel."

Up ahead, strolling casually, Corey Boynton stopped to gaze in the window of a tobacco shop. Hatless, cashmere overcoat unbuttoned, a cigarette bobbing in the corner of his mouth, he looked—jaunty. At one point, tossing down the cigarette butt and stomping on it, he twisted around and spotted Noel and me on the corner, headed in his direction. His head flicked back and forth for a second, then, agitated, he started to rush away, stepping in front of an old man and woman.

"He's avoiding us," I told Noel.

He grumbled, "Why would anyone do that? People seek us out."

"Maybe you," I said, laughing.

Noel yelled over the heads of strollers. "Mr. Boynton. Corey. Wait."

Reluctantly he paused, waited for us to catch up. Watching our faces, he lit a cigarette, then immediately changed his mind, tossing it into the street.

"A surprise." He grinned at us.

"I'll bet," I told him.

Corey stammered as he stepped away. "I was headed…"

I spoke over his words. "You haven't been around much. Dougie tells me you've become a stranger."

Corey looked over my shoulder as if expecting Dougie to appear out of the shadows, a child's wind-up jack-in-the-box, wagging a censorious finger. "I've been busy."

"We're all busy." I stared into his face.

"Why haven't you seen Dougie lately?" Noel asked Corey bluntly. The young man started to say something but then became quiet. "Friends?" Noel sniped.

Corey shook his head, once again scanning the street. A light changed and I expected him to dart away, weave madly through cabs and buses. Resigned, he rocked on his heels. "He moved out of the Stanhope, as you probably know. He's back with Lady Maud. It's easier for him."

I rolled my tongue into the corner of my mouth. "And, I guess, for you, as well. I don't know about living with Lady Maud. That can be a trial. He has nowhere to run to."

Corey's voice had an edge. "But c'mon, folks. It got to be easier there—like hiding away in a mansion—than enduring the hostile looks of people accusing you of murder."

"True," Noel added, "but Dougie feels abandoned by his friends."

Corey shivered from the cold, his coat still unbuttoned. Strangely, beads of sweat dotted his brow. "I haven't abandoned him," he said hotly.

"That's not how he sees it," I went on.

He crossed his arms defiantly, then dug both hands into his pockets, hunching up his shoulders. "You know, right after the… the murder, I stopped in at the mansion. Lady Maud refused to see me, even to *allow* me upstairs. I *did* try to be a friend. Sort of. I don't even know if Dougie was home then."

That surprised me. "Good for you then. A point in your favor."

He locked eyes with mine. "But, Miss Ferber, I'm uncomfortable with the whole—with the murder thing. I have to tell you that."

"So you think he's a murderer?" I asked quickly. A gust of wind buried my words, but I could see he understood. "I believe you told me folks like you didn't commit murder."

"I don't want to answer that." Then, his voice high and thin, "Sometimes I believe he did it. A jealous rage. Maybe." He backed up. "Belinda didn't deserve to die like that."

I watched him closely. "I agree with that. We all agree with that. But a friend of yours stands accused…"

He stopped me. "I can't follow what's going on here," he stammered. "Frankly, I don't know what to say to him. I can't find the words." He arched his head back. "In prep school they don't teach you how to be civil to those heading to jail."

"Given the corruption with high-placed politicians and top-of-the-heap executives these days," I seethed, "I would think such a course would be mandatory for the future leaders of America in your Ivy League warrens."

Silence, Corey debating what to do. Then he confided, "Kitty is moving to Hollywood." He actually laughed out loud. "Movies. Musicals. Busby Berkeley. She wants to get herself into that world. New York is too cold and heartless."

"And Hollywood is utopia?" I asked.

"Sunshine makes even bad people look good."

"When is she leaving?"

"She hasn't decided."

Noel probed, "You going with her?"

That startled him. "Lord, no. We are *not* a couple, Mr. Coward. Are you out of your mind?" He sucked in his breath. "My father, scrimping and whining these days, says I have to leave the Stanhope."

"Where will you go?"

He shrugged his shoulders. "The family homestead in Scarsdale." He shrugged. "God must really hate the wealthy class of America."

"Yes," I told him, "he picks on them all the time."

He stared into my face. "Look, I'm sorry about Dougie. I really am. An old college friend, yes, but never close..." He took a step away. "I really have to leave." He shuffled his feet.

Noel reached out and touched his sleeve. "It might be good for you to see Dougie, Mr. Boynton. For one night. Edna and I are taking him out to dinner at Chambord's tonight. An eight o'clock reservation. You're a man who likes fancy restaurants, no? Why don't you join us? Come to my place. Drinks first. Six o'clock. Our treat." He looked at me. "Actually, Edna's treat. Expense is no object. After all, she wrote *Show Boat* and has a boatload of money. The only woman to survive the Crash. My apartment on Beekman." Noel slipped a card from his breast pocket. "My address. Join us, Corey. We'll share a cab to Chambord's."

"No, I don't think so." He waved goodbye and rushed across the street, against the light. A cab swerved, a horn blared.

"That's a sad story." Noel watched his retreating back. "I don't understand who he is."

"I do. Maybe. A craggy barnacle on a pleasure boat that sank."

Noel laughed. "You don't like him, do you?"

"I don't suffer fools, Noel." I raised my voice. "And neither do you."

"Actually I find some fools diverting."

"That's where you and I differ then, Noel, my dear."

He narrowed his eyes, amused. "Yes, darling Edna, the only wrinkle in our friendship."

For some reason, perhaps unsettled by the encounter with Corey, we decided to wander, enjoying the cold, arm in arm, companionable. We strolled through Times Square, idling, drifting, caught by the hoot and howl of tourists jostling one another. Noel whispered lines from his *Bitter Sweet*: "Though there may be beauty in this land of yours, skies are very often dull and gray."

"Don't try to cheer me up, Noel."

An itinerant drummer stood on the corner of Forty-second Street hawking gigantic New Year's Eve hats. Red, white, and blue, with streamers. Happy New Year 1933. He kept honking a flimsy paper horn.

"Buy you a gift, Edna?" Noel said.

"Can you give me a happy new year? Let's welcome 1933 with whistles and horns."

"At least you Americans will be able to drink without the law breathing down your neck. Maybe, if FDR has his way."

I laughed. "And when did we ever stop drinking, Noel?"

Lazy, enjoying each other's company, we lingered in a booth at Child's, too many cups of coffee. We watched snow showers drift against the window. "Edna, you bring out the worst in me," Noel said. "Indolence. The pure joy of it."

It didn't matter—we were content.

It was snowing as the cab approached Beekman Place. Idling at a light, the cabbie grunted and pointed at a policeman who was shooing a man off an upturned soapbox. Through the wispy snow, I discerned a disheveled, bearded man shivering in a spring jacket and perched atop the wooden crate. In the darkness, lit only by a snow-shrouded streetlight, he was waving a cardboard sign. I barely made out his message: "Unite Workers. End Slavery." The burly cop would have none of it, jostling the man, pulling him off the box, boxing his ears. An amazing sight, this lone protestor who'd chosen the quiet, privileged neighborhood on this cold night. As we watched, he stumbled out of sight, his makeshift sign dragging behind him. Irritated, the cop kicked the soapbox and it splintered into pieces.

"He should be in Union Square with the other protestors," Noel said.

"No," I said, "this is exactly where he belongs."

"At the entrance to my rarefied kingdom?"

"Exactly."

The light changed. The cab sputtered forward.

"Gonna be a snowy night," the cabbie said, craning his head back to look at us. A thick accent, Russian. "Might be a blizzard, they're saying. Bad for business."

"Look, Noel."

A taxi had pulled up in front of Noel's apartment. As we watched, Dougie stepped out, looked up and down the street. Bundled up against the cold, he wrapped his arms around his chest, bent into the wind. Then, looking in our direction, he waved his hands in the air as he danced an exaggerated two-step.

"He's assuming we're in the cab," Noel laughed. "Otherwise his song and dance is lost on strangers."

A sudden blast of icy wind from the East River, a belt of fierce snow smacking the windshield. I shivered. Looking up into the streetlights, I watched the thick snow swirling and dipping.

"Edna." Noel's voice broke.

I looked.

A dark figure lumbered from between two parked cars, hunched over, stumbling, turned from the wind. Dougie didn't notice as the creeping figure approached his back. He was still dancing for us.

Suddenly in the still night a shot rang out. Then another. *Boom boom.* Both shots sounded like cannon fire as they echoed off the buildings.

I screamed out, "Dougie."

Dougie swiveled around, banged into a parked car, careened into a pole, then slipped to the icy ground, his face buried in a snow bank. The dark figure leaned over the fallen Dougie, seemed to be reaching for something, then disappeared back into the dark night, shielded by the pelting snow and a line of parked cars.

Springing out of the cab, Noel and I reached him just as we heard a horrid gurgle and watched the snow turn dark crimson. Under the awful streetlight, a deep red halo circled his head. Noel reached down to touch him, but I staggered back, my mind reeling. I closed my eyes.

From a faraway place I heard Noel's wretched voice. "The boy is dead."

Chapter Seventeen

Lady Maud sat in my living room, her back stiff in the chair, her jeweled hands folded decorously in her lap. Her face a grim mask, she was staring at me.

"Tell me who killed my son, Edna."

I'd spent the morning working on a short story, hidden in my workroom, exhausted, craving a forbidden cigarette. Dougie's horrible death two days earlier had drained me. My typewriter was a feeble refuge in my Spartan workroom with the eighteenth-century writing desk I cherished. Work always my salvation. My three-finger pecking at the keys. Scribbled hieroglyphics. Meetings with police, late-night coffee with Noel, who was shattered, my own troubled sleep. My snow-covered terrace. Shadows on my midnight wall. My only therapy: work. Work. My lonely rooms.

A quiet rap on my closed door, something Rebecca knew I frowned upon when working.

Impatient, I'd called out, "Rebecca, what? You know…"

The door cracked open, and Rebecca discreetly nodded her head back to the living room. "You have a guest."

Haggard, hair askew, nails bitten, I balked. "Impossible. Tell whoever it is to go away. Why would you let in…"

She cleared her throat. "Lady Maud." She backed up, twisted her head to the side, a look that suggested visiting royalty.

Lady Maud sat stiffly in the red moiré armchair by the piano. She didn't move as I approached and sat down quietly in a chair opposite her. "Lady Maud, my deepest condolences. Dougie was…"

She held up her hand. Her lips thin, pale. "Tell me who murdered my son, Edna." The voice stentorian, fierce.

I fumbled. "Lady Maud, I don't know. The police are…"

"Are simpletons in the pay of shantytown rabble."

"I can't tell you anything. I don't know."

Behind her, stealthy like a house cat, Rebecca mouthed the word "coffee" with a question mark. A barely perceptible nod from me: yes. Now. Right now. She disappeared into the kitchen.

"You were looking into the murder of that saloon singer. You must have learned about enemies or love affairs or…" She stopped. "What?"

I sucked in my breath. "You told me to stop."

No smile, those lips in a razor-thin line. Then, a nod. "I doubt if a woman like you would take orders from anyone."

She interlocked her fingers, for a moment carrying them to her chin, her fingertips a pyramid.

"Would you like to take off your coat?"

She didn't answer me. In my hot apartment, her floor-length mink was draped over her shoulders like a luxurious cloak. Dressed in a black satin dress, a black silk scarf around her neck, a choker of pearls slightly visible, and a pillbox black hat with the veil thrown back, she looked frightfully funereal. A contrast to the brilliant gleam and shine of the ostentatious rings on her old fingers. A silver filigreed hairclip embedded with diamonds caught the overhead light. A marvel, this grande dame. John Singer Sargent's mysterious and compelling Madame X perhaps, had that lovely and regal image aged a good forty years—and wore a face shattered by grief. Here was a woman used to being looked at—but from a cool and respectful distance.

I ventured a thought. "I was told the police believe that the killer lifted Dougie's wallet from his breast pocket. I did see the killer bend over and…"

Her hand shot up, her voice biting. "And you believe that?"

"I don't know what to believe." Then, considering my words, I added, "Of course, you're right. I don't believe it was a simple robbery gone horribly wrong."

She made a harrumph sound. "Exactly. Which is why I am here this afternoon disturbing you."

As we were talking, Rebecca quietly entered the room and placed a coffee pot on the table. A tray of freshly baked macaroons. She nodded at me and I nodded back. "Coffee, Lady Maud?"

"Of course."

Rebecca poured cups for both of us, adding a dollop of whipped cream to mine. She placed a cup in front of Lady Maud, but the woman never touched it. I sipped mine slowly, watching her.

"I'm waiting." Imperious, her eyes riveted to mine.

"I don't know who murdered Dougie," I said, exasperated. "I liked Dougie, as you know. Noel and I both did."

"He had no friends," she said coolly, a remark I resented, given what I'd just stated. "I am talking about long-time friendships, the wonderful camaraderie of young men doing the Grand Tour together. Venice, Paris, Vienna. Polo at Yale. Hunting parties in the White Mountains in New Hampshire. I must tell you—my late husband went hunting with Teddy Roosevelt out west in his younger days. Buffalo fell like bowling pins. But not for Dougie. My son refused membership in the Cloud Club in the new Chrysler Building. A coveted invitation, of course. Power brokers, men only. A sacrosanct world of cedar humidors and ticker-tape machines and private business tête–à–têtes. No thank you, he said. Chrysler, Benton—vandals, he termed them. An impossible boy sometimes."

"He must have had school chums."

She barely shook her head, though her eyes flickered. "You would think so, yes? But in boarding school the teachers considered him—odd. A bump on a log, they informed me. Sitting alone, staring off into space like a defective child. A dreamer, they said, and they shook their heads. I had big hopes for college.

My husband insisted on Yale, of course. Everyone in his family going back centuries. Henry insisted on him pledging a fraternity, though Dougie balked at that. But for once he listened to his father."

"What about Corey Boynton?" I asked. "At Yale, the same fraternity, I gather, rediscovering each other in the city—rooms across from each other at the Stanhope."

She pursed her lips. "A gadabout fool, that boy. A family impoverished by the Crash, blaming everyone else. This young Corey hasn't a dime to give a beggar on the street. A hanger-on." A thin smile. "A younger version of Buzzy Collins. You know him, right? He hangs on the sleeve of every moneyed soul in town. But Corey is a leech, Edna. Dougie flashes cash, and Corey puts up his paws like a lap dog getting a treat. Disgusting. I never liked him. I never liked his family. Pretenders, really. *Poseurs.*" A sigh of resignation. "But I understood that Dougie needed a companion in the city, so I allowed Corey into our world."

I sat back, annoyed. "I think it was Dougie who allowed Corey into his world."

She reached for the coffee cup but then changed her mind. "Think what you want, Edna."

"I always do."

"That is unfortunate for those listening to you, I imagine."

I smiled. "Good for you, Lady Maud."

She ignored that. "His father indulged him too much. Once he discovered that Dougie had an affinity for finance, as he himself did, it was as though God had given him a younger version of himself—to be molded into a Wall Street tycoon. The Midas touch. And Dougie responded—money was his way of hiding from people."

"I'm afraid that never works."

A sharp rebuke. "Of course it does." Her fingers grazed the coffee cup. Then, not missing a beat, she said, "The detective I hired was an abject fool. Whatever were the Vanderbilts thinking? His reports about that girl's murder simply mimicked what could be found in the *Daily News*. Yet perhaps I dismissed him too early." She drew in her breath. "Tell me who killed my son, Edna."

I said nothing, watching her, waiting.

"Please have some coffee," I said finally.

She glanced at the cup but didn't move, that spine still rigid, that mink coat draped over her shoulders like a thick, furry blanket. For a moment she looked away, nervous. "Dougie told me he thought he was being followed. Lately."

That was news. "What? He never mentioned that to me or Noel."

"Perhaps he had his reasons." A smirk. "I *am* his mother." A pause. "Of course, he had no proof, but he felt a presence now and then, a shadow, he said. A sudden movement behind him. A trail of cigarette smoke. A whiff of strong cologne. I paid it no mind. He'd become a walker in the city, to my horror. A man who wandered down to the rotting piers. He'd be lost in Central Park. From my upper windows I could see him in the park." She shivered. "What was he thinking? I'd be in the car and the chauffeur would point. 'Your son.' Humiliating, really. A wanderer, crazy."

I was alarmed. "Followed? That bothers me."

"He laughed it off, said, 'I'm seeing ghosts.'"

"But who?"

She was talking to herself, lining up facts in an order she could make sense of. "I admit that lately—for some time now—Dougie has been out of focus. Ever since he met and wooed that girl. He lost his center. The family business suffered dreadfully. My husband dead, Dougie ran the works. The vast monies that survived the Crash. But I tell you, Edna—his lack of focus was *not* good. I have enemies—anyone in our world does. Business rivals, especially now with rich folks hurling themselves out of windows in despair, money-grubbing, trickery, takeovers, vicious disregard for old-guard civility. Gone, all of it. There are those who would take our wealth."

I was puzzled. "So someone murdered Dougie—maybe murdered Belinda too—because of the family investments."

A patronizing smile, unhappy. "Rich folks don't want to stop being rich, Edna."

"I understand that, but…"

"Of course I believe his murder has to do with his crazy involvement with theater. With that dreadful woman, herself murdered."

I watched her face tighten. "Then you must have some ideas, no?"

"Suspicions that the police will not entertain."

"Like?" I was impatient.

Her eyes got cold. "Cyrus Meerdom, for one. You do know that the old letch resented being abandoned by that hussy—who'd set her sights on Dougie. Vast money and pretty youth. A tantalizing combination for a schemer such as she. Meerdom's a powerful man, travels in some of the same financial circles my family does, of course, and wields undue influence."

"But murder?"

Again that tone that she must have honed on generations of skittish help. "Don't be naïve, Edna. The old man mooned over that girl, and Dougie told me how they'd had chance encounters on the street. Murderous eyes, Dougie said about the look. Those were his words. 'Murderous eyes.' Meerdom followed her—he had to know where she was. Always."

"But how?"

"Spies. Cash."

"Servants?"

A slippery smile. She had no intention of answering me. "Think, Edna. The rich and the poor need cash. Victims of the Crash. Everybody in our world knows everyone." A purposeful pause. "Even her so-called friends. A few dollars here, there."

"Incredible."

"Welcome to the real world, Edna. This isn't a page out of your romantic novels, this new world out there."

"But it's one thing to *think* murder—I've considered killing George Kaufman on a daily basis—but the actual act takes a certain madness."

"Or passion. Use *that* word." She considered her words. "Lord, Edna. I don't mean that old codger lay in wait with a gun or a kitchen knife. He hires someone. People need—work. A job. Read a mystery novel, my dear. Agatha Christie, maybe. That's how it's done. Lackeys will do your bidding for a handful of gold coins."

"But risky for such a rich man."

"But one who was miserably besotted with the memory of that dead girl—and doubtless believed, as does the *Daily News* and the *Mirror* and those other subway rags, that my Dougie did it."

"So you think it's someone in the theater then. You haven't mentioned Belinda's brother, Lady Maud. The actors at that struggling theater."

"Of course, I thought of that sad crowd. Jackson Roswell immediately came to mind, so said the inept police captain. His theater floundering, him and that brassy actress yelling at the cops as though they're mindless children."

"Yes, there was resentment there, Lady Maud."

She eyed me closely. "Except for one thing, my dear. Jackson would be foolhardy killing my son. You see, Dougie, coming out of his haze one morning, suddenly waxed sentimental about the dead Belinda and those…those failed actors. The brother who allowed my Dougie to find Belinda. Or some such circuitous thinking on his part. Giving money to beggars wasn't enough. So he actually sent Jackson money. A pile of it. Too much—to produce a new show. A check I fought him over. He wouldn't listen to me. A lavish Christmas day present. Frankincense and myrrh and dollar bills. A note that regretted the delay. All this blather about keeping Belinda's beautiful memory alive—return to the source. Stuff and nonsense, that boy. My dear boy, against my wishes. So Jackson is flush again. A mistake, I told Dougie, but he insisted. Hicks from Podunk doing square dances in the family barn, the cows keeping time." She looked over my shoulder and shrugged. "No, not Jackson. Why would you shoot up the bank?"

I sipped my coffee, watching her over the rim. "Then you have no proof of anything. No suspects. The police have to do their job."

She arched her head, looked down at me, her eyes dropping. "That's why I'm here, Edna."

Surprise in my voice. "Visiting me? What do I…"

"You know these theater people. I told you once before that Dougie's investment in theater sealed his doom. That Noel Coward. I saw his play *Private Lives*, reluctantly dragged there last year by misguided friends. A British nothing, frivolous chatter and idle quipping, empty as a drained cocktail glass. And questionable—effete, airy men in purple ascots who sail above the clouds. A bad example for my Dougie."

I hardened my voice. "I will not defend my talented friend to you."

"I don't expect you to. But I do wonder if you have any thoughts."

I sat back. "No, I'm afraid not."

A trace of sarcasm laced her words. "I don't know if I believe you. You are a perceptive woman, sharp, opinionated, smothered in fame and money, but you're an orderly woman, disciplined. I imagine you find murder—messy. Disorder probably upsets you. Your own instincts demand you run through the possibilities."

I smiled. "You do read one part of my character well."

She spoke over my words. "You have a foot in theater but another foot in"—she swept her hand around my lovely rooms——"in luxury, in taste, in an Upper East Side reserve." She pointed to a small marble sculpture on a stand. An original Lipchitz. A gift from Herbert Swopes. "Quite the dichotomy. I imagine you have some sleepless nights."

I bristled. "Lady Maud's one-stop psychoanalysis?"

She shivered. "Oh Lord, don't bring that crippling faddist obsession up with me. Friends of mine lying on strangers' couches when all they need is a trip to Newport. Sit on a rocking chair on a veranda, for heaven's sake, not lie on a couch and bleed out your imagined sins."

I laughed out loud.

Her eyes got a sudden faraway look. "Anther thing I failed to mention. Tommy Stuyvesant, Belinda's rich paramour, so far as we know."

"So?"

"So the death of that girl has caused his show to flounder, so my spies inform me. Folks went to *Tommy's Temptations*"—she scrunched her mouth in disgust—"to see Belinda Ross. Her alone, sensational. Her being gone turned his revue into a ho-hum show, with no shining light. Attendance is down, the show might close. Times are tough—people spend their nickels elsewhere. Tommy is furious."

"So he murdered Dougie?"

"Anything is possible."

I noticed a faint hint of color rising in her parched face.

"Lady Maud," I began, "perhaps you shouldn't be here."

She wasn't listening. "Let me tell you about my family, my dear. We trace our roots back to early Boston. Settlements in Concord. My husband's side. My side. Frankly, most D.A.R. members are newcomers to the shores. Old New England. Founders of towns in Connecticut. Rhode Island. My family's Harvard, my husband's Yale. An uncle a member of Grover Cleveland's cabinet. Another an ambassador to Spain. You get the picture."

"Why are you telling me this?"

Her voice became raspy. "Because the line ends with Dougie. An only son, the period at the end of that long American sentence. My husband and I hoped he'd marry well, produce a son with his name, carry on for another hundred years. We are America." Her words like rapid gunfire now. "It...ended... with...Dougie. Do you understand what that girl took from us?"

I counted the seconds. "I'm very sorry."

Her foot stomped on the floor. "Do you know what's it's like to have to face your friends? They stare at you with wonder— maybe accusation—in their horrid looks. Blame. That horrible word. Blame. The old lady in the castle. Alone now. Dougie and I were so close. We did everything together. I've been done in by that girl. Then by murder. *His* murder. How do you hang that painting over the family hearth? I step out of my car and eyes accuse, fingers point."

I sat up, gobsmacked. "Lady Maud, you're firing your guns in every direction but…"

"But what?" A harsh laugh. "Are you going to blame me?"

"I never said that."

"You think I haven't woken in the night and wondered—what did I do to create this failed boy? This boy who ran off with the…I almost said circus. Virtually the same thing, no?"

"You blame yourself," I said quietly.

"Of course not." But her voice faltered.

Suddenly, perversely, I understood the reason for her visit: she was seeking absolution, someone to take away the nagging sting that let her believe, if only for a heartbeat, that she contributed to her son's death.

I wanted no part of that.

"Lady Maud." My voice low. "Go home to grieve for your son."

She seemed not to know what to do, planted so deliberately in that chair, the mink covering her shoulders.

"Yes. Much to do."

I looked into her face. "Lady Maud, if I might say something completely candid to you—Dougie made his own choices. Like it or not, he was a grown man, and maybe some of the choices he made were not the best. But they were *his* choices. Maybe the coddled boy wanted to declare himself a man. Yes, a man hopelessly in love. But he tackled his own world. Finally. Maybe his own demons. Maybe…"

I stopped because Lady Maud's eyes got wide.

"Yes." One word, emphatic. "You're right, Edna. A life separate from mine. His choices."

For a moment she looked triumphant, as if slammed into a welcome epiphany. Her eyes flickered, her chin jutted out, and one of her jeweled hands caressed the side of her powdered face.

"Yes," she repeated.

But in the next instance her lips quivered, her eyes got moist, and she turned away, staring out the window. I waited. Her hand trembled. Then, finally, she turned back to face me. The moment had passed. Her body was rigid again, in control, her face set in a grim countenance, her eyes pinpoints of clarity. Grandly, she pulled the mink tighter around her and stood.

"You've been absolutely no help, Edna."

Chapter Eighteen

Sitting with a cup of hot tea in my workroom, staring at the blank sheet of paper in the Remington, I ignored the ringing of the phone. Then it rang again. Rebecca was out shopping and, against my nature, I answered. Muted, swallowed words, a man's tremulous voice. I waited.

"Miss Ferber." The sound of men laughing in the background. "Please."

"I'm here."

"Corey Boynton."

"I know. What's the matter?"

A deep intake of breath. "The police have been questioning me. Over and over. That makes no sense. Why would they stop at the Stanhope? Everyone here…They asked…" His voice trailed off, but then, clearing his throat, he stammered, "I have nothing to do with this. Dougie—*murdered*. Murdered? I never wanted anything to do with this."

"You were a friend of Dougie." Annoyed, I cut into his blather. "It's expected that the police question his friends. Those who knew him."

A long silence, someone calling his name from behind, which he ignored. "They mentioned you—and Noel Coward. There. At the scene. Hours after you left me on the sidewalk, it seems. All of us."

"I'm not following this, Mr. Boynton. All of us?"

"Everybody involved." Panic in his voice. "Can you meet us in a while?"

"What do you mean—'us'?"

"Kitty and me. They've been talking to her, too. Both of us. She's terrified, Miss Ferber. She's been on the phone with me over and over. Each call is worse—hysteria. Why? This is not the kind of world we want to be involved with. Lord, I can't tell my father any of this."

"It's routine. Now stop this nonsense."

He whined. "Do they think that I killed Dougie?"

That gave me pause. I tapped my fingers on the table, considering. "Did you?"

He cried out, "Christ, Miss Ferber, a low blow."

"Then why this over-the-top panic, Mr. Boynton?"

The sound of a radio in the background. Men laughing nearby. "Well...I was...sort of...there. At Beekman Place. Mr. Coward's place. Around the same time. I..."

My mind went blank. "I will meet the two of you."

Late afternoon I sat opposite Corey and Kitty at the Taft Coffee Shop on Seventh Avenue, a large sunny room where the waitresses left you alone. Both Corey and Kitty were late, rushing in, flustered, bumping elbows, searching the tables for me. Sliding into the seat opposite me, Kitty grasped my hand, squeezed it, and mumbled, "Thank you."

"For what?" I answered, unhappy. I pulled my hand back and buried it in my lap. My hasty gesture irritated Kitty, who frowned at me, but then forced herself to smile.

I signaled to a waitress, though Corey at first waved her away with the flip of his hand. "Not now," he told her. But I persisted, and the waitress, narrowing her eyes at Corey, smiled at me, a look that commiserated and communicated—a nice middle-aged lady like you forced to put up with spoiled louts. I smiled back at her.

Despite both their panicky states, which I still didn't quite comprehend, they were nattily put together. Corey had slipped off his Chesterfield overcoat and revealed a navy blue double-breasted suit with a creamy white silk necktie. Hair slicked back from his temples, parted sharply in the middle, so shiny his head seemed a polished museum piece. Immediately he lit a cigarette, closed his eyes in narcotic bliss, and seemed ready to fall asleep. Kitty wore the sleek expression of a Ziegfeld girl fresh from finishing school. She'd hung her velvet bouclé coat with the fox collar on a hanger but kept eyeing it, as though fearful someone lurking nearby would abscond with it. Dressed in a tight-waisted yellow dress with vague periwinkles dotting the fabric, with an oversized rhinestone brooch on her collar, she looked ready for high tea at the Ritz.

She looked around the eatery. "I've never been here before."

Corey ignored her. "You know, Miss Ferber, everything started that night the four of us went to the automat. The night Belinda died. The four of us. That *cursed* excursion."

"What are you saying?"

He looked into my face, fear in his eyes. "That…that fated night." Corey blew a smoke ring across the table. "Because we were there, the police believe…I don't know what they believe. But we were *there*. And now *two* of the four are dead." His hand slapped the table. "Two."

Kitty actually yelped, an unpleasant blurt of noise that sounded like a colicky baby spitting up milk. "I'm frightened, Miss Ferber."

Perplexed, I watched the two of them. "I don't understand your craziness. No one is accusing either of you." I stared into their jittery faces. "Am I missing something here?"

"Two murders," Corey said, and waited.

"Yes," I said, angry, "I know how to count."

The waitress put coffee on the table and Corey, grabbing his cup, gulped down the drink, smacking his lips. He nodded at the waitress. "Another."

"Mr. Boynton," I began, my eyes on him, though his own shifted, avoiding mine, "on the phone you mentioned that you were at Beekman Place. I don't understand."

His eyes blinked wildly. "That's the problem. I *told* the police that. They'd find out anyway, right? They tend to force things out of you, you know. I'm not a stupid man."

"That makes no sense."

He sat back, looked impatiently for the waitress who was chatting with another customer at the counter. Abruptly, he snubbed his cigarette in the ashtray and pushed it away. I pushed it back at him, away from me, a move that confused him. "After you and Mr. Coward met me, and, you know, talked of my neglect of Dougie's friendship"—Kitty swung around to look at his profile, question in her expression—"I felt a little squeamish. Maybe embarrassed. I don't know. You shamed me, Miss Ferber. Mr. Coward, too." A sliver of a smile covered his face. "I'm not used to that emotion."

"I imagine." My lips set in a thin line.

He ignored that, though he twisted his head to the side and shot a sidelong glance at me. "I thought—okay, join all of you for dinner. An evening at Chambord's sounded—desirable. Fishing in my pocket for matches, I found Mr. Coward's card. His address. I thought it a good sign, if you know what I mean. You mentioned Beekman place. Six o'clock. Drinks and all. It sounded—civilized. I have friends who live at Sutton Place, just a stone's throw away. I debated, changed my mind, but finally thought—why not? Make Dougie feel good."

"So altruistic."

"Please don't patronize me, Miss Ferber."

"I didn't realize that was what I was doing."

He tightened his face. "I imagine you always know what you're doing. Every step of the way."

Kitty was making a face that I couldn't interpret. Repeatedly, she glanced toward the door.

"So you caught a cab?" I prompted.

"So I caught a cab, we got stuck in midtown traffic, the snow picked up, chaos, but I arrived there in time to discover a commotion. The street was blocked off. Police cars everywhere. Chaos. The wail of a siren. Flashing lights. A nightmare scene.

I had the cabbie back away, take me home. I had a bad feeling about everything. Of course, I didn't know anything, but, you know, I had this…my gut instinct. Just too many cops swarming the street. In the morning I read the papers." He started to cough, reached for another cigarette. "I was there."

"So was I," I answered. "And I didn't kill poor Dougie. Neither did Noel. If what you're saying is true, neither did you. The police will investigate."

He broke in. "That's the point. *Investigate*. My name will be splashed all over the papers. The wretched *Daily News*. The four of us started out in that automat, and now I'll be on the front page of the tabloids. Do you know how this looks?"

I sat back. "Stop fretting, Mr. Boynton."

Kitty had been fiddling with the buttons on her dress but now jumped in, impatient with Corey's ramble. "You don't understand, Miss Ferber. There is a reason someone killed Belinda and Dougie."

My eyes got wide. "What are you saying? That someone will go after you—or Mr. Boynton?"

"Preposterous," said Corey, rolling his eyes.

She turned to face him. "Is it?"

"But there's no reason to believe that—" I began.

"How do you know?" she screamed.

Nearby, a table of women stopped to watch us. A waitress, approaching with a coffee pot, took a step back.

I folded my hands into my lap, watched the two as they squirmed in their seats. "I don't know. But tell me, the two of you, what exactly do you think is going on? There's a reason I'm sitting here. Something is not being said here."

My question stunned them into silence, and for an awkward moment we fiddled with our cups, drummed fingers on the table, glanced around the restaurant.

Corey started to speak but stopped. "I…nothing. My mind's all foggy."

"Tell me the truth. Why would anyone kill Dougie?" I asked bluntly.

Corey's voice was low, hesitant. "That's all we've been talking about. You know, he must have known who killed Belinda."

I looked into his face. "Didn't you tell me you thought Dougie might have killed her in anger? In a jealous rage?"

He stammered, "I don't remember saying that."

"I do."

A helpless shrug. "Well, yeah, true. Dougie *was* crazy with jealousy. Do you know how many times I had to listen to his fears about Belinda's fidelity? Over and over, ad nauseum, frankly."

"But you were the one who whispered to him in the automat that she was planning on leaving him for a richer guy, no?"

He looked away. "I don't remember that."

"I do." I ran my fingertip around the rim of the coffee cup. "Did Dougie know you didn't like Belinda?"

My question stopped him cold. "I thought her…a floozy, if you must know. I told Dougie *that*. A schemer. A money-grubber. Growing up a rich boy, I met so many girls who saw dollar signs when they batted their eyelids at me."

"But Belinda was in a position to make her own money, no?"

Sharp, nasty. "I don't really care. Lord, her weasel brother, that …that Jackson—we all know this is true—maneuvered the meeting with Cyrus, which led to Tommy Stuyvesant, then to Dougie. A chain of fools, one after the other."

"Dougie? A fool?"

He hesitated. "A misguided fool. Perhaps that's what I mean. Yes, I told him that. Somebody had to. Inexperienced in the ways of love, Miss Ferber. I kept warning him. Be careful. Yes, she's beautiful and talented, but beware. Girls like her…"

"Yet he didn't listen to you."

He scoffed, "No, obviously. He kept running to me, so in love but unable to understand what was happening. And you see where it got everyone. Of course, I didn't anticipate his marrow-deep jealousy of *every* little move she made. Christ, the green-eyed monster that ate his soul."

"It doth mock the meat it feeds on," I added.

Kitty got wide-eyed. "What in the world are you two talking about?"

"Friendships," I said to her.

She rolled her eyes.

I deliberated what to say next. Then, quickly, "Did Dougie know you also disliked him?"

A shocked voice that broke at the end. "How can you say that?" He spoke through clenched teeth.

I turned to Kitty who was unhappy with the drift of the conversation. Every minute or so she looked toward the doorway. Escape? Trying to ignore us, she'd taken a compact from her little Bienen-Davis silk purse—she'd placed it on the table so I'd notice and admire it—checking her lipstick. But her face closed in as she ran her tongue over her crimson lips, spotted a smear of lipstick stuck to a front tooth.

"I'm sorry, my dear," I addressed her severely. "You seem very unhappy."

"I'm frightened. Not unhappy," she pouted.

"But I don't understand—why frightened? That's irrational. You and Mr. Boynton were background players in this horrible little drama. A chattering Greek chorus in the wings, dipping into scenes with gossip and ill-timed advice. The stars of the play are both dead, yet you think the play is still going on." I pulled my tongue into the corner of my cheek. "The understudies are no longer needed."

"It *is* going on," she said. "Nothing will be over until the murderers are caught." Her voice trembled. "I sort of understood Belinda's murder." A quick, nervous glance at Corey. "I mean, all the sniping at each other, the reconciliations, lovey-dovey, sickening really, the sloppy cooing that led to—to murder. In some stupid way that made sense—love gone awry, you know. The stuff of stories from the days of cavemen on." She interlocked her fingers. "Yes, maybe. But Dougie's murder?" She shivered. "That *scares* me. That doesn't make sense."

"Maybe it does make sense. Maybe it's connected with Belinda's murder."

Kitty squirmed. "Lord, if it isn't." Again, her voice broke. "Maybe there is something we don't know." She started to sob. "I want to go to Hollywood. I should have left days ago. A new life there. None of this craziness."

Corey breathed out, melodramatically. "Yeah, land of cocaine and naked starlets." He grinned. "I read *Hollywood Tatler*. Fatty Arbuckle and gold-plated roadsters."

I ignored his rambling. "Tell me, Kitty, what you know about the man Belinda was leaving Dougie for? What do you know? You mentioned him to me. No one has a name. He may figure in this, too."

She avoided eye contact. "I don't know anything."

"But you must have talked about it with Belinda, no? Even with Dougie?"

"He"—she pointed at Corey—"he talked about it with Dougie. I kept my mouth shut."

"But you and Belinda did chat about it." I watched her closely. "For one, all the stories about builder Wallace Benton. You were the one who told me she had her sights on another man."

She fidgeted in her seat, looking over my shoulder. "Not really. It's just the rumors you hear. Friends at *Tommy's Temptations*. Backstage gossip. Lots of talk—stupid. There was even talk of William Paley of CBS. *His* attention. He does like pretty young things. Big-time, powerful men in this city. People *talk*."

"Perhaps it wasn't true," I suggested.

She got adamant. "Of course, it was true. Belinda was ready to move on."

"How did you know that?"

She faltered. "It's just that...girlfriends pick up on things like that. Little things said, suggestions, hints." She laughed. "Powder room chatter."

"Did Belinda actually ever tell Dougie she was leaving him?"

She waited a long time. "No." She whispered, "I don't know."

"Did Dougie ask her?" I looked at Corey.

His stony eyes told me the answer.

I got dizzy as I watched the two of them, both refusing to look at each other. "It seems to me that the star-crossed couple was plagued by jealousies other than theirs."

"And what does that mean?" A flash of fire from Kitty.

Corey whispered into Kitty's neck. "Why are you so riled, Kitty?"

Staring at the two of them as they talked and exchanged furtive glances at each other, each one intent on impressing me, something happened to me: my head started to spin, crazily, waves of sudden flashes that stunned me. For a moment I closed my eyes. It was as if I'd entered a long tunnel. Distant voices echoed and clashed—then silence. I watched Corey and Kitty, but nothing came out of their mouths, though their lips moved. A silent movie, without dialogue lines. Panicked, I leaned forward, but nothing helped. Something was not being said, despite their moving mouths, their animated shoulders, their flickering eyes. Something—I stopped: these two, puppets performing for me.

Rattled, I shook myself out of the trance.

"Are you all right?" Corey asked.

I said nothing.

Kitty added, "You look like you seen a ghost."

I found my voice. "I may have."

They looked at each other. Corey shrugged and turned to me.

"Miss Ferber," Corey said, "we brought you here to ask for your help. With the police."

I stood up, fumbled with my purse and dropped some bills onto the table, struggled into my coat. Two sets of hostile eyes glared at me.

"Then you've wasted an hour of your afternoon. Goodbye."

They shot glances at each other, flummoxed. "I don't follow." From Corey.

I rushed out of the restaurant.

Outside, light-headed, I buttoned my coat. A sharp wind swept the street and I turned my head away. Ice pellets pinged my face. I took a few steps, stopped, and idly gazed at the window display of a haberdashery. I had trouble moving—my head pounded. What had just happened? When I looked back to the sidewalk, I got alarmed—swarms of faces coming at me, moving, moving, faces red from the cold, hooded faces, scarves wrapped around faces. Hidden faces. Coming at me: staring through me.

I couldn't budge.

Something had happened in that restaurant. I felt it to my core. What? Corey and Kitty, two selfish people, privileged leeches, swept with petty jealousies and their own dim confusions. Something had been said to me back there. Walking away, I rushed through their words, but nothing came to me. Truth, I suddenly thought. Is anyone telling the truth in this story? Corey and Kitty—they'd written their own diabolical scripts and plugged hapless Dougie and Belinda into them. But for what gain?

What had Jackson Roswell told me? Something about myths. Legends? Truths? Lies? The words of Chauncey Waters, that actor who'd disappeared out of Manhattan. What had he said? *Jackson created a life for her and was furious when she wouldn't live it.* Half-truths. Personal agendas, vicious desires. Other people orchestrate your life—a selfish act. What had I missed?

Dizzy, I drifted up the sidewalk.

At the corner, not paying attention, I bumped into a man perched over an upturned trash barrel and found myself staring into his weathered face. A surprisingly kind face, I realized, this fortyish man with an unshaven chin, watery hazel eyes, and untrimmed hair under a battered felt fedora. An expensive hat. But a crumpled Brooks Brothers pinstripe suit jacket, baggy, torn at the elbow.

He didn't say a word as he watched me right myself.

I fumbled in my purse and handed him the only quarter I could find. At first I had no idea what he handed me, but his grimy hand held out a cold-stung tangerine, small, blackened, hard as a golf ball. Numbly I dropped it into my pocket.

I stepped away.

"Thank you," he said to my back.

I looked back to catch his eye. He was smiling at me. His cold lips trembled.

A whisper. "No one believes that I had a life before this."

Chapter Nineteen

No one believes that I had a life before this.

I wrestled with the man's troubled face all night long. Before this…a life no one knew about. A new life created for you. Sleeping fitfully, I startled myself awake and thought: Everything is a lie at some level. But then my mind roiled with confusion: what does that mean? What had I missed? Words, words, words. Shakespeare's lovely litany. Words that are—Lies, lies, lies. The modern Manhattan landscape.

Lies.

Jealousy. A horrible thing.

I needed to make a few phone calls, including Noel who was methodically packing his bags for Cleveland. "Darling," he said into the receiver, dragging out the word so that I smiled, "when I arrived in America weeks ago on the *Empress of Britain* I had two dozen steamer trunks. Unloading the ship looked like a scene from a Cecil B. De Mille epic, nubile slave boys at the ready. I lost a perfectly wonderful blue smoking jacket that was given me by Somerset Maugham."

I broke in, anxious. "Noel, take a breath. You're not onstage now."

He laughed. "I'm always onstage." Then, deliberately, he added, "My dearest."

"Look, Noel. There's something you have to do. I know Cleveland is waiting. Lynn Fontaine and Alfred Lunt are waiting. *Design for Living* is…"

"Going to be a smash hit."

I breathed in, inpatient. "Noel, you have to give me part of today." I explained what I wanted and I could hear him tapping the table with his fingertip. The striking of a match. An intake of cigarette smoke. "I think I understand something now."

His voice was sober now, reflective. "Good for you, Edna dear. Of course. Just tell me where."

"You need to invade a sacred male province, forbidden to mere women, Noel. I understand from a call I made to his office that Cyrus Meerdom is hold up for the day at the Union Club on Park Avenue. No women allowed entry into that rarefied world. I can't even call him to the phone. Men are fearful that the presence of any woman in those hallowed halls will point up their obvious inferiority."

He laughed out loud. "Go for the throat, dear Edna."

When I hung up with Noel, I phoned the New Beacon, asked to speak with Tommy Stuyvesant. His secretary hemmed and hawed, whispered that he was busy—"A hit show, you know"—but when I identified myself a second time, my voice firmer and lamentably attaching the words "Show Boat" to my name, she made a quirky sound and scheduled me for a brief meeting late that afternoon. "Only for you," she breathed into the phone. "At the theater."

Noel called back an hour later, obviously delighted with his part in these sudden machinations. "Male province indeed," he said gleefully. "The man who answered the phone dripped privilege and haughtiness. What are they hiding?"

"They?" I asked. "Who—men?"

"I still find my own species bizarre and—sometimes impossible."

"Aren't we lucky then that we both escaped that purgatory?"

Noel didn't answer that, but I heard papers shuffling. "Cyrus Meerdom agreed to meet us at noon in a private dining room at the Savoy Hotel on Fifty-ninth. Yes, he has that estate in Dobbs Ferry with his patient-Griselda wife. Yes, he maintains a not-so-secret *pied-à-terre* somewhere on the West Side, probably over a speakeasy, and yes, he spends most of his time at the

Union Club where he doesn't have to talk to the likes of us. Shelter from the tempest that is the Depression. Edna, it took some arm twisting—I actually had to use that toadstool as an intermediary—Buzzy Collins, sycophant extraordinaire—to broker the meeting. Buzzy knows all, and for some reason seems to have control of Cyrus' expensive ear."

I sat back. "But it's done."

"It's done." A pause. "But a caution, Edna. I told Cyrus that we want to talk about Dougie and Belinda, as he expected. Not surprisingly, he immediately became distant. He'll be difficult to deal with."

Grimly, I said, "We have no choice."

Up until his amorous devotion to Belinda Ross, Cyrus Meerdom relished his reputation as a hard-nosed businessman, a fierce negotiator, a slick entrepreneur reinventing Manhattan. He was also a formidable force in Shubert Alley. A string of successful shows financed by his family's oil refinery interests, spotlighting the career of Helen Hayes, for one, and he became a fixture on Broadway.

His theatrical sense, however, was not always unerring— witness the short-run flop he created to spotlight Belinda. Of course, he would have gladly paid for her to read out loud the Manhattan yellow pages perched on top of Grant's Tomb up in Washington Heights—and expected the world to genuflect in awe. Since the caper with Belinda ended so badly, his reputation was tarnished, if only a little. He retreated back into his wealth and private men's clubs.

● ● ● ● ●

Noel and I sat in a surprisingly small room off the lobby at the Savoy. A long mahogany table surrounded by chairs upholstered in striped burgundy-and-white fabric, green-shaded table lamps, a black walnut floor-to-ceiling bookcase crammed with evenly-lined volumes. I examined the books, a persistent habit I never lost. The books folks surrounded themselves with told me a lot about their lives. Of course, these days I visited homes where nary a volume could be found. Persnickety matron that I am, I paid no second visits there. Here, in this claustrophobic chamber with dimly-lit wall sconces and an emerald green Tabriz Oriental, I ran my fingers down the burgundy spines of a complete set of Bulwer-Lytton, another of Charles Dickens' bound in calves' leather, and a wonderfully decorative set of the complete works of Marie Corelli, that British romancer who once proclaimed her superiority to Shakespeare. I chuckled out loud. I pointed out the set to Noel.

"I met her years back," he told me. "She floated into a room in gossamer and tulle, a specter out of the Arabian Nights, and talked in a breathy voice."

I smiled. "A look I've never cultivated."

Noel eyed the severely cut wool suit I was wearing, charcoal gray, a hint of black piping, a rigid Eton collar that I'd accented with a sapphire brooch.

"Edna, you look almost like a man."

I counted a heartbeat. "So do you."

He roared until the door suddenly opened, and Cyrus and Buzzy walked in, both alarmed by Noel's laughter.

They sat down opposite us, grim-faced, their shoulders almost touching, and immediately the door opened and a young waiter, probably eighteen or nineteen, pimply and all Adam's apple, placed a tray of coffee on the table. Bowing deferentially, a grand salaam, he backed slowly out of the room, behavior that annoyed me. The mimicked trappings of old-guard European royally here, I thought—and particularly unwelcome in the grand old Republic. Neither Buzzy nor Cyrus even looked into the young man's face.

Buzzy was the first to speak. "What's this all about, Noel?"

Noel deferred to me. "Edna has some questions, if you don't mind." He was looking at Cyrus.

Cyrus' voice was thick and harsh. "Let's get this over." He shot a quick, unhappy glance at Buzzy. "I still can't get over Belinda's death." He shivered. "Murdered. Poor Dougie—gone. Murderers all over the place."

"Mr. Meerdom," I began, "ever since Dougie was murdered at Beekman Place, I've been…" I stopped because he held up his hand. "What?"

"You certainly don't believe I killed that hapless young man?" A fingertip smoothed the lapel of his suit jacket. A small gold pin in the buttonhole. A diamond chip.

"No, I don't," I told him, but suddenly thought *maybe yes, maybe no.* "And after Belinda's sad death, we"—I indicated Noel who was watching me closely—"we thought it best to ask questions."

Sarcastically he replied, "We do have a police force, you know."

"Of course." His stare was unnerving. "Of course. But Noel and I were friends with Dougie, liked him, and we…"

Buzzy broke in. "I heard Lady Maud told you two to step aside. To mind your own business."

Beside me, Noel fussed, tapping his foot nervously.

"She did, indeed." I glanced at Noel, who nodded back at me.

"And you didn't listen?" Buzzy checked with Cyrus, who refused his stare.

"I make my own choices, Buzzy," I said.

"She makes her own choices," Noel echoed, relishing the moment.

"What do you want from me?" Cyrus stared into my face. His forehead glistened, and he extracted a huge white handkerchief from a pocket and ran it across his forehead.

"I need you to help me put events in order. What happened when. I'm trying to understand Dougie and Belinda's relationship. I have the feeling that I'm missing something, that some things were not true. Idle rumors, maybe, converted to truth. It dawned on me that everyone has told me a self-serving story. Dougie and Belinda had their own—perhaps ignored."

"I'm not following you." Cyrus took a cigar from a pocket and lit it. A cloud of smoke filled the room. "Everyone knows what happened. Lord, the subject of their romance entranced parties and gossip fests all over town."

"But I'm still missing pieces."

"I'm not sure I can help."

"I believe you can." I breathed in. "Could you please tell me how you met Belinda? And—even Dougie. Yes, his family is part of your social world, but…" I stopped.

Frustrated, his face tight, he put down his cigar in an ashtray. "Important?"

"Maybe."

Resigned, he sat back after glancing at Buzzy, who hovered near him like a lawyer who knows he's lost his case but needs to act the part for his client.

Cyrus didn't talk for a long time, and the room got uncomfortable. Buzzy, rattled, rolled his head back.

"You're making everyone goddamn nervous." Cyrus' eyes darted to me. "Pardon my French, Miss Ferber."

"I've heard worse, sir."

The rebuke didn't please Buzzy, whose body gyrations only intensified. Finally, Cyrus laid a hand on Buzzy's forearm, and the man settled down.

"I find talking about Belinda embarrassing," Cyrus said at last.

Noel looked puzzled. "Embarrassing?"

Cyrus' eyes landed on the wall of leather-bound books. Softly, his voice hesitant, he laughed lightly. "An old fool." A heartbeat. "Still an old fool. Frankly, I would not be sharing these thoughts with you had not—Belinda died like that. And even poor Dougie." For a second he shut his eyes, then sighed out loud. "I'll never understand the loss of that boy."

I felt a tick inside me. Me too, that horrible loss. A life, wasted. Two lives, wasted.

"How well did you know Dougie?"

"Not very, frankly. Of course, the young son of an old friend. Away at school. I don't pay attention to other people's children." A thin smile. "Until he was in my sight."

"With Belinda?" Noel asked.

"I guess so." Cyrus sucked in his breath. "Part of the business world earlier—but…just there. But when Belinda came into sight…I can't explain my…my infatuation with that poor girl.

I'm a married man, and happily so, grown children. A wife who indulges my peccadilloes, such that they are. You know how it is in the theater, Noel. Fresh new faces stepping off the bus from Topeka or Peoria, fluttering eyelids, whispering. Flattering, to have a beautiful girl on your arm. We all do it."

I winced at that. "All?"

He shook his head. "Maybe not all. But…flattering. And harmless. A decoration accompanying you to parties, to openings. But never a step into dangerous indiscretion."

"Until," I commented wryly, "Belinda came along."

"No." Emphatic, forceful. "No, Miss Ferber. Yes, we went places, the two of us. I wanted her on my arm. But that girl was—circumspect."

I protested, "But all the rumors."

"The hell with the rumors," he stormed. "I know what I know." A trace of a smile. "Okay, I heard the rumors and let them go unanswered. A boost to my ego, maybe. As I say, I'm embarrassed by my…" He stopped, his gaze drifting from me to Noel. "Anyway, I fell for her. Hard. I wept with the pleasure of her company. I was drunk with her. I was used to the…we men at the club call them five o'clock girls. They stop in when day is done. Showgirls. Secretaries, the pretty ones. You know…"

Icily, "No, I don't."

"Noel?"

"Really now?"

Cyrus looked baffled as he fiddled with the stub of his cigar. "Of course, I'm not a stupid man. I know that was the intention of her mendacious brother, Jackson. A slime-bag, completely. He maneuvered her into my sight, and she was complicit. Yet it had to be—her success. The girl was monumentally talented, and beautiful, and funny, and—she was made to be a star."

"But she left you for Tommy—and his successful revue."

He made a pinched face. "That was business. My revue failed miserably within weeks, so she disappeared from my arm. No time for me to mount another revue. Waiting in the wings, a move plotted out, Tommy swept in, a vulture. It's the way things are in this business. Stupidly, I mooned over her, unable to let go of the fascination. I swear it was new for me, such abject hunger. I couldn't even explain it to myself. An old man acting like a randy farm boy. But spurred by Jackson, Belinda moved on."

"Yet you followed her around. I'm confused."

A hint of color in his cheeks. "As I said, a foolish old man, obsessed with beauty—and, I suppose, rejection. The ornament disappeared from my grasp."

"How did you know where she was all the time?"

An embarrassed chuckle. Suddenly he tapped Buzzy's forearm. "A spy in the house of love."

Buzzy fumed. "Not true, no." A fiery look on his face. "Cyrus, why do you tell them all this?"

He sighed. "Because it's all over, that's why. I know when the game is over." He grinned at me. "Buzzy reported in—for a fee."

Buzzy sighed. "Goddamn it to hell."

"A contract," Cyrus added. "A few dollars here. There. Some, in fact, dropped into the sweaty palm of a girl named Kitty Baker."

"My God." I looked at Noel who was smiling.

"Belinda was Jackson's tool, but his grip failed. Finally."

"Greed is a democratic vice," Noel said.

I was bothered. "And how did Dougie fit into all of this? When did he appear on Belinda's arm?"

He seemed surprised at the question. "Frankly, Dougie was there from the beginning."

"Meaning?"

"I'm not sure what you're getting at, Miss Ferber. She met Dougie a day or so after she was in rehearsals for my revue."

"I didn't realize she knew him that far back."

Noel spoke up. "When I got back from Europe a month back or so, they were already a couple. I thought…" His voice dropped out. "What was I missing?"

I looked into Noel's face. "I met Dougie through you, Noel. After you returned. I never questioned…"

Cyrus' voice rose. "What you don't realize, Miss Ferber, is that Belinda and Dougie went out for coffee that same afternoon. Suddenly she was happy to be with him. And, wildly, unexpectedly, Dougie, the cold-blooded financial wizard, was giddy as a puppy."

"Then…" I tried to form words. "Then they were involved…"

He nodded at me. "From the very beginning. She didn't leave me for Tommy—he enjoyed squiring her to fancy clubs, too—then jumped into Dougie's eager arms. I was so moonstruck over the girl that I closed my eyes to her real love—that boy."

Noel was sputtering. "But Dougie never said anything."

He laughed out loud. "I don't know if Dougie understood what was going on. He'd see her on my arm, and shrug. On Tommy's arm. His jealousy came later. His temper. In the early days he spent long hours watching her, eyes glassed over, not realizing she was watching him, eyes glazed over."

I sputtered, "But all the rumors suggested…"

"No, all the rumor-mongers played with it all, mocking me for my all-too-public infatuation." He grit his teeth. "I'm still mortified by the way I acted at your party, Noel. When I called her that horrible name. I was—stunned to see her. If I could take back any moment, it would be that. The look on her face." His voice hardened. "I deserved to be slapped. You know, I still mourn that girl. My heart still breaks. She did something to me." He tapped his heart. "In here. A tick that I thought was long dead. But no, Juliet only had eyes for her Romeo. And she was singing to him from the front of the theater nightly."

Noel was grumbling. "As the Bible tells us, a loose translation, 'Tattlers and busybodies blab things they should not say.' Welcome to the world of the theater."

"Welcome to the planet," I added.

Noel was anxious to say something. "And that story about Belinda leaving Dougie for some rich tycoon. Maybe a smitten Wallace Benton?"

Buzzy was nodding his head. "Everyone said that. I heard it more than once."

I bit my tongue. "But not from Belinda, I gather. I bet no one believed it—those fabricators." I was thinking out loud. "Kitty, for one." I paused. "Or maybe she made it all up."

Noel tapped my elbow. "One person did believe it. Dougie."

Cyrus frowned. "That was unfortunate."

Buzzy, his eyes flitting around the room. "It didn't matter because everyone knew she was a gold-digger. Her plot with her scheming brother. The path to riches. To—to *this* world." He pointed around the elegant room. "She was at fault. Her behavior brought about those rumors, Miss Ferber."

"Rumors." I let the word roll off my tongue. "A death sentence."

Cyrus' eyes focused on Buzzy. "You're as much a fool as I am, Buzzy." But he smiled at the end of it, though Buzzy, caught off guard, squirmed. "Do you know what I think happened, Miss Ferber?" A wide engaging smile, genuine, Cyrus pleased with himself. "I think Belinda surprised herself by falling in love with Dougie." The smile disappeared. "But that, too, was ultimately unfortunate."

• • ● • •

Tommy Stuyvesant was late arriving at the theater. Noel and I sat in a tiny makeshift office at the New Beacon in front of an old chipped oak desk. Probably once a dressing room, the office smelled of old rotting wood, generations of mouse droppings, and the sour odor of old rags and water stains. A young woman had led us in, insisting Tommy would arrive any moment. An indulgent smile. "He likes to spend as little time in this cramped room as possible."

"He does have offices in the Woolworth," I noted.

"But his heart is here. In theater."

"A contradiction then, my dear."

She didn't answer but scurried out of the room.

When Tommy appeared, he strode past us, settled into a swivel chair, leaned back, unbuttoned the top button of his vest, and opened an enamel Frankart box on his desk and fingered a cigarette. A big man, such a contrast to the miniature and bony Cyrus, Tommy was broad-chested with a florid face and loose jowls, a drinker's face, and his high forehead gleamed under the overhead light. His salt-and-pepper hair was styled in an expensive cut. An old-fashioned gold watch fob. Although I couldn't see his legs, I had no doubt he sported Gentleman Jim Dandy spats. Probably four-button mustard yellow. Once a fad among the swell men about town, but the younger crowd sported flannel slacks over pointed Italian shoes.

He offered Noel a cigarette but not me. Noel took one and laboriously inserted it into the ivory holder removed from a pocket. A deliberate performance, so slow and mannered, that Tommy, ready to speak, simply watched, mouth agape, probably waiting for some dramatic finish. Noel waited for Tommy to hand him a lighter. A curious pantomime, the two men, that ended when both men sat back and blew smoke rings into the air. Smoke signals, I thought—yes, it's time to hear what the woman has to say to us. Let's listen to her.

I waited.

Finally, Tommy made a clicking sound with his tongue. "I haven't seen the two of you in a while. A lot has happened."

"And none of it good."

"You don't have to tell me that."

"Is the show closing?" I asked.

He swung his head back and forth. "Not yet. We're floundering, true. But the loss of Belinda is…lethal. That's the problem when everything revolves around one star. You take Mary Boland out of Irving's *Face the Music*, and the show is crippled. She'd become that show. Same thing here."

"What will you do?" I asked.

A fatalistic shrug. "Move on. What choice do I have? Hide out in my family's bank account till the dust of this down turn ends."

I exchanged a glance with Noel. "We just came from talking to Cyrus Meerdom."

Before I could finish the sentence, he was chuckling softly, speaking over my words. "That old reprobate. Lord, I still recall that resounding slap Belinda delivered at your killer-diller birthday party, Noel."

"Yes," Noel grimaced, "party favors and boogie-woogie floor shows. It beats blowing out the candles on a cake we never got around to slicing."

"I hear he took Belinda's death really hard." Tommy rolled his cigarette between his thumb and index finger.

I shot him a look. "And you didn't?"

He sat up. "That's not fair, Miss Ferber. Of course I did. I was shattered by it. And, if you must know, by Dougie's strange murder. The thought of that boy dying like that—a sleepless night for me."

"Belinda's wasn't strange?"

He hesitated. "Poor choice of words maybe. You're playing with me, madam. His death seemed to come out of nowhere. But Belinda...the automat. Dougie in a fit of anger..."

"So you also believe Dougie killed her?" Noel questioned.

He nodded. "Sadly, yes. Who else? I've actually given it some thought. Of course, who *hasn't*? I mean, those of us who knew them. The two of them sniping at each other was famous—maybe I mean infamous—gossip around Schubert Alley. It was only a matter of time before he snapped."

"Because of her infidelities?" Noel asked.

He squinted at us. "Are you suggesting something about me and her?"

"Yes," I said, simply. "After all, you took her from Cyrus' arms."

Again, the soft, almost inaudible chuckle. "No, Miss Ferber. Lord, you talk like a radio song lyric. The truth of the matter is that Belinda was the unfortunate creation of an avaricious brother, his wonderful molding of an untutored girl into a temptress. I was fond of her, liked her company, enjoyed the game she played with me—the attention, the cooing, the flattery—but no, she practiced those maneuvers with me but I didn't fall prey to them. I'm surprised you're saying that to me." He pushed back his chair, cradled his hands across his big belly.

"Cyrus says she was taken with Dougie from the start."

"That's true."

I looked at Noel. "So…"

"So," Noel finished, pointing a finger at me, "you and I were watching a different play, Edna."

I frowned. "It seems lots of folks were watching that play. And perhaps they were also writing the script for it."

"What are you two talking about?"asked Tommy.

For a while I said nothing, my eyes focused on a line of glass-framed stage posters behind him. Helen Hayes in *The Lilac Garden*. Ruby Keeler in *Red Shoes*. None, I noted, of Belinda in *Tommy's Temptations*. Somehow that bothered me.

"You know, I'm getting a different picture of Belinda now. Yes, a woman who was a driving woman, really, her sights set on money, perhaps prodded by her brother. But I met her after she was already taken with Dougie. Before that…"

He held up his hand. "All true, I'm afraid. When I first met her, on the arm of Cyrus, in fact, her eyes screamed greed. A look I'm familiar with in this business. It was uncanny. She was robotic, I thought. Take this step, now take that one."

"But that changed?"

He pulled out his watch and checked the time. He tapped a sheet of paper on his desk, puffed out his lips and made a we-have-to-make-this-fast gesture. "That's what was strange. You know, I'd locked her into some ironclad image, and found it amusing. Like at your party, Noel. A diversion. Lord, how many times have I seen it in this world! Step your way to the top. But one day, talking with her about something, some new arrangement for one of the numbers in the show, I looked into her face. And there it was." He stopped, his eyes wide.

Noel leaned forward in his seat. "What?"

Tommy closed his eyes for a second, then popped them open. "Weakness. That's the word. She always had this…this hardness about her, steely, fierce, even a little unnerving. But one day it was gone."

I sat back. "Dougie?"

Tommy suddenly looked very melancholy. "Yeah, Dougie."

He pointed to his gold watch, straightened up, and said, "I'm sorry, but I have to end this."

"Thank you," I said to him as I stood up.

Standing in the lobby, I looked at the giant poster of *Tommy's Temptations* dominating the wall. There was Belinda Ross, gorgeous, a siren with a come-hither look in her eyes, that beautiful smile on her face. Her name in bold letters.

"The Newest Light on Broadway."

A run of critical quotations.

"The surprise of the season is the joy of the season."
—F.P.A. in "The Conning Tower."

"Jazz baby comes alive. Oh you kid me not!"
—Walter Winchell in the *Mirror*.

"Stop, look and listen—and dance the night away."
—Brooks Atkinson in the *Times*.

"This can only be the art of something great!"
—Dorothy Kilgallen.

I shivered.

Noel cradled my elbow, a worried look on his face. "Edna," he began, "tell me your thinking."

"Noel," I said quietly, "we've been lied to. I've been a foolish—and not a very good reporter. Our view of that pair was filtered through others' prisms. I asked all the wrong questions."

He got defensive. "There was no reason for us to question the stories. What I saw when I returned to New York was a full-blown romance, though a shaky one. Those outbursts colored a lot of my thinking. We simply saw Dougie fretting and worrying. We accepted his *doubt* as fact."

"And believed it all." I slammed my fist into my palm. "How could I be so stupid!"

He spoke bitterly. "Corey Boynton and Kitty Baker."

"Exactly."

"They produced a scenario that served no one but…"

"Themselves." I stressed the word. "Lord, Noel. Jealousy. Manipulation. Falsehood. All to the end of ruining lives they envied, coveted. Or simply because it was fun to play games. The face of false friendship. Kitty and her stories of other loves. She was the one who kept bringing up Wallace Benton and that darn skyscraper. Corey and his whispering in Dougie's ear. 'She's leaving you.' Lies." I shook. "A game to them."

"A deadly game."

"I don't like being so foolish, Noel."

"But none of this leads to murder, does it?" He looked worried.

"Of course it does, Noel." I stared at the poster of Belinda. Dead now. Dougie, dead. "The end result was the death of two love-struck souls."

"They lied to us, Edna."

"Yes, but we can live with that. You. Me. What is worse is that they lied to Belinda and Dougie. Kitty with her hints and rumors, Corey with his frat-buddy confidences."

"But what does it tell us about their murders?"

"It tells me who killed Belinda."

Chapter Twenty

Lady Maud couldn't disguise her anger at me. She stood by a window on the fourth floor of her mansion, her back to the splendid view of Central Park, and glowered. I'd disturbed her, but worse—I'd barged in uninvited, the ragtag usurper of her serene afternoon. I'd rung the bell downstairs, waited an untoward amount of time, bothered the maid who answered and then hastily dismissed me, a look of wonder in her face that told me no one dared step into Lady Maud's fiefdom so brazenly. But I persisted. No, I would not leave. Sorry, she was spending her afternoon writing notes to friends and others. Doubtless thank-yous for condolences, for flowers, for sympathy. The proper response. Black-lined stationary. *The death of my dear son… Thank you for your…*

"Tell her I'm here."

The maid, stymied, headed to another room and left me standing in the front room under a French rock crystal chandelier. I expected it to fall on me, triggered by a butler in Lady Maud's Satanic kitchen.

Lady Maud was not "at home," I was told. "Lunch at the St. Regis with friends."

"Of course, she is," I demanded. "You just told me she's writing notes. Which is it?" My voice echoed back at me in the high-ceiling foyer.

A guttural voice erupted from behind the trembling young woman. A social secretary, I assumed. A ghoulish horse-faced woman in a schoolmarm's smock, though she'd accented it with a single strand of pearls and a rhinestone clip in her graying hair. "Good afternoon, Miss Ferber."

Not happy, but then neither was I.

Upstairs Lady Maud sat at a tiny writing desk by the rear window, her face turned away from the doorway, her hand clutching a fountain pen. A stack of envelopes and cards spread before her.

I cleared my throat. "Lady Maud."

She turned quickly, her face set in anger, her eyes stony. "You do not take no for an answer, do you, Miss Ferber?"

"I try not to."

"Manners learned in a hen house?" She sucked in her cheeks.

"Actually no manners at all. A lesson learned from my days as a reporter in Milwaukee as I hounded folks who refused to talk to me."

"I'm not surprised." She stood and walked to a window, turned to face me.

She was not dressed for entertaining. A deep black silk wrap-around housecoat over a loose charcoal-tinted morning gown. A thin trim of ermine around the collar. Japanese sandals speckled with green and blue bamboo reeds. A run of jangling bracelets on one arm. One simple ring, a wedding band. Gone the ostentatious array of rings she'd worn before. A little self-conscious, her hand fumbled with her hair, pulled up and tucked casually under a lace bonnet. She looked grandmotherly. Or, I supposed, a Robber Baron matron from an era when James Garfield assumed the presidency. She saw me surveying her clothing.

"I'm not dressed for company."

"No matter."

Idly, stepping away from the window, she glanced down on the writing desk, her fingers grazing the stack of sealed envelopes. "I'm busy."

"I'll take as little time as I need to."

A flash of fear in her eyes. "What does that mean, Miss Ferber? What do you want from me?"

"Answers."

"And I have them?"

"I believe you do."

She sighed, glanced back out the window. She searched the room, as if her possessions were new to her, alien. Her eyes drifted to an overgrown spider fern in a huge Chinese urn. Red lettering against a soft brown glaze. Tendrils of pale green and white vine spun out, cascaded over the sides. She took a step forward and her fingers clipped off a yellow leaf, crumbled it between her fingers. Then another. Another. She muttered to herself, "Everything dies in this room. There is no morning light."

"Lady Maud," I began, "you have to understand that I liked your son." I started to say, but stopped—she crushed a brown leaf and let the pieces fall onto the carpet, trickling from between her fingers.

Her fierce look stopped me. "You'll not let me grieve in peace, will you?"

I said quietly, "There has to be an end to this story, no? Two murders."

She gasped. "I lost my only son." She banged the side of the urn.

"And," I stressed, "don't you want to know what happened?"

Distracted, she circled the urn, but then she sank back into her chair and folded her hands into her lap. "You know this house is so still now. The servants tiptoe around me like I'm a museum piece. But their whispering is so loud it echoes off the ceiling. I can't escape it."

"No family to visit?" I asked softly.

She swung her head to the side. "Distant cousins from Chicago. In town for the funeral. Annoying people. My husband's family. I don't want to be with them. They reek of disaster—and hunger."

"I'm so sorry. So you're alone."

"And will be from this point on." A bitter smile. "Dougie and I talked. At least we did before his world spiraled madly out of control. Sunday mornings in this room, in fact. A house of twenty or so rooms, echo chambers. Fifth Avenue out there. At night the gear-grinding taxis startle me awake. The backfire of trucks. Each time I think—gunfire. Dead." She pointed. "Here—silence. This room. Tea in the afternoon. Confidences. A young boy, fifteen or sixteen, home from boarding school, wanting to be with me." Her voice sailed over the room. "Mommy." She closed her eyes. "This room is my tomb now."

"Lady Maud."

"Don't you dare feel sorry for me. It's the way I want it, Miss Ferber. Don't you understand? This is the only room that will allow me the memories I demand." Her eyes shot to the fern. The crumbled dead leaves. "I hate that plant."

I didn't know what to say so I waited. As quietly as I could, I sat down in a chair across from her. She'd not invited me to sit.

"Dougie's chair. His favorite. Mornings." She glared at me. "Why are you here?" she asked bluntly. "Why won't you tell me?"

A horn sounded from the street. She jumped and swallowed a sob.

"Because I suddenly realized I didn't know who Dougie was. Dougie and Belinda—their life together."

That confused her, though she bristled at Belinda's name. "No." One word, meaningless.

"Nobody believes that I had a life before this." I repeated the line from the homeless man on the street. Lady Maud's eyes got wide, startled. I rushed on. "A dreadful line I heard recently. It got me thinking—so easy to create someone else's life in your head, a life that perhaps has nothing to do with the life actually led."

Her eyes got cloudy. "I don't understand a word you're saying."

I nodded. "I'm sorry. What I mean is—Dougie and Belinda had a different life from the one everyone talked of. Convinced me of. The life we saw, for one. Negative, harsh. A gold-digger, a Broadway jazz baby seducing your inviolable boy. That life. But that wasn't true." She started to interrupt but I said quickly, "A life so many of us came to believe was written in stone."

"I still don't understand."

"Only this—we didn't allow them the life they wanted."

I watched Lady Maud shift in her seat, twist toward the Chinese urn. She stood up and plucked another dead leaf and crumbled it between her fingers. The brown bits fell onto the black-lacquered teak table. For a moment she looked out the window, but then, undecided, sank back into her chair.

"Lady Maud. I've come to realize how unfair the world was to Dougie and Belinda."

She half-rose from her chair. "To them? To them? Honestly, Miss Ferber, your choice of words. Unfair is hardly…"

I locked eyes with hers. "They loved each other."

She gasped. "For heaven's sake. Nonsense. Do you hear yourself?"

"Let me finish," I insisted. "That's my horrible conclusion because it's a conclusion that brings a dreadful ending to this play. I think it was a surprise for both of them, this unplanned love. Oddly, Dougie came into his own as a young man, something that, despite his financial wizardry, you suppressed. He could no longer be the prep school boy on his mother's arm at high tea at the Ritz."

She stormed, "How dare you!" Her fingers curled around the fountain pen on her desk.

I went on. "Belinda, for Dougie, was liberation. Yes, a showgirl with all kinds of fireworks blazing. But Dougie fell in love with her. Crazily so. Hopelessly. Yes, he may not have understood what that meant, so new an experience for him, but no matter—intoxicated, driven, swept off his feet. He was too old for the novelty of it all. Perhaps he was happy for the first time in his life."

She simmered. "Do you know how offensive you are?"

"I can imagine, Lady Maud. But hear me out."

She looked ready to press a bell at her elbow, but resisted. I fully expected burly wait servants, those rough-and-tumble men in stevedore shirts who shoveled the coal in her basement, to rush in and hoist me out like a sack of old potatoes. But I also realized something else: Lady Maud was eager to hear what I had to say. There was something in her eyes. Wariness, yes, but also curiosity. She was waiting.

Her voice was a low rumble. "Effrontery, Miss Ferber."

I folded my hands in my lap and sat back, comfortable now, purposeful. I knew where I was going. "But I've come to believe the bigger surprise was the one that flooded Belinda Ross. You see, she came to care about Dougie, probably loved him back. A surprise because she'd been fashioned by Jackson Roswell into a tool for his own—of course, *hers* as well—success. A maniacal man, that Jackson, who took a young girl and told her he could make her rich and famous. A hardscrabble Pygmalion. And he almost succeeded. But he misjudged. Cold-hearted himself, severe, narrow-minded, wildly stupid, he thought her landing a rich husband—or a lover—was an easy maneuver. Take this step, take another. Giant steps."

"Belinda was compliant." She spat out the words. "His help-mate."

I nodded at her. "Agreed. At first. A robot jerking her head up and down. May I take one giant step? Cyrus Meerdom. Tommy Stuyvesant. Dougie Maddox. But recently I learned—to my amazement, talk about the power of rumor—that Dougie was actually at her side during all of this maneuvering, that those two men were simply bit players in the drama. And Belinda, herself surprised, found herself in love."

"With Dougie," Lady Maud whispered.

"Exactly. A harmless young man, guileless, charming, maybe bumbling. But seductive to the girl. Two babes in the woods. Wolves everywhere, liars, dissemblers, folks ready to destroy them. So she started to distance herself from Jackson."

"But…" she said, faltering, breathing hard.

"But it was too late. The two lovers were already entangled in a fabric of lies and deceit. Corey Boynton. Kitty Baker. Millie Glass. Jackson."

"I don't understand." Her hands were nervous, clasped, then unclasped. A furtive look at the Chinese urn.

"Jealousy, maybe even dislike, masquerading as companion-ship, friendship. Brotherhood. Sisters. Shared confidences. Lies, lies, lies. Words, words, words."

"I never liked Corey. A grubbing family."

"Stung by his family's loss of money after the Crash, he insisted he still be a part of that playboy life. He'd got used to money, and the loss twisted him, made him reckless. He resented Dougie's happiness. So he sabotaged it, possibly unwittingly at first. A few words here, innuendo, whispering, lies. He was abetted by a partner-in-crime named Kitty Baker, a failed actress, unemployed, in Manhattan to find the success she saw Belinda achieve. Another casualty of the Depression. A pinched life, resented. As she watched Belinda on the arm of Cyrus, then Tommy, then Dougie, she burned. A fabricated story, doubtless about Belinda's leaving Dougie for Wallace Benton. Maybe William Paley of CBS, now that his scandalous mistress Louise Brooks is taking her clothes off in a warmer climate of Hollywood. Jealous."

"What if those stories were true? Belinda had a roving eye."

"Stop," I thundered. "Not true. I've sat with them, listened to them, sympathized at first, but finally realized I'd been duped. Lied to. Fooled by fools. Noel and I. Others. In these awful struggling times, the worms crawl out of the woodwork, infest, infect."

"My Dougie." A rasp in her throat.

"Yes, your Dougie. Belinda's Dougie. A naïve young man, he dumbly listened to the ugly rumblings in his ear. He nodded at Corey's poison. He believed what was said about Belinda. Poor Belinda fought him, denied over and over, watched his temper tantrums, and became exhausted by it all, maybe protested too much. But Dougie refused to listen to her. He'd made up his mind. Sick with love, feeling betrayed, desperate, haunted, trailing after her for crumbs of affection. Watchful, bewildered. A welter of conflicting emotions that ruined his days. He imagined her squired off in a Rolls Royce to a secret penthouse apartment on Park Avenue while he bayed at the moon in the streets below."

She spat out her words. "You don't know what she was up to."

"I'd hazard a guess. Nothing. Yes—*nothing*. She was torn— battling with her brother over her freedom. She hated that life but didn't know how to embrace the new one. She was coming into her own, as well. The two of them." My mind reeled. "I'll tell you something else, Lady Maud. I'm happy Dougie found love. A short life, as it turned out. I'm glad he had that moment. Yes, a bad ending, but for a while he was happy. And that counts for something."

"Dougie was weak," Lady Maud declared. "I hated that in him."

"I imagine you told him that more than once. Not like his powerful father. A weak man."

She lashed out. "I tried to make him a strong man." Her hand slapped the desk. "I fought every bit of weakness in him—hammered at him. He *knew* he was weak."

I'd had enough. "Oh, I don't believe a word of that. You wanted a docile boy at your elbow, sitting in this sunny room surrounded by over-watered ferns in Chinese pots."

She closed her eyes. "You've never been a mother, Miss Ferber."

I debated my words. "Perhaps you never were one either."

She cried out, "In my own rooms…in…" Her hand grasped her chin.

"I'm sorry, but I have to say all of this."

She laughed. "You relish it."

"I hope you don't believe that. Lady Maud, Dougie believed that Belinda was unfaithful. The idea haunted him. That awful night in the automat. You know, I was with them all the earlier part of the evening. Bickering. Love pecks. Forgiveness. Back and forth. I love you. I hate you. I didn't know what to think. You could see the chaos—maybe madness—in his face. Kitty and Corey, watching, probably savored the street show they had somehow fostered."

"No."

Suddenly she stood and crossed to the window. She stared down into the street. Quietly, "They're tearing down another mansion," she said, her voice shaky. "They're all going. The Astors. The Vanderbilts. The Mellons. Soon—me. This grand home. So beautiful, so fragile. I'm left like an anachronism in this mausoleum. The wrecking ball banging against my nighttime sleep."

"Lady Maud."

She turned and watched me, quiet, quiet. Her face a frozen mask.

Her voice low, horrible. "You know his last days he did nothing but wander these streets. Out *there*. He'd bring back bags of ugly, gnarled, ice-stung apples. Odd bits of clothing he bought from derelicts on corners. You walk on Fifth Avenue and someone begs for a nickel. One after the other. Dougie spilled his coins into their dirty palms. I'd be driving in the car and the chauffeur would point—'Your son.' A smirk on his face. There was Dougie, disheveled, bent over against the wind, talking with people in breadlines."

I waited, said nothing.

"'Why?' I asked him. I begged him for an answer. Do you know what he said? 'They smile at me.' What kind of an answer was that?"

Her fist banged the window and I thought she'd smash the glass.

Time stopped: my breath quickened: my mind a blur of black lightning.

"Dougie killed Belinda, Lady Maud."

Her eyes closed, then opened wide, a sweep of fear in her eyes. "You know?"

I nodded. "There could be no one else."

She wrapped her arms around her chest and swayed back and forth. "Yes."

"Tell me."

"A day before he was killed I walked into his room and he was crying on his bed. Just sobbing like a sad child. When I caught his eye, I knew." A sliver of a smile. "But I suppose I always knew. The detective I hired was a fool, but I knew that when I handed him a fat check. But..."

"What did Dougie tell you?" My heart beat wildly.

"The stories he heard. The last straw. A penthouse on top of the new Wallace Benton building, built especially for her." She paused. "It was an accident."

"No."

"Please. Yes—an accident."

"No."

She whispered, "He told me he'd returned for his scarf, but he was worried about leaving her alone in that place. Late at night. An automat. But she wasn't there. His scarf was. He waited and then she stepped out from the back hallway, spotted him, backed out of view. He followed her. And he said he joked with her, tried to make her laugh. She was nervous. But then she laughed. He said he playfully put his scarf around her neck, toying with her—'This way I won't forget it again'—and she laughed, gave him a peck on the cheek. Yes, she said everything was all right, but she still wanted him to leave. To be alone. Just that night. They would talk in the morning. He got—angry, pulled her toward him, grabbing the scarf. She panicked, saw something in his eyes. And…"

"My God." I breathed in, hollowness.

Lady Maud looked toward the window. "And then she was on the floor. He rushed out the back door and left it open. He ran through the streets. He ran to his rooms."

"My God," I said again.

Lady Maud took a step toward me. "Can you understand how horrible it is to listen to your son tell you that he murdered someone?" Her voice cracked. "Can you? Can you understand the chill that goes deep into your soul? Can you understand that you walk into a wall, you stumble, you don't know where to turn? A nail in your coffin. Blackness, an abyss of horror. Life can never be the same."

"Then he was murdered."

Suddenly Lady Maud erupted, sobbing, her hands fluttering in the air like wild birds.

As I watched, stunned, she raged on, stumbling around the tight room. Then, her face drained of color, her hair broken free of that bonnet, she thrust out her arms. The Chinese urn of ferns toppled from its stand, fell to the carpet. It shattered into pieces, dirt spilled everywhere. The raw scent of rich soil.

She stood back, triumphant. "There!" Her voice broke. "There!"

Chapter Twenty-one

He created a life for her…

The morning of New Year's Eve.

I woke with a start, disturbed from a restless night of sleep, that phrase roiling around in my head. Chauncey Waters confiding about his erstwhile boss, Jackson Roswell, the man who ironically set into motion this long Elizabethan tragedy of love and revenge, greed and ambition, decline and fall. Jackson Roswell, watching the world he created crumble around him as he hid in that squalid apartment over a stumblebum vaudeville theater in Hell's Kitchen.

He created life for her…

And how had Chauncey finished his grim epitaph?

…and was furious when she wouldn't live it.

The hollow-eyed man on that street corner: *Nobody believes I had a life before this.*

Something was wrong with the story, some stage direction missed, a stage manager slipping up, perhaps words that should never have been said. I lay in bed, snuggling under the warm fleece blankets, my eyes focused on the ice-streaked window, nineteen stories up, isolated. The sky over Central Park deep white with the promise of snow.

Cocoon. Moss Hart all over again.

Then I remembered something else, and I sat up like a bolt of lightning. Of course.

Bathed, dressed, contemplating Rebecca's sumptuous buttermilk pancakes, I fiddled with a pencil and notepad. A half-hour later, antsy, I phoned a friend at the *New York Times* who promised a quick journey into the paper's dusty morgue, the buried files. An hour later, as I sat in my wing chair by the terrace window, the phone rang.

I was right on the money.

The money—yes, it was always about the money.

I headed down into the street, determined to take my mile-long walk despite the chill. The doorman nodded at me, wished me a happy New Year, though I saw in his eyes what was always there whenever I ventured out in driving rain and snow blizzard and brutal August heat—Who was this maddened rich lady who missed the news that cars were invented to get from point A to point B? I agreed—yes, maddened. But especially this morning as I contemplated what to do, where my thinking led me. That news from the newspaper morgue. Yes, important. Grimly, I thought—morgue. How aptly we name the dark recesses of a journalistic grave.

Back upstairs I reached for the phone. "Noel, what are you doing now?" I heard banging in the background. The whistle of a teakettle.

A long pause, a chuckle. "Darling, have you been following anything I've told you for a month? I leave for Cleveland this very evening. Probably on a train packed with frantic revelers who will not understand that New York's white-haired boy is famous and demands silence."

"Noel, a note of caution. When you step off the train and see marching bands and tubas oom-pah-pah-ing around you—it isn't for you."

"I imagine New Year's Eve in Cleveland is a desperately lonely event. A hope of heaven for the following year."

My voice was grim. "That's New Year's around the world, dear Noel. Forced frivolity that ends in melancholy."

He laughed. "You're chipper, darling. Someone stole your lunch money?" A pause. "What task do you need of me?"

Quietly, I told him of my visit to Lady Maud and the horrid truth of her confession to me. Listening, Noel gasped, and for a moment I could tell he held the phone away from his ear. Finally, his voice hollow, he whispered, "I suppose I knew it all along. It's just that you don't want to believe the worse of the best of your friends." Then, quietly, "Why did he ask us to help him? To clear his name."

I waited a long time. "Because he thought he was dreaming and we would wake him up and say it never happened."

"He couldn't believe he could do such a thing."

"He wanted it to…never have happened."

"It must have been awful for you, Edna. Just awful."

I didn't answer, fumbling with the telephone cord, twisting it, wrapping it around my fingertips.

"Edna, what?"

I counted a heartbeat. Then, my mouth close to the receiver, I told him what I needed from him.

He debated refusing me, a moment of awful silence, but I knew he wouldn't. I could hear the quick snap of a suitcase closing. "Edna, I'll meet you there. A cab."

I hung up the phone, yet I sat there, paralyzed, my eyes focused on the wall.

When I arrived at Eleventh Avenue, I noticed a cab idling in front of the Paradise, billows of exhaust smoke clouding the sidewalk. Inside, Noel's long aristocratic head was leaning forward as he engaged the cabbie in some chatter. I smiled because that spirited conversation would doubtless reappear in one of his plays, a few smart and throwaway witticisms that critics might decry as rarefied, snobbish—but downright riotous.

Spotting me, he insisted I greet the cabbie, a string bean Cockney lad with freckles and a bushel-basket of flowery ginger hair that made him seem an unlikely harbinger of spring. "Harry tells me next year with FDR as president life will be…a bowl of cherries. I should write a song with those lyrics, Edna, though I believe I've heard them before."

The cabbie leaned over and addressed me. "Next year, you wait and see."

"Noel, must you engage the whole world in your tomfoolery?"

He acted shocked. "I try, endlessly. It's a mistake to be witty, dear Edna. Such souls as I are always waiting for someone to say that they *like* them. A horror!" He leaned back into the cab where Harry was listening to the exchange. "Do you like my wit, Harry?"

Harry grunted. "Okay, so long as it comes with a dollar bill."

Paid, grinning, he sped off.

Noel linked arms with me, the smile disappearing. "Edna, is this the last act?"

"Yes."

He swiveled to look into my face. "Smile, Edna. I like happy endings."

"Yes, happy. The tragic loading of these gritty streets."

The breadline up ahead, unwavering on the arctic day. Beggars bunched by light posts. Young boys in slough caps hawked what looked like spools of twine wrapped around sticks. A squawking baby was lost in the folds of its mother's shawl. A handwritten sign in the window of a store: Out of business. A newspaper kiosk at the end of the block, shuttered, its opening tarpapered, one corner loose so that it flapped in the wind.

The doors of the theater were unlocked, which surprised me. As Noel and I strode down the aisle, I could see the stage illuminated, someone standing on a ladder center stage. The sound of hammering. The shadowy figure had paused when he heard the door open at the back of the house, stepped down, and moved downstage to watch Noel and me walk through the dark orchestra seats. We stopped at the apron.

"Miss Ferber. Mr. Coward." Jackson's voice was hesitant. "Can I help you?" He pushed the ladder aside and dropped the hammer onto the floor. "Dammit," he swore. The thud echoed throughout the theater.

"Questions." I looked up at him as he stepped back.

He glanced into the wings, seemed flustered, but then he threw his hands into the air in a kind of what-the-hell gesture. He waited. Noel and I climbed the steps and walked out onto the stage. Noel's eyes flickered, his body rocked back and forth as he faced the empty house. He mumbled softly to me, "I love being on any stage." With the curtain up, the space seemed vast, a little intimidating. Noel looked out over the orchestra and tipped his hat. He pointed a finger at me. "Nancy Drew. The Secret of the Old Theater."

Jackson, watching, was unhappy, his face set, tight, hard. "What?" Too loud. His voice went out over the house seats.

I fixed my eyes on Noel. No more humor. "Act five, dear Noel."

Jackson saw me looking at the ladder. "I'm planning to open a new revue the middle of January. A reinvented life for us. Turning a corner." But he was nervous, his voice cracking as he stammered, "Is this about Belinda and Dougie?"

"What else?" Irritation in my voice. "Why else would we be here?"

"I can't help…"

I broke in, sharply. "Of course, you can. You may be the only one with answers." I backed off that statement. "Or maybe— some answers. Others…" I faltered.

"You're not making much sense." He grinned an unhappy grin.

I breathed out. "'He created a life for her and was furious when she wouldn't live it.' Someone told me that about you."

A puzzled look on his face. "Just wait a minute now. You're not going to accuse me of anything." Wildly, he swung around, looking to the wings, pushed the ladder away from him, then looked back at us.

"Another thing you told someone some time ago. 'Nothing gets past this city boy.'"

He squinted at me. "Yeah?" He punched the air. "I say a lot of things, lady."

Enough. Watching his face contort, I chose my words carefully. "Jackson Roswell died three years ago up at Harlem

Hospital. He's on a list of folks buried in a pauper's grave in Queens. Just a name in a column."

Silence. Long and awful.

"What?" From Noel, startled.

I watched Jackson's face. Suddenly a bemused smile, though his eyes betrayed wariness. "You do your homework, Miss Ferber."

"Who are you?" I asked, and waited.

He didn't answer for the longest time, biting his lips, a faraway look in his eyes, but finally, spreading out his palms in a gesture of surrender, he hissed, "I should have known you'd discover that because of your nosiness. Lord, do you invade everyone's life with such impunity?"

"Only the ones with something to hide."

"How did you know?"

"I had an idea." I counted seconds. "And actually I do have an idea who you are, in fact."

"You could be wrong."

I pursed my lips. "I doubt it."

Noel smiled at him. "She allows herself to be wrong only when I point it out."

I ignored Noel as I held Jackson's eye.

"Tell me," he said. "I can see you can't wait."

"The nameless suitor who swept Linda Roswell off her feet back in Sayville, whisked her off for a marriage that didn't take, and then, probably cowering before her father's shotgun, someone who disappeared for good."

He laughed a long time. "Not exactly for good. Obviously."

"Bingo." Noel nodded to me.

Jackson made an exaggerated stage bow, then curled out his hand in a melodramatic flourish. "Eliot Pittman, at your service."

I smiled back at him. "You were your own first creation."

"Unintentionally, ma'am."

"Tell us what happened."

He rocked back on his heels, unhappy, but, oddly now, a part of him savoring the moment. Mistaken identity. Playing a part.

The actor in his moment. "If you must know—and the look on your face suggests you're unrelenting and a little forbidding, actually a horrid woman—this all happened by chance. Yes, that ill-founded romance in that hick town, running off, a foolish marriage. I was older, early twenties, headstrong, delirious with the girl. I loved her—*thought* I loved her. We eloped, so romantic, only to have it end with a thud. A welcome thud. Together in a fleabag hotel in Hartford we realized we'd made a mistake. It's amazing how a spark can turn to cinder in a flash. Luckily, her one-brain-cell daddy come a-knocking with the sheriff and the marriage that lasted a day or so was dissolved. A quickie divorce that seemed a dream come true. Sand through your fingers."

"And so you left town?"

"I was from Bridgeport." He smirked. "The big city I obviously mentioned to someone in passing, who spread the news to you. I wanted theater, New York, Schubert Alley, Times Square, acting, directing. I came here."

"And you met Linda and Jack?" asked Noel.

A strange look came into his eyes, annoyance maybe, mixed with a little anger. "Christ, I was wandering the forlorn streets of Morningside Heights, way uptown, near Harlem, staying in a flop house, dirt poor, the world crashing down on me and on the whole damn country, when I spotted Linda and Jack grubbing for food in some local eatery. Jack was sick—he was always sick. Linda was surprised to see me—friendly even, but by then she was desperate. Leaving Sayville was a mistake for them. Of course, Jackson couldn't stand me. After all, I'd violated his little sister, but he was suddenly too sick to do anything about it. One day he collapsed, died the next day, and Linda discovered that he was the one who took whatever money the family had squirreled away. Dollars and cents, hidden in a soup can. My eyes lit up, let me tell you. Linda had no idea he'd taken it. Jack was aiming his sights down here—Broadway. But refusing to spend a plug nickel to survive. He was waiting for the right time."

"So you took over his dream."

A smug expression. "Exactly. It was already my dream. But I realized—I already knew—that Linda had the talent— that angelic voice, those looks, even that zany comic strain. Everything. A godsend, that girl. She was so young, trusting. A little...stupid. It was then that I decided to make her—and as a corollary, me, in fact—rich off her talent. I talked to her through the nights, convincing her to play my game. I created Belinda Ross out of simple Linda Roswell. I used the money to rent this deathtrap theater, an old forgotten vaudeville house. Those rat-infested rooms upstairs. But close to the Great White Way, near enough to get someone—like that old fool Cyrus Meerdom—to wander in to listen to Linda."

I thought of something else. "Another thing I recalled, sir. Your life as an acrobat—fit, able-bodied."

He rolled his eyes. "Yeah, good one. Jack was a fragile vessel, always dying. Thank God he finally did. Conveniently."

"And you began the journey?"

He nodded. "Galatea and Pygmalion. Myths and legends."

"But," Noel began, "why did you take on Jackson's persona? Why not be—Eliot Pittman?"

"Simple. You know this unforgiving town. You know America with its puritanical codes. Vestal virgins. Wink wink. Lord, haven't you been aware that we've lived under tight-laced Republicans throughout the twenties? Belinda had to be the young, untouched ingénue, the pretty young thing of men's desires. You couldn't have her be a girl who was once married and then—horror of horrors—divorced. Living upstairs with ex-hubby. Christ, imagine what that ass Winchell would have made of that in his 'Broadway Calling' column?"

"The Roaring Twenties?" Noel said. "Flaming youth? What am I missing here?"

"You're missing image. There's a boundary line, you know. Divorce? Never. Not for what I wanted to create." A sly chuckle. "Of course, once famous she could be as carefree with her favors as could be."

"So you became the dead brother."

A ta-da motion with his hands. "I had all the documents, of course. Step one, step two. Each calculated step. According to plan. Getting Cyrus Meerdom to discover Belinda and carry her to Broadway. I knew that he was a doddering letch, so that sale was effortless. The rest was history. I sat back, counting the pennies that flowed my way. My plan was to abandon this hole-in-the-wall dump and manage a legitimate theater. Like the New Amsterdam. Classy, noticed. I'd be able to keep my dream of being in theater in these horrible times."

"Belinda went along with it?"

Noel added, perplexed, "She willingly followed your orders?"

He fretted. "Blindly, at first. To be sure, she wanted fame on the stage. I gave her that. Cyrus and the other fools loved her—she laughed at that, drifted through their lives like she was soaked with laudanum. Fame is a powerful aphrodisiac, my friends."

"Then there was Dougie."

"A wrinkle in the fabric I wove."

"She fell in love with him."

He clapped his big, beefy hands together, a sound that reverberated throughout the theater. "And he with her. Money, yes, but she suddenly had reservations. She didn't *want* to be the girl I created for her. She backed off."

"And you were furious."

He eyed me closely. "But I didn't kill her." His words thundered across the stage. "If that's where you're headed with this interrogation."

"I know that," I said.

"Then what?" Puzzled, his brow furled. "Why are you here now? The story is over."

"Dougie." I waited. Then I said his name louder. "Dougie. Dead now."

"Christ, you can't think that I had anything to do with that horrible death."

"Did he ever suspect the fraud—that you were not Jackson?"

He reached into a breast pocket, took out a cigarette wrapper. As we watched, he rolled loose tobacco from a pouch into the paper, carefully licked it, and then, with a flourish, lit it. He breathed in, closed his eyes. "What did it matter? I know Belinda threatened to confess to him 'I want no secrets,' she babbled. But I made her promise."

"No one else knew?"

A voice from the wings yelled out, "I knew."

Millie Glass charged onto the stage, her face contorted. "Lord, Eliot, you have a big mouth." She poked him in the chest. "Put a ham actor on a stage and he sings all his sins to the known world."

Startled, I jumped, bumping into Noel's sleeve.

"For Christ's sake, Millie," Eliot swore. "You'll give us all heart attacks. Every time I turn around you're at my back, watching, watching. You gotta give me some room to breathe."

Her glance shot from me to Noel. "You've done enough breathing on your own. I've been listening to you spill the beans to these two. Do you think that's a good idea?"

I ran my tongue over my lower lip. "I don't think he had any choice, Millie, my dear. He gave himself away long before today. This is just the unpleasant denouement."

That perplexed her, though she stood close to Jackson—or Eliot—and linked her arm into his elbow possessively. Involuntarily, his body pulled away from hers, his eyes dark, but she leaned into his side and stared up into his face. "Yeah, I suppose so. What does it matter now, anyway?" she said to me, her eyes cloudy.

"Perhaps it doesn't," I told her. "But there are still many questions."

"But not about this," she said, hurried. "It was a game we played when Belinda was alive. The curtain has come down."

Noel stared at her. "How long did you know about the ruse?"

She considered whether to answer, but finally, clicking her tongue, "Not at first. I was just"—she spat out the words—"the hired hand around here. Not until Eliot and I fell into a relationship."

"When was that?" I asked.

"When Belinda moved out." Her voice swelled, joyous. "Or maybe earlier. Yes, earlier. We kept it a secret, of course. It didn't matter—Eliot and Belinda were brother and sister. Supposedly. So the world thought. So you two thought—but we were afraid you would crack the secret. Too many questions. That visit to Connecticut. But…" She lingered on the word.

"What?"

She frowned. "Belinda didn't like me. She didn't approve of me and Eliot."

"They were no longer married, right?" Noel said, puzzled. "What did it matter?"

"No matter. But she was spiteful. She thought me—common."

Eliot smirked. He blew a smoke ring into the air. Millie glowered and stepped away from him. "Talk about your revelations and confessions, my dear."

Millie drew in her cheeks. "She didn't care about *us*. There was no *us* to her, that selfish bitch." She pointed at Eliot. "She simply couldn't stand me."

Eliot suddenly dropped his cigarette, stomped on it. His face was flushed and he flicked his head toward Millie. "Millie, enough."

She preened. "Funny how life turns out, really. Him and me— we're a team now. Together we'll build a life without Belinda."

"You really have no choice," I commented.

I caught Noel's eye as he nodded back at me. Eliot was unhappy with what was happening, but, more so, his expressions hinted a problem with Millie. Oblivious, she strutted about, cocky, commanding the stage. Watching his transparent face, it dawned on me that Eliot had reconsidered his decision to get involved with Millie. A man used to being in control, a man purposeful—and solitary. A convenient romance, perhaps, pleasant at one time, probably shelter from the unraveling Belinda scheme. But the bitter look on his face suggested Millie wrote herself a large speaking part in that bedroom farce, and the only critic that mattered wanted the show closed on Saturday.

"What does that mean? No choice?" Millie stared into my face.

"You know, dear, there's still the mystery of unsolved murder."

She rolled her eyes. "That has nothing to do with us. Do you mean that weasel, Dougie? He murdered Belinda. Everyone knows that. Then someone kills him. Karma, as they say. An underworld of thugs in this city. You play with the hookers and thieves, you get a knife in the back. Fat-cat money men. Dougie betrayed us. A fawning, annoying suitor—and benefactor. Charity begins in the theater aisle. He was a man of empty promises. Where was he when we had to shutter our doors? The creditors pounding any hour of the night."

"My doors," Eliot said quietly.

She snarled at him, "I'm part of this world, too."

"I only mean…"

Millie's voice sailed out over the theater, echoed back. "How dare he treat us like that? Do you see the breadline out there? The soup kitchen? Beggars with dead eyes." Her voice quivered. "I don't care what happened to him—not after what he did to us."

Quiet on the stage, Eliot's face got tight as he watched Millie's gyrations. "Quiet, Millie, for God's sake."

She seethed. "No, I won't. They say it's impolite to speak ill of the dead, but so be it. I've never been one for proper behavior—fighting my way to this damn stage. Pulling myself up from every Podunk dance hall."

Eliot, eyes dazed. "Stop it, dammit."

"Someone needed to murder Dougie." Noel's words filled the room.

Millie twisted her head to the side. "So what? I'm not sorry."

Eliot's face suddenly looked sad.

I looked at him. "You never told Millie about Dougie's check?"

He shook his head.

"What?" From Millie.

I took a deep breath. "Millie, Dougie didn't abandon you. Just before he died, he sent Eliot a check so the theater could go on. Lady Maud told me so. In Belinda's memory. He'd just forgotten it. He was paying his debts at the end."

"What?" She lunged at Eliot. "He gave you money?" Her mouth fell open as she pounded her fists into his chest.

"Yes." Eliot's face closed in.

"Why didn't you tell me?"

Eliot stepped back, folded his arms over his chest, his voice cold. "Because it was my money."

At that moment something happened to Eliot. His eyes got glassy with fright, his shoulders dropped as his hands flew up to face. An awful moan escaped from deep inside his throat. Wildly, his eyes sought mine, then Noel's, and finally, panicky, he groaned out loud. "Oh, Christ, no." He stumbled backward. "Oh, Christ, no." He grabbed the edge of the ladder he'd carried onto the stage, gripped the rungs, staggered, bent over it. He started to heave. "Oh, Christ, no."

Millie watched him, her face stony. "You goddamn fool."

Quietly, I said to Millie, "You shot Dougie, Millie."

A flash of fire as she sucked in her breath. A ragged voice. "I hated him. We were gonna have to be in the street. Me—Eliot. We'd lose the theater, the..."

I faced her. "That had nothing to do with Dougie."

She screamed at me. "It had everything to do with him. I *hated* him. It wasn't supposed to be like this. He broke my dreams into little pieces. How the hell did I know what was going on?"

"Oh, Christ, no." Eliot's body shook. Crazily, he stepped toward her and reached out to touch her shoulder.

"Don't you dare touch me, you damn fool." With both hands she pushed him away. She spun around, her eyes looking into the wings, then to the back of the orchestra. "I don't wanna be touched by you."

"You followed him?" I said to her.

"Day in, day out. Whenever I could get away from here. The crazy man wandered the streets. Lost in Central Park among those people. Finally, I had my chance."

Eliot's voice broke. "Christ, Millie. No."

She rushed at him, thrust out her hand, and slapped him across the face. He winced, swung his head to the side, and swore. "Christ, no. Belinda. Dougie." He looked back at her, pain in his voice. "Did you kill Belinda, too?"

Her laugh went on too long. "No, of course not. There were other people in line ready to do that dirty little job."

Eliot's voice was thick with anger. "But how could you…?"

Suddenly, her head dipped into her chest, Millie looked frightened. Her body shaking, she looked over her shoulder toward the wings, as though expecting a squad of police. A strange gurgle came from her throat. Then she started to sob. An awful wail, so loud we all backed up. She bent over, clutching her sides, and the wailing grew louder. On that old stage, facing the empty house seats, her crying filled the room, echoed off the old walls. Eyes closed now, rocking, rocking, she slipped onto the floor, her body writhing. When Noel leaned over and reached out his hand, she slapped him away.

"Don't you touch me, any of you. Don't nobody come near me."

Eliot turned his back to her, but his shoulders trembled.

Noel faced me. "Over."

"Over," I echoed.

• • ● ● •

Twilight fell on my terrace. Icy snow beneath my feet, crunchy, as I stepped out of the apartment. Cold, shivering, I stared down nineteen stories to the street below. A line of slow-moving cars snaked along the avenue, idled at a red light. Specks of gold drifting into pockets of blue and black. In the distance the new Chrysler building, Art Deco splendor. illuminated. Glittery and spangling on this festive New Year's night. But oddly quiet now, hours before the midnight crowd teemed into the streets, horns blowing, screaming, laughter, hoopla, and embraces. Times Square madness. Dancing the night away at Roseland. At the Hotel Pennsylvania. But at midnight I would be in my bed. It was no night for celebration.

Cold. Time to go in. But not yet.

A short time before Noel had called to say goodbye and to wish me happy New Year. "I'm off the Cleveland, but I feel like the New Year is already old."

My voice had shook. "There are no heroes in this story, are there, dear Noel?"

I'd heard him drag on a cigarette. "If I don't return from Cleveland, send out a search party."

I laughed. "You have to come back. I need you."

A sweetness in his voice. "I love you, darling."

"I love you, too."

Then the line went dead.

Cold, my eyes moist from the arctic wind that swept over the terrace.

Leaning over the balustrade, though I gripped the railing carefully, I could discern a slight whisper of music from the apartment below. A radio on perhaps. Notes that drifted up and then away, faded to nothing. A hint of a song, staticky and then smooth. A mellow refrain. Jazz, I realized. Ellington's mournful elegy on the death of things in the purple haze of late-night revelry and early-morning goodbyes. Darkswept, and inviting.

A bittersweet voice.

...in the evening when the lights are low
I'm so lonely I could cry...

My chest tightened, I cried out loud, I turned away from the distant music.

My eyes sought the dark park below me: a purple forest starred with gold. Like the sun turned upside down.

I stumbled back into my quiet rooms but my mind raced with a haunting refrain from another lifetime:

What of soul was left, I wonder, when the kissing had to stop?

To see more Poisoned Pen Press titles:

Visit our website: poisonedpenpress.com/
Request a digital catalog: info@poisonedpenpress.com